CAN'T TAKE MY EYES OFF OF YOU

~ Summer Lake, Book 2 ~

New York Sullivans Spinoff

Bella Andre

CAN'T TAKE MY EYES OFF OF YOU

~ Summer Lake, Book 2 ~

New York Sullivans Spinoff

Sign up for Bella's New Release Newsletter

www.BellaAndre.com/newsletter

bella@bellaandre.com

www.BellaAndre.com

Bella on Twitter: @bellaandre

Bella on Facebook: facebook.com/bellaandrefans

Christie Hayden escaped to Summer Lake to heal from heartbreak, but found so much more than that: a job she loves as an innkeeper, a close-knit community of friends, and a chance at the perfect romantic future she's always longed for. But nothing is as it seems, especially when it comes to Liam Kane, the gorgeous millionaire who sweeps into her life from out of the blue…and instantly turns it—and her heart—upside down.

From the first time Liam Kane lays eyes on Christie, he's a total goner. He knows he should keep his distance, because he's not capable of giving her the happily-ever-after she's looking for. But when it comes to her smiles, her laughter, her kindness—and her sweetly sinful kisses—for the first time in his life, he can't hang on to his self-control. Not when the love she offers him is everything he never thought he could have, but now craves with every fiber of his being.

But Liam has been keeping a secret for twenty years, one that nearly destroyed him—one that has the potential to tear his whole family apart too. When Christie can't stop herself from trying to help out of pure love, will Liam be able to let himself heal? Or will they both end up broken, leaving her to pick up the pieces all over again?

A note from Bella

Welcome back to Summer Lake! Calvin Vaughn found his forever love in *The Best Is Yet To Come*, and now it's Christie Hayden's turn. The path to true love, however, is rarely a straight line. Especially for Christie.

As for Liam Kane...well, let's just say that I might have a bit of a crush on him. He's the embodiment of the heroes I love—not only sexy and brilliant, but also a man who will do whatever he needs to do to protect the people he loves. Even if keeping them safe has the potential to destroy him.

I hope you love watching Christie and Liam fall for each other, against all odds!

And then get ready for Alec Sullivan, the hero of *You Do Something To Me (New York Sullivans #3)*. This fall, I promise we're all going to have the best time watching him try to keep his heart safe from the only woman on earth who could possibly sneak inside the walls he's built up and steal his heart away.

Please be sure to sign up for my newsletter (bellaandre.com/newsletter) so you don't miss out on any new book release announcements.

Happy reading!
Bella Andre

CHAPTER ONE

"You are such a beautiful bride." Christie Hayden smoothed out the cuff of Sarah Bartow's long-sleeved wedding gown and smiled at her friend in the full-length mirror. Summer Lake, still mostly frozen and lightly dusted with snow, was reflected through the large-paned window in the mirror.

Sarah's eyes were full of excitement and anticipation for her wedding day. "Thank you for everything you've done to help us. I could never have pulled this off so quickly, or so beautifully, without you."

Christie was pleased by how smoothly the wedding preparations had come together. Her final walk-through downstairs half an hour ago confirmed that the Summer Lake Inn had been completely transformed into a tasteful, elegant wedding venue.

"I've absolutely loved helping you," Christie said, "but we both know you could have single-handedly planned a dozen weddings in the past two weeks and gotten a spread in *Brides* magazine while you were at it."

Sarah grinned. "That was the old me, before I decided to start playing with yarn all day at the store."

Christie was happy to let Sarah say whatever she wanted. After all, this was her wedding day. But both of them knew that moving back to Summer Lake and becoming engaged to Calvin Vaughn hadn't changed the core of who Sarah was. She had always been driven. Brilliant. And on top of that, she also happened to be one of the most loving, caring people Christie had ever had the good fortune to know.

Business at Lakeside Stitch and Knit was more brisk than ever now that Sarah had taken over the store for her mother and grandmother. Not only because Sarah was a phenomenal businesswoman with a background in management consulting, but also because she was truly passionate about knitting *and* the women who shopped in her store.

As Sarah turned to look into the antique mirror in the inn's wedding prep room, she seemed almost surprised by the wedding gown, the soft curls brushing against her collarbone, the pretty makeup, and the lacy knitted veil over which she couldn't stop running her fingers in wonder.

"I never thought today would come," Sarah said softly, "but I always wanted it." She lifted her gaze to meet Christie's in the mirror. "I've loved Calvin my whole life."

Christie blinked quickly to push away the tears threatening to fall. "You and Calvin both deserve the love you've found again. Especially since this time, it's forever."

She smiled as she looked at Sarah's slightly rounded stomach, and the lump in her throat was replaced by the joy of knowing there would soon be a new baby to cuddle. Her friend's fingers spread across the growing life inside her in an instinctive gesture of protectiveness and nurturing, and a bolt of longing hit Christie so hard that she nearly stumbled back from the force of it.

"Christie?" Sarah reached for her arm. "You know you can talk to me, don't you?"

Christie knew she'd just given too much away. She always did. Some people had poker faces, but hers would cause her to lose everything in a casino because she didn't have the first clue how to play the game. Especially when it came to love.

Still, knowing the last thing she should do was dump her fears and hurts and baggage all over Sarah on her wedding day, Christie was intent on finding a way to deflect her friend's concern and lighten the mood. "I always get emotional at weddings. You should have seen me at each of my sisters' ceremonies. I cried buckets. The guests in my row were all wishing for raincoats so I wouldn't soak them."

But Sarah didn't so much as crack a smile. "You

don't have to pretend with me." Regret flashed across her face. "Ever since I got pregnant, my brain has been fuzzy and I want to sleep all the time. That's got to be why I didn't see it more clearly before—we never should have scheduled our wedding for this weekend." Sarah's words were said softly, and while there wasn't pity behind them, Christie believed that was due only to their close friendship.

Unfortunately, there was no escaping the fact that *Christie* was supposed to have been the one to get married this weekend. Only, instead of wearing a long white gown and saying *I do*, she was going to be sitting in the audience, watching her friends make their vows of love to each other.

It hadn't been easy walking down Main Street these past three weeks, going to the grocery store, getting a coffee at the café, knowing people were whispering about her. Sure, they all smiled and exchanged pleasantries. But either they had to be feeling sorry for her, or they were trying to figure out just what horrible thing she'd done to make Wesley Kane call off the wedding—and disappear from Summer Lake the very next day without a word to anyone.

Including her.

Only the women in the knitting group had remained the same as always. Warm. Gossipy. And yet, utterly nonjudgmental. No matter how busy she was,

Christie made sure to keep every Monday night open for drinking too much wine at Lakeside Stitch and Knit, and usually doing more talking and laughing than knitting.

She'd found her home in Summer Lake, liked to imagine growing old on an Adirondack chair on a dock while she watched her future grandchildren playing in the clear blue water. She hated to think that she'd been accepted by the locals only because she was engaged to a man whose family had lived here for generations. She wanted to believe that she belonged on her own merit, because people liked her and thought she contributed something valuable to the community.

But regardless of how off-kilter she was feeling after the break-up, she refused to taint Sarah's wedding in any way. "Really, it worked out perfectly," Christie insisted. "You needed a wedding venue on short notice, and I had one all ready to go. It was meant to happen this way. I'm certain of it."

Anyone else would have stopped talking there, would have held something back, would have hidden the rest of her feelings. But Christie had never known how to do that. Especially when a dear friend was looking at her with such deep concern. Besides, she'd finally stopped lying to herself about her ex-fiancé three weeks ago. So what was the point in trying to hold back with Sarah now?

"You know Wesley and I weren't right for each other. Not as anything more than friends. The truth is, I enjoyed putting the finishing details on your wedding far more than I ever enjoyed working on it when it was my own." Christie shook her head. "I guess that should have been my first clue that something wasn't right. After all the weddings I've put on at the inn, after spending time with Drake and Rosa and Suzanne and Roman whenever they're staying in town, and then watching you and Calvin together..." She made herself smile. "You two were supposed to be picking out cake toppers a few weeks ago, but couldn't stop staring into each other's eyes. That was the day I finally realized I couldn't marry Wesley. And that he shouldn't marry me either." Not just because she wanted that kind of love for herself, but because it also wasn't fair to him. "And I will always be grateful to you for helping me see the light." Long after she should have seen it on her own.

Sarah hugged her tightly, and even though Christie longed to tell her friend more—she could swear that her secrets were actually eating her up inside—there was one thing she couldn't tell anyone.

Specifically, what had happened three weeks ago when she and Wesley had broken off their engagement.

CHAPTER TWO

Three weeks earlier...

Christie was so twisted up inside her head—and heart—on her way to Wesley's suite of rooms that she didn't think to knock before opening the door. She literally froze in place when Wesley and John, a mutual friend of theirs from college, pulled away from each other so quickly that she almost thought she'd imagined their embrace.

Their kiss.

Wesley cursed and came toward her, hands outstretched, his face ravaged with guilt. "Christie, I didn't want to hurt you. I swear it."

She waited for betrayal to kick in, for anger to burst forth. Instead, all she felt was relief. Because this had to mean Wesley didn't want to marry her either.

Maybe she should have been shocked by his kiss with John. Only, she wasn't. Not when all of the warning signs, everything that hadn't added up from the first time Wesley had asked her out, suddenly made perfect sense.

Christie had always dated tall, dark, and mysterious men who made her heart race. Men with a core of danger and secrets that she wanted to heal. Whereas Wesley had been safe. Gentle. A calm lake instead of a roaring sea. He had been her best friend since their freshman year in art college, when they'd bonded over giggles during a nude-drawing class. Many years later, when they'd started dating, their kisses—which, honestly, had been few and far between—had been nothing to write home about. But she'd told herself fireworks were overrated. Lord knew she could live without the careening emotions that had gone hand in hand with her previous relationships.

Now, as she stood in Wesley's living room with John waiting awkwardly by the window, she finally realized why their engagement had always felt so wrong. They'd both been desperately lying to themselves. Both been wanting to believe in something that could never make either of them happy.

"Why didn't you tell me?" She wasn't angry, but as his closest friend, she was hurt that he'd felt he needed to keep his true feelings from her.

"I wanted so badly to make things work. You and I are such close friends that I thought I could be with you, but seeing John brought up so many old feelings. Feelings I thought had gone away. Feelings I'd convinced myself had never existed in the first place." His eyes looked wild, as if he was only just barely keeping it together. "I'm just so confused about everything. You must hate me. But I swear I didn't cheat on you. Just that kiss." The tears that spilled down his cheeks, along with his confession, broke her heart. "I'm sorry, Christie. So, so sorry."

"Please, Wes." She took his hands in hers. "Don't cry. Not over me. And don't think I could possibly hate you. Especially when I came here tonight to call off our engagement."

His eyes widened in shock. "Are you kidding?"

"No." She swallowed hard, then admitted, "I should never have said yes when you asked me to marry you. Should never even have dated you. Not when we both knew we could never be more than friends."

He squeezed his eyes tight, as if he was trying—and failing—to process everything that was happening. When he reopened them, instead of looking calmer, if anything his panic seemed to have heightened.

"Please keep my secret. About that kiss. About John." He gripped her hands so tightly that she winced. "I need to figure things out before I deal with my family. With our friends. With this town."

They both knew she was no good at keeping secrets. But it was the fear, the pain, the confusion in

Wesley's eyes that had her promising, "I won't tell anyone what happened tonight." Knowing he must be desperate to talk things through with John after their kiss, especially if it was their very first, she said, "Tomorrow, we'll figure out how we want to break the news to everyone. That we've decided to just remain friends and call off the wedding."

But the next morning, Christie was surprised to find his note.

I have to leave. I need some time, some space away from Summer Lake, to think things through. I'll come home as soon as I can, but please don't come looking for me.

Mere minutes later, his mother, Susan, burst into the inn's reception room gripping a similar letter in her hand. Tears were fresh on her cheeks—and she didn't bother to hide the accusation in her eyes when she looked at Christie.

* * *

Present day...

A bird chirping loudly outside the inn's window brought Christie back into the moment. One where Sarah's look of concern had morphed into full-on worry.

"Have you heard from Wesley yet?" Sarah asked.

"No. He hasn't been in touch with any of us."

"He's family, and you know I love him," Sarah said. Her grandmother Olive and Wesley's grandmother Jean were sisters. "But that doesn't mean I always understand him, or his brother Liam, who never even responded to our wedding invitation."

Christie turned her gaze to the window, as if she could somehow spot Wesley out there if she looked hard enough. But she sensed he wouldn't be back so soon. He was dealing with a lot right now, but every now and again, she felt a little miffed that he'd left her here to deal with everything on her own, for who knew how long.

Sarah gripped her hand tighter, and Christie felt moisture tickling her eyes again. *No.* The only tears she'd cry today would be happy ones.

Just then, the church bells chimed. Christie opened the door and held out her hand to her friend. "I can't wait to see Calvin's face when you walk down the aisle. He's going to be the happiest man alive."

* * *

Oh my. What a lovely wedding it was. Beyond anything Christie could have prepared herself for.

Of course, the bride was gorgeous and the groom was handsome. Pink and white and red hothouse roses were in bloom all over the room. But Sarah and Calvin could have been standing in the middle of an open field wearing jeans and T-shirts and it still would have been one of the most beautiful ceremonies Christie had ever witnessed, simply because the love between them was so big and true that it reached out to wrap itself around everyone in the room as they said their vows.

Sarah was at once strong and completely vulnerable as she looked into Calvin's eyes. "Calvin Vaughn." She smiled as she said his name, and even if she said nothing more today, everyone in the room already knew from the raw, pure emotion that infused her words just how much she loved him. "There isn't any part of my life that doesn't have you in it. When I was five years old, you were there with me on the playground, pushing me higher on the swings than I thought it was possible to go. When I was fifteen, you kissed me for the first time and made me feel more than I thought it was possible to feel. And even when I wasn't here for ten long years, every single second that I was gone, you were with me in my dreams, in my hopes...and in every single part of my heart." Tears spilled down her cheeks, but Calvin caught them, gently brushing the wetness away with his thumbs. "My love for you is unconditional. My love for you is breathless and passionate. My love for you is everything I was, everything I am, everything I want to be.

Anything you need, I vow to give you. Anytime you hurt, I promise to heal you. I love you, Calvin Vaughn, now and *forever.*"

An audible gasp sounded in the room when he dipped his mouth to hers and gave her the sweetest kiss in the world. "I love you, Sarah." His deep voice resonated with boundless emotion. "I can't remember a time when I didn't love you—and I know there will never be a time when I won't. Your love is what has always been, and will always be, at the foundation of who I am—and who I want to be. Your devoted husband." He placed one hand over the slight swell of her stomach. "The best father in the whole wide world to our children." She covered his hand with hers as he said, "And your partner in all of the adventures we're going to have together." He drew her even closer, so close that Christie knew that despite the wedding guests watching them say their vows, he was seeing only his bride. "Past, present, future—you have my heart."

Christie didn't bother to hide her tears, not when everyone else in the room was dabbing at their eyes. Thankfully, she really had thought ahead and put pretty little boxes of tissues at the end of every row of seats. Boxes that were currently being passed back and forth as Calvin's ten-year-old sister, Jordan, reached into her basket of rose petals and threw them over her brother and new sister-in-law as they kissed and the crowd cheered.

The guests were mostly Summer Lake locals, with a few of Sarah's friends from the city having made the trip as well. Suzanne Sullivan was there with her boyfriend, Roman. Drake Sullivan was there with his girlfriend, Rosa. And Alec and Harry Sullivan were there too, along with their father, William. Christie always marveled at how even though so many of the Sullivans were famous or billionaires—or both—they made sure never to overshadow their friends. Instead, they always managed just to fit in with everyone else in the small town.

Just the way Christie so desperately longed to.

And as she watched the new bride and groom pull each other even closer to kiss again, Christie couldn't help but make a silent wish for her own happy ending one day. Even if all the signs pointed to it being the most impossible dream in the world…

CHAPTER THREE

Liam Kane heard the applause and cheers as he walked through the inn's front door. From the flower petals drifting out of the event room, he could easily guess it was a wedding.

It instantly struck him as strange. Why would Wesley schedule another wedding at the inn on the same weekend as his own? And how exactly did his brother plan to clean up this wedding party and still have time to set up for the rehearsal dinner tonight?

Liam had been planning to head straight upstairs to his suite to take a shower after his red-eye flight from China. It had been a crazy three weeks of constant flights, of hotel rooms he'd barely had time to check into before he was leaving for the next airport, the next meeting. But he hadn't been back to the lake in so long that curiosity had him dropping his bags behind the registration counter and walking toward the large room that overlooked the lake to see who was getting married.

As he stopped at a side door behind a large potted

plant, he was stunned to realize that Sarah Bartow, to whom he was related through his grandmother, was wearing a wedding dress and holding hands with her old boyfriend, Calvin Vaughn.

As far as he knew, they'd broken up after graduating from high school. When had they gotten back together? And how come he'd had no idea they were getting married today? Admittedly, he hadn't done a great job of keeping up with his family, or the Summer Lake locals, over the past few years. But that didn't mean Sarah would deliberately leave him off the guest list, did it?

There must be a rational explanation why he hadn't known about the wedding. As Sarah and Calvin kissed to seal their vows and the crowd cheered, Liam could see that they really were in love. For now, at least. It was what happened later—ten, fifteen, twenty years down the road, once they had kids and were supposed to be a cohesive family unit who all looked out for each other—that he had no faith in. In fact, the only thing he knew for certain was that the people who got hurt when love failed weren't just the man and the woman who had once made vows to each other on their wedding day. No, the net was cast much wider than that.

Which was why, in nearly twenty years of dating, Liam had never wanted to get married, had never been even remotely tempted to get down on one knee and ask one woman to be his for eternity.

Normally, he never let rogue emotions get the better of him like this, so he pushed them back down deep as he scanned the occupants of the room. It had been a long time since he'd been back to town, but he recognized nearly everyone. The old football coach. The owner of the general store. Several people he'd gone to school with. The Sullivans he'd gotten to know during the summers when they'd come to the lake from the city to help their father, William, build his log cabin.

And then a flash of movement caught his gaze—and held it.

Golden hair was gliding like silk across a woman's shoulders as she moved from behind a tall elderly man. And when she turned toward Liam, his breath actually lodged in his chest. Her eyes were glittering with tears, her cheeks flushed. She was biting her lip, her hands covering her heart.

And she was the most beautiful woman he'd ever seen.

He'd never been drawn to a delicate woman like this, who looked like she could sprout fairy wings and fly away. He'd always carefully chosen the women who shared his bed, making sure they were realistic enough never to make the mistake of falling in love with him or thinking they could change him.

But there was no denying his elemental reaction to

this woman.

The bride and groom were starting to make their way up the aisle and out of the room. He should head over with the rest of the crowd to offer his congratulations. But he couldn't tear his gaze from the woman who was not only taking his breath away, but who was making his heart beat faster too.

Her green dress was well tailored, but not at all flashy. The pearls at her earlobes and around her neck were elegant, but not intended to draw a man's eyes. Neither were her shoes, low-heeled and silver. He got the sense she wasn't the kind of woman who drew attention to herself.

Even though she had every ounce of his.

By now, everyone had followed Sarah and Calvin out of the room through the opposite door, but the woman hung behind, bending over to pick up stray flower petals strewn around her seat. Something jogged his brain, a prickle that was more than just awareness of a beautiful woman. A warning that he knew her from somewhere. But where?

She was picking up another handful of flower petals from the floor when she looked over and saw him standing at the side door. She was closer now, near enough that he could see just how delicate her features were, from her high cheekbones to her slightly pointed chin and the tiny indentations in each cheek as she smiled.

"Oh, hello." A bunch of the rose petals fell out of her hands and fluttered to the floor. She gave him a wry smile as she bent to pick them up again. "These smell good, but they're so messy."

Liam knew she was expecting him to say something, to tell her who he was or what he was doing standing there staring at her. But he hadn't yet found his voice.

She was the first woman ever to leave him speechless.

"With the wedding, I wasn't monitoring the front desk," she continued, her welcoming smile still in place. "Can I help you with something? Are you visiting a guest at the inn, perhaps?"

Finally, he told her, "I'm Liam Kane."

In an instant, her smile disappeared. Her mouth opened slightly and her cheeks grew flushed. She took a quick step backward and bumped into one of the covered folding chairs.

He waited for her gaze to drop to his scar and hold there, certain that must be the reason for her sudden, too-strong reaction. But her eyes never left his, never once raked over the mark that bisected the lower half of his left cheek from earlobe to chin.

"Oh my gosh. Of course you're Liam." She bit her lip, drawing his attention to its full, soft shape. Despite the conservative nature of her dress and shoes and jewelry, her lush mouth and the deep green of her eyes seemed to show a deeper truth about her. A sensuality she couldn't hide. Sensuality that wrapped around him from nothing more than his name on her lips. "I knew something about you looked familiar. I should have realized it earlier, but the wedding must have scrambled my brain. Sarah was wondering why you didn't respond to her invitation, but you ended up making it after all!"

As she spoke, her big green eyes were stealing away his brain cells one at a time. It felt like a hammer was pounding inside his head. How did she know exactly who he was when he couldn't for the life of him think who she was?

"I've been on the road for the past month," he explained, "and I'm guessing that their wedding invitation must have been misplaced in my pile of unopened mail. I actually had no idea they were even getting married. I'm here for my brother Wesley's wedding."

Her eyes grew even bigger. And, if he wasn't mistaken, more than a little horrified. "You don't know what happened?"

The hammer pounded harder, joined by a warning bell inside his brain that told him something was definitely wrong. Hadn't he known it from the minute he'd walked into the inn and realized there was another wedding taking place?

Something bad must have happened to his younger brother, whom he'd always looked after when they were kids but hadn't been around to check on much over the past few years. "Like I said, I've been on the road continuously and my cell phone doesn't always work reliably in some of the countries I've been in. If Wesley tried to get hold of me through my staff, I certainly didn't hear about it." Concern for his brother had him putting his hands on her shoulders to make sure he had her full attention. "What happened? Where's Wesley?"

Her eyes were wide enough now that he couldn't help but memorize their exact color of green, like fresh growth on bare trees in spring. "I don't know where he is."

Suddenly, he could feel her tremble beneath his hands. What the hell was he doing manhandling her? "I shouldn't have grabbed you like that." He was lifting his hands off her when he finally realized why she looked familiar. He blamed the red-eye for it taking him this long to put two and two together. "You're Wesley's fiancée."

Wesley had sent a picture of her back when they'd announced their engagement, and Liam's secretary had laid it out on top of the rest of his business correspondence. He'd been late to a meeting and barely had time to look at the picture before it was filed away—and then he'd been in Asia when they'd had their engagement party, so he hadn't had a chance to meet his brother's fiancée before now. But from what he recalled, while she had seemed pretty in the picture, nothing about her had drawn any special notice.

He could hardly believe this woman before him was the one beside Wesley in the staged photo. Same hair, same eyes, same face, same features—but totally different. As if she'd somehow come into focus since that photo had been taken.

"Yes," she said. "I'm Christie. I was his fiancée."

He couldn't miss the *was*. She hadn't intended he should. "You're supposed to be getting married tomorrow."

"Yes," she said again, but she was shaking her head even as she agreed with him. "We were, but—"

A door was flung open and Liam heard his mother's voice. "Christie, have you seen my wrap? I think I left it at my sea—" The words fell away as she realized her oldest son was standing there.

Christie jumped out of his grasp so fast he swore he felt a blast of cold air in the spot she'd been standing.

"Liam?" His mother moved toward him, her gaze immediately going to his scar and holding there for several seconds. "Oh, honey, I'm so glad you're finally home. It's all been such a mess. For all of us. Your father and I kept trying to reach you, but your secretary always said you were in a meeting or on a plane somewhere." She lowered her voice. "I didn't want to leave such a personal message with a stranger."

"So there's no wedding?" He directed the question to Christie rather than his mother.

"No," she said softly, "I'm afraid not."

"Why?" Again, he directed the question to Christie, but before she could reply, his mother reached for his hand to get his attention.

"Wesley left me and your father a note saying he needed to go away for a while to think about things, even though he didn't say what those *things* were. Isn't that right, Christie?"

Christie tilted her chin slightly to face his mother, who was several inches taller. "Yes." He was struck by her surprising strength as she turned back to him. "Wesley and I agreed a few weeks ago that the engagement and wedding were a mistake, but that we're still friends. There are no hard feelings between us. None at all. We both just want what's best for each other." She paused. "Unfortunately, the next morning he was gone."

Her earnest words seemed genuine, but Liam still wasn't satisfied. Not when he sensed there was a heck of a lot more going on than what she was telling them.

"I just wish Wesley had come to tell me that himself," his mother put in, "instead of disappearing in the middle of the night with only a note saying he'd left Christie in charge of the inn. I just don't feel right about it."

Yet again, the woman who had trembled in his arms stood strong in front of his mother as she said, "Wesley is a wonderful man. I'm sure he'll be back soon to let us all know what's going on."

"When?" Susan asked. To anyone else's ears, his mother's question was simply full of worry for her youngest child. But Liam could hear the ice at its core. Ice that was directed at Christie.

"I wish I knew, Susan. But I don't." Christie turned to him again. "Are you sure he didn't try to reach you, Liam?"

His name on her lips sent another jolt through him. Telling himself it was simply that he was feeling every one of the two hours of sleep he'd managed on the flight—or rather, the twenty-two he hadn't—he ran a hand over his face before answering. "Not as far as I know."

Damn it, if Wesley was in trouble, why hadn't he come to his older brother? Had Liam done so bad a job of being there for him these past years that Wes didn't know his door was always open? Wesley was the one person Liam had always loved with his whole heart.

The only person he knew he could trust wholly and completely.

But now, out of the blue, his brother had done a runner.

"He left the rest of us letters," Christie told him. "Perhaps yours got lost in the mail."

"I'll have my assistant go through my mail—and email—again tonight."

The door creaked again and the clicking of high heels sounded on the old wooden floorboards. "Christie, I've got a tear in the seam of my dress, and I was wondering if you could—" Sarah skidded to a stop halfway into the room, looking shocked—but pleased—to see Liam. "You're here!" She threw her arms around him. "We only sent out invitations a few weeks ago, but when I didn't hear back from you, I wasn't sure you got yours."

"I didn't." He might not believe in love for himself, but if Sarah did, he was damn well going to be happy for her. "But I'm glad I lucked into being here anyway. Congratulations, Sarah."

"Thank you." Her smile was so full of joy that he could almost feel it melting a hole through the frustration in the room. "It's been forever since we've been able to chat, and I really want to catch up with you on everything, but I think I'd better stitch up my dress before it turns into a full-on tear."

"I've got a sewing kit upstairs," Christie said. "I can do it right away."

"Thank you, Christie!" Sarah turned back to Liam to give him one more hug, then said, "Come find me at the reception so that we can talk before you leave town again."

After Sarah headed up the stairs with Christie, Liam and his mother were left standing alone in a room full of empty chairs and hundreds of rose petals.

"It really is good to have you home, honey." His mother's hand felt cold on his arm. "We've all missed you."

The truth was that he'd missed the lake, the mountains, the clear air. But he hadn't missed the way the knot in his gut always tightened, how it grew bigger and harder than ever inside him, whenever he was here.

When he was a child, his mother's arms had been warm, and he'd loved to sit with her while she read him books and told him fairy tales before bed. But he hadn't been a child for a very long time.

And he'd learned the hard way not to make the mistake of believing in fairy tales.

He knew she wanted him to forgive her for what she'd done so many years ago, to tell her everything was okay, that what had happened in the past didn't matter anymore. Instead, he asked, "What exactly did

Wesley's letter say, Susan?" Her eyes flashed with hurt at the way he'd used her given name. He hadn't called her Mom since he was fourteen and everything had gone to hell. He wasn't about to start now.

"Just that he was sorry, but he and Christie had decided not to get married. And that while he was gone, he trusted her to run the inn as she saw fit."

She looked away too quickly, and his chest tightened, the way it always did when he spoke with her. After all these years away from Summer Lake, he'd believed he could be in complete control of himself during Wesley's wedding weekend. But that had been when he thought it was no more than a couple of parties and the ceremony.

He was nearly certain that she was hiding something from him. "Is that all his letter said?"

His mother was an attractive woman, but as they stood together, the sunlight disappeared behind a cloud. She looked worn and sad. "I don't want to hurt you, honey. Don't you know that? I've never wanted to hurt you."

He didn't say anything in response to this non sequitur. They both knew he couldn't say anything, not if she wanted him to continue keeping her secrets, just as he had for the past twenty years.

Her shoulders rounded even further as she sighed. "Wesley said none of this was Christie's fault and that if anyone should take the blame, it was him. But you and I both know he wouldn't hurt a fly. He's always been such a good boy."

Another wave of exhaustion swept over Liam. "Don't worry," he finally told her. "I'll find out what's going on."

Looking relieved, her gaze went back to the side of his face. "Your scar looks much better. You must be using that cream I sent you. I know how much it's always bothered you."

Actually, he'd never really cared about the scar, but what was the point in clarifying things twenty years after the accident that had sliced up his face?

Before he could respond, his father poked his head into the room, obviously looking for his wife. "Liam!" Henry Kane pulled him in for a bear hug. "Welcome home. I'm glad you were able to make it after all."

His grandmother Jean was there a moment later, giving him a kiss on the cheek, then holding him still so that her wise eyes could take in far more than he'd planned to give away. Just like she always did.

"I found Liam talking with Christie a few minutes ago," Susan explained.

"Christie is a lovely girl," his grandmother said with a smile. Something about her expression shook him. The glint in her eyes looked far too much like *matchmaking* for his peace of mind.

"You've heard about Wesley and the wedding, I take it?" his father asked.

Liam nodded. "I was planning to head upstairs right now to start making some calls to see what I can find out."

"You can't stay at the reception a little longer?" his mother suggested, a hint of desperation pulling at her words. "Sarah and Calvin would love to have you here."

Knowing she was right, he pulled out his phone to send a quick text to his secretary to see if there was a note from Wesley waiting for him at his house or in his email spam folder, then went to congratulate Calvin on his new marriage.

Liam hoped his friend and his cousin could pull off the impossible—and actually make love stick.

* * *

"Was it kind of tense down there, or was it just me?" Sarah asked as Christie carefully sewed the hole closed on her wedding dress.

"It wasn't just you," Christie agreed. "Especially since Liam didn't know that Wesley and I split up. He came here expecting us to get married tomorrow."

Sarah whistled softly. "And of course Susan had to get right in the middle of it all, didn't she?"

Christie bit her tongue. She might not be marrying

into the Kane family now, but she still didn't feel right saying anything about how uncomfortable Susan made her feel. She had never been particularly warm and embracing. "Susan is just concerned about Wesley."

"I know she is. We all are. But I still don't get it," Sarah said. "You're every mother's dream daughter-in-law. She should have been thrilled that you and Wesley were engaged, instead of always acting so weird and stilted around you."

The thing was, Christie had noticed Susan acting strangely around Liam too. Completely different from the way she behaved around Wesley. Susan had always taken care of Wesley, almost to the point of being suffocatingly nurturing. With Liam, on the other hand, she'd seemed tense. Worried.

Not knowing how to fake either a smile or an easy response, Christie pretended to be busy tying off the thread on Sarah's silk gown.

"Even though we're related, I haven't seen Liam in years," Sarah mused as Christie finished up. "But Wesley and Liam were always close. I'm really surprised he didn't know about the wedding being off."

"Me too."

That was all Christie was going to admit. Definitely not that her reaction to finding Liam standing there staring at her had been more powerful than any reaction she'd had to another man.

Ever.

Even realizing he was Wesley's older brother hadn't been enough for her to stop feeling like fireworks were shooting off inside her stomach just from being in the same room with him. One look at him and she'd dropped the entire handful of rose petals she'd been holding. And when he'd put his hands on her...

Thrill bumps moved across her skin again, just from remembering how electric his touch had been.

"He sure hasn't gotten any worse looking," Sarah said. "Back in high school, pretty much everyone had a crush on him. All the girls in town wanted to be my friend in the hopes that they'd get invited to a family gathering, even though he rarely came to any of them." Sarah smoothed her hand over the fix-it job Christie had done to her dress. "I swear the scar from the car accident only made the girls want him more. Probably because of all the danger and mystery swirling around him."

"I didn't notice a scar. Where is it?"

Sarah shot her a surprised look. "It's on his left cheek. Lower down. It's hard to miss."

Christie tried to think back to those moments when he'd been holding her close, questioning her about Wesley. But all she could see in her mind were his intense eyes staring into hers. And all she could feel were butterflies. In as light a voice as she could manage, Christie asked, "Was he a total heartbreaker in high school?"

"Nope. They all wanted him, but he never dated anybody in town." Sarah shrugged. "Honestly, Liam's always been hard to read. Which only ever seemed to make women want to try to uncover his heart. It's the same old story we've all heard a million times—some poor, delusional girl out there thinks she's going to be the one to make him fall. The reformed rake brought to his knees by love."

"Definitely delusional," Christie agreed. She knew firsthand all about girls like that.

Because she'd been one of them her entire life.

Heck, she'd wanted so badly for things to work out with Wesley that she'd actually accepted his proposal of marriage. And before Wesley...well, she'd been even *more* delusional with her previous boyfriends. She'd seen only what she wanted to see—and ignored all of the warning signs.

Never again. Especially given that warning signs had started flashing bigger and brighter than ever before when she'd been talking with Liam. He was just Christie's type, in fact.

The very type that always ripped her heart out of her chest and stomped all over it.

CHAPTER FOUR

Six hours later, Christie had seen the bride and groom off on their way to the airport for their honeymoon and was saying good-bye to the final wedding guests—many of whom couldn't resist addressing the huge white elephant in the room.

"Such a lovely wedding, Christie. We're just all so sorry you won't be up there tomorrow marrying Wesley."

Ugh.

"Oh, honey, it must be so hard at your age to have to start over. We're all trying to think of any single men we can introduce you to."

Double ugh.

"You must be so overwhelmed running the inn without Wesley. I heard Liam was back home to help."

God, no.

Liam hadn't come home to help her with the inn. Ten minutes in the same room with him was enough to send her head spinning and her heart racing. Working together would surely do her in completely.

Only William Sullivan had known the right thing to say. "It doesn't matter what anyone else thinks. All that matters is that you're happy. Let me know if you need to get away in my rowboat for a little while. Sometimes there's nothing better than sitting in the middle of a quiet lake with the water and the birds and the mountains for company."

She'd hugged him so hard that he had to have been more than a little surprised by it. But he had no idea how much his words of support helped.

Finally, she was back in her room, where she was desperate to take a long, hot bath.

She reached for the zipper of her dress, knee-length green satin that played up the best of her figure and hid the worst. She hadn't told anyone that it was supposed to have been her rehearsal-dinner dress. Figuring it was better to get some use out of it after the amount of money she'd spent on it, she'd decided to wear it today.

Still, after ten-plus hours running around in it, she couldn't wait to get into a pair of leggings and a T-shirt. But when she tried to pull the zipper down, it wouldn't go. She tugged and pulled at it until her index finger was scraped sore by the small metal tab.

Was this dress cursed?

Just as she had the thought, the window in her bedroom that looked out on Main Street began to shake.

She hadn't noticed the wind earlier in the afternoon—in fact, it had been unusually still out on the water—but the weather changed so fast in the Adirondacks that the sky could go from bright blue to pelting hail in seconds.

With some help from the moonlight, she could see that the treetops weren't blowing. And the flag on the town hall was limp. But, strangely, the window was still shaking.

Wesley had fixed up this suite of rooms high under the inn's roof especially for the two of them to move into after their wedding. Sixty years ago, this bedroom had been the honeymoon suite. But only a few years later, for some reason that no one seemed to know, it had been converted to storage.

Wesley had insisted she move in a month ago, and she'd agreed, glad to have the chance to make the rooms feel like home before the wedding, rather than returning from their honeymoon to an impersonal space. But as she stood in the middle of the bedroom, she felt cold, despite having turned on the heat earlier. The small hairs on the back of her neck prickled, and a rush of air moved over her, almost as if someone had walked by.

Spinning around, she saw that she was still completely alone.

Or was she?

She'd always had a vague sense that something wasn't right about the bedroom. She'd even heard rumors during the months she'd worked at the inn that it was haunted. And though she'd laughed it off, over the past few weeks since she and Wesley had called off their wedding, she wasn't sure it was completely ridiculous anymore.

But when her stomach growled, she decided low blood sugar was the only reason she was thinking about ghosts and spirits. Her bath would have to wait until she went back downstairs and had a snack. There was leftover cake, and considering she hadn't eaten much all day, she figured she deserved a big slice. Maybe two. Plus, even though her employees had all gone home, if she was lucky she might find a guest in the common rooms downstairs who could help her unstick the zipper.

So the dress was staying on for the time being. Shoes, however, weren't going to happen again tonight. Just the thought of putting her heels back on had her wincing.

Her feet bare, she left her living room and walked out into the private hallway. Well, not so private anymore, since Wesley insisted on keeping a small suite here for Liam's visits to town—which had never happened until today. Hurrying past his door and down the stairs, she was soon pushing through the inn's kitchen door.

Where Liam was sitting on one of the stools, tucking into a piece of wedding cake.

"Hi," Christie said, wishing her voice didn't sound so breathy. "I didn't realize you were still up."

Liam's eyes quickly took in both her slightly wrinkled dress and her bare feet. For some reason, not wearing her shoes around him made the moment feel almost intimate.

Far more intimate than she had ever planned to be with Wesley's brother.

"I got hungry and thought I'd come down to get a snack," she told him when he didn't say anything, "but I didn't think anyone would be here. I don't know where you flew in from today, but since Wesley says you're always traveling overseas, I figured if it was a long-haul flight, you might be really jet-lagged."

Oh God, she was babbling. *Stop talking, Christie. Just stop.* She clamped her lips shut and tried to lift her feet to back out of the room, but they were stuck as though she'd stepped into quick-drying cement.

Liam gestured to the cake. "There's plenty."

It wasn't exactly an embossed invitation to sit down with him, but it didn't take a social genius—which she was not, by any stretch of the imagination—to see that if she ran now, she'd look guilty of something.

Like, maybe, breaking his brother's heart.

And, probably, single-handedly driving Wesley out of town.

As if she needed any help from her stomach, it growled so loudly that Liam's eyes actually widened. "When was the last time you ate?"

She looked down at her wrist, but she'd already taken off her watch in preparation for the thwarted bath. "A long time ago."

She couldn't have been more surprised when he stood up, got a clean plate off the rack, and put a large piece of cake on it. For her. "Sit down and eat. You were on your feet all day."

He'd noticed? She tried not to flush. It was so embarrassing, but with her light coloring, if she blushed it didn't just cover her cheeks, it also covered her chest. A chest that was on much better display in the green dress than usual.

Realizing she was still standing there in the most awkward way, she tried to put a smile on her face and move toward the cake. Toward Liam. Thankfully, her limbs obeyed her this time—unlike her heart, which was racing out of control again.

What was wrong with her? Why did he make her so nervous? Well, not nervous exactly, but like she was buzzing on the inside. And even worse than the fact that she clearly had no control over her stupid feelings, was that she was certain he could see her attraction to him written all over her face.

Her unfortunate reverse-poker face.

Taking the stool to the far side of the one that he had been using, she was pleasantly surprised again that he didn't sit down until she was seated. He was obviously a gentleman, like his brother and father. It should have made her more comfortable. Instead, her nerves ratcheted up another notch.

There was nothing quite like a bad boy who acted the part of a gentleman. It tended to do all sorts of ooey-gooey things to her insides.

She'd eat as fast as she could, and then she'd flee.

She was reaching for the fork when a pang landed in the pit of her empty stomach at the thought of running again. Her instinct had always been to run. From bad jobs and bad boyfriends.

But when she'd gone to break things off with Wesley, she'd vowed that she was going to change her life for the better. She'd started by throwing herself not only into Sarah and Calvin's wedding, but also into focusing on something that was all hers: the Tapping of the Maples Festival. In two weeks, she was going to put on her first big event in the Adirondacks. Even before Wesley left, she'd watched the details line up one after the other and knew in her heart just how great the event was going to be for the entire town.

Yes, she was uncomfortable sitting in the inn's kitchen with Liam. But that didn't mean she was going to let herself fold under the pressure, darn it. Not only was she going to make herself sit here and enjoy every single bite of what was supposed to have been her wedding cake, but she was also going to force herself to relax. After all, for years she'd listened to Wesley's stories about his beloved older brother and she'd wanted to meet him. At last, she was getting her chance.

"So," she said to Liam, "you said earlier that you've been on the road for a few weeks?"

"I was."

While she waited for him to say more, she finally took a bite of the cake. *Mmmmm*, it was good—half a dozen layers of chocolate cake surrounded by coconut and chocolate frosting. So delicious that she couldn't hold back a small moan as she closed her eyes to fully appreciate it. When she finally swallowed it down and opened her eyes, she was surprised to find a glass of milk in front of her. Provided by Liam.

After drinking half the glass in one gulp, she smiled and said, "Thank you. That was the perfect touch."

"You're welcome."

She swore one half of his mouth had almost quirked up as he said it, but she couldn't have proved it for a jury. It was just a sense that he might be loosening up the slightest bit.

"Where were you traveling, if you don't mind me asking?" One of the things she loved most about her job was talking to the inn's guests about their travels. She very much wanted to visit all those wondrous places she'd heard about. It was another vow she'd made to herself—that one day she would see the seven wonders outside of a book or a cable TV program.

"I've been all over Asia these past weeks."

She could tell he was a big traveler, simply by the way he said it, like it was no big deal to visit Asia. She would have been gushing like crazy about her trip and pulling out pictures.

"I've always wanted to see that part of the world," she said after another bite of cake. "Do you have a favorite country in the Far East?"

"Japan. Especially in the spring."

She leaned forward, guessing, "Were the cherry blossoms in bloom?"

"Everywhere."

She closed her eyes, trying to imagine what it must be like to stand beneath the pink blooms. "How lovely it must have been," she said, a smile on her lips at the vision in her head.

"Lovely," he echoed.

She opened her eyes and found his gaze locked on hers. His eyes were darker than she remembered them being a few minutes earlier. Even more intense. Which was saying something, because he was one of the most intense men she'd ever come across.

Wanting to go back to that space they'd just been in where things had finally felt somewhat comfortable, she said, "Wesley told me you have your own business."

His almost-smile disappeared. "I just sold it."

"Oh." She wasn't sure what she was supposed to say to that. "Is that a good thing?"

"It was time to move on."

Yes, she knew all about moving on. "Any thoughts about what you want to do next?" Feeling borderline comfortable again, she picked a chocolate crumb from the stainless-steel countertop with the tip of her left index finger and licked it off.

Of course, that was right when he said, "Look, Christie, you seem like a nice person, but I don't understand what happened with you and my brother. I need you to explain it to me. Now."

CHAPTER FIVE

Christie nearly dropped the fork in her right hand at his abrupt conversational switch. But really, how could she blame him for asking when they hadn't had a chance to talk much about it earlier? It was easy to see how much his brother meant to him.

"I'll do my best." She wanted to be honest with him, despite knowing she had to keep Wesley's secret. It was a heck of a position to be in. She put down her fork and pushed her plate away, not hungry anymore. "You probably know that Wesley and I have been friends since college."

"He always said you made him laugh."

She grinned at that. "He made me laugh too. Did he tell you the first time we met was in a nude-drawing class?"

His lips twitched a little bit again, and she found herself wishing he would let himself actually smile. But, again, his mouth flattened out before that could happen. "No, he didn't mention that."

"I probably should have known right then and

there that I wasn't cut out to be an artist when I couldn't keep a straight face while sketching the nude." When he raised an eyebrow, she realized she was getting off track. "Anyway, fast-forward ten years and I needed a job." And an escape from her mistakes. "Wesley offered me one here at the inn." She looked around the inn's kitchen, at all the upgrades she'd helped make in the past nine months. "I absolutely love working here."

"Did you and Wesley date in college?"

"No. We were just friends."

"When did that change?"

She dreaded this next part. Because this was where things got sticky and didn't totally add up—even in her own mind. But she owed him the fullest explanation she could give. "It didn't. Not really. That was the problem, in the end. I think we were both far more enamored with the idea of getting married and settling down than we were of each other."

"So you didn't love him?"

Christie knew what he was thinking, that she'd set out to hurt his brother on purpose. "Of course I love Wesley. I've loved him practically from the moment I met him." She was sitting straighter on her stool now, her shoulders back, her chin up. "But as a friend."

"How could it have taken you so long to realize this? You were engaged for months."

"You're right," she admitted. "It shouldn't have taken so long for me to figure out that marrying your brother was wrong and that neither of us should settle for anything less than the kind of love that Sarah and Calvin have for each other." A part of her couldn't believe she was saying these deeply personal things to a man she'd met only hours before. But she was sick and tired of trying to pretend that she felt something she didn't.

"So when you realized this," Liam said, "you broke it off with him."

"I was going to, but before I could, he told me he'd also finally realized he couldn't marry me. So we agreed to call off the wedding and stay friends. But then I found his note the next morning." She hated this. Hated knowing without a shadow of a doubt that Liam was going to keep pushing and pushing and pushing at her until she broke. But all she could do tonight was shake her head, feeling trapped in a terrible web. One that she'd helped to weave. "I thought we were going to have a chance to talk about things more, that we were going to stand together to tell everyone about calling off the wedding."

"Do you really expect me to believe that he left without telling you why he was leaving?" His voice was still smooth, but there was steel behind every word. Along with a determination to learn not only

Wesley's secrets…but every single one of hers too. "You've just told me he's your closest friend. So why wouldn't he have confided in you, even if you both made a mistake about getting engaged? I get that you made a promise to him, but I'll never be able to forgive you if he's hurt and you didn't give me the information I need to help him."

"I've told you everything I can!" She couldn't keep her cool any longer. She shoved away from the counter and dropped her plate and cup into the sink with a clatter. "Even things that you have no right to know, frankly, about my relationship with your brother."

But she could see from the hard, closed look on Liam's face that he didn't care about what she'd told him. Only what he was—rightly—assuming she hadn't. Didn't he realize how bad she felt about having to keep his brother's secret?

Well, no, of course he didn't. Which was why there was no point in her spending another minute down here with him. Why hadn't she just ignored her stupid grumbling stomach and stayed upstairs to take a bath?

Which was when she remembered her dress. And the stupid zipper.

Of all the people to have to ask for help. She almost groaned out loud. But knowing it was either Liam or the scissors, she turned around to face him one more time tonight.

Wishing the earth would open up and swallow her whole, she made herself say, "This is really awkward, but I'm afraid I need your help with something." She lifted her right arm slightly. "The zipper on my dress is stuck. That's partly why I came downstairs. I was hoping to find someone who could help me. Since we're the only ones up, I'd really appreciate your help."

Her request hung in the air between them for a long moment before he finally moved toward her. She shouldn't have felt like a lamb being stalked by a lion, but she most definitely did. And as he came closer, ten feet dissolving to five, then three, then a handful of inches, she had to firmly resist the urge to back up.

He'd touched her only once before now—when he'd grabbed her shoulders after the wedding to ask about Wesley—and she hadn't been able to forget the feel of his hands on her yet. She really didn't need round two to make things worse.

"Lift your arm a little more," he said softly.

That was when she made the mistake of looking up at him, and his eyes caught hers. She'd heard what he said, but her brain couldn't seem to comprehend the meaning of it. Not when he was standing this close. Not when she could finally see the faint line of a scar that cut across his face, cheek to chin. Not when she was breathing in his deliciously masculine scent, reminiscent of cedar chips and summer bonfires.

Finally, her brain registered his words and she lifted her arm. He held still just long enough for her to wonder if he was as reluctant to touch her as she was to be touched by him.

And then she felt his fingers lightly brush the side of her rib cage over her dress. She could feel her body reacting to his nearness, heat creeping across her skin, a fierce rush of desire that had no business swamping her system from nothing more than the lightest brush of his fingertips.

He worked the zipper slowly, steadily. Feeling lightheaded, she realized she was holding her breath.

"I see what's stuck. But I'm going to have to get at it from the inside." His low tones wrapped around her like velvet.

"From the inside?"

"I'm afraid so."

How she wished he was like her sisters' husbands. They made her laugh, made her groan at their jokes and love of football, and she loved them because they loved her sisters, but that was it. There were no hidden currents. No reasons she wouldn't want to be alone with them in a dark hallway. And if one of them had to reach inside her dress to fix a stuck zipper, even if they got a feel-up by accident, they would've simply laughed about it later.

But neither she nor Liam was laughing.

And she honestly wasn't sure she'd survive even one more second of his fingertips brushing over her skin.

She had to stop thinking this way. There was nothing between her and Liam. And there never would be. He was simply Wesley's brother. Getting all weird about his fingers inside her dress was crazy.

"Okay," she said as firmly as she could manage. "Go for it."

She tried to think of something, *anything* but Liam's lightly callused fingertips sliding over her. She focused on the problems they'd had ordering new silverware for the inn's dining room. She reviewed her mental files on the guest last week who'd "accidentally" packed the room's alarm clock. Heck, she went all the way back to the time when she was five and had the mumps so bad she could hardly recognize herself in the mirror.

But nothing, not one single thing she could think of, could distract her from the sensation of Liam's warm touch on her sensitive skin.

Finally, the lining of her dress shifted out of the zipper's teeth, and in one smooth motion, he pulled it all the way down, then back up.

Abruptly, he moved away. So fast that he half spun her around. She blurted, "Thank you," then shot toward the door and up the stairs to her room.

She'd vowed not to keep running. But if ever there was a time and place to run, it was now.

Because with only the slightest brush of his fingers across her skin, Liam Kane had made her feel things no other man ever had.

* * *

What was wrong with him?

If Liam had been the least bit in control of any of his senses, he would have gotten the hell out of the kitchen the minute Christie walked in. But every second he spent with her had his brain working less and less on a rational plane. Which was crazy, because he was *always* rational. Hell, he'd used his analytical mind to make millions upon millions of dollars.

She looked soft, warm, sweet. But finding out just how smooth her skin actually was…

Sweet Lord, he couldn't believe how close he'd been to kissing her. She'd just told him that she and Wesley didn't love each other. That they were just friends. So there was no barrier there.

But there were others. Big ones, like the fact that he was certain she wasn't telling him the full truth about Wesley's disappearance.

Yes, she seemed like an open book. It looked like everything she felt was written on her face. In fact, when she'd been talking about wanting love, her wistful longing had almost gotten to him. To the heart he swore he didn't have.

But he knew better than to be fooled by it. Not when painful experience had taught him that people held back as much as they could get away with.

Liam's early years as a venture capitalist had been exciting, but over the past year or so he'd tired of the scene, of dealing with people who were in it only for the win. Just as he always had been. He'd come back to Summer Lake for his brother's wedding and to prepare for his next career move, but now he realized he should have come back sooner.

His brother had needed him. And he hadn't been there for Wesley. Liam wouldn't make that mistake again.

Just as he wouldn't make the mistake of letting Christie's big eyes and sweet mouth turn him into the gullible idiot he'd sworn he'd never be for a woman.

CHAPTER SIX

Despite a late night reading through business proposals and contracts, Liam was up early. Not as early as Christie, however, who was on the phone at the registration desk. He found it hard to believe how fresh and bright she looked, considering how hard she'd obviously worked putting on Sarah and Calvin's wedding, while also keeping the inn running without Wesley.

She hadn't yet noticed him standing by the door as she said, "Mom, I'm fine." There was a little frown between her eyebrows. "Please stop worrying about me. I've told you before, it's not like I'm all alone out here. I have a lot of wonderful friends." She gave a little shake of her head, her blond hair moving around her shoulders. "Please don't come right now, and don't let any of my sisters drive up either." She lifted her eyes to the ceiling as if looking for divine intervention. "No, it's not that I don't want you to visit. Of course I do. But when you come, I want it to be for a vacation, so that you can relax on the lake. Summer will be a much better time for that. Besides, I have so much to do right now with the Tapping of the Maples Festival that I'm afraid I wouldn't get enough time to spend with you." Finally, her lips curved up slightly at the corners. "It's going great. But I'm crazy busy trying to run the inn too." Her smile fell away at whatever her mother said in response. "Wesley would be here to help me with everything if he could."

It sounded like she meant it. At the same time, there was a slight thread of irritation, but whether it was at her mother or his brother—or both—he wasn't sure.

"I know I made another bad decision," she was saying into the phone, bristling a little as she defended herself, "but I'm staying this time." Christie's voice had risen, and she was pacing the small area behind the counter. "Even though things didn't work out with Wesley, that doesn't mean I have to pack up all my things and leave my friends and my job. I really love being an innkeeper. And I love Summer Lake." Remorse—and heightened frustration—flashed across her mouth as she said, "Of course I love you all too! But I've made my decision. I'm staying." Before her mother could say anything else, Christie said, "Give my love to everyone. I'll call again soon."

She'd been firm without becoming nasty. Yet again, she'd surprised him with her strength of will.

She was a great deal tougher than anyone would ever guess, given how sweet and gentle she looked. It wasn't just her angel's face that gave that impression; it was the picture of those pink-painted toes he'd seen the night before that wouldn't leave his brain.

The inn was clearly home to her. That was why she felt comfortable coming downstairs to the kitchen without shoes on. Whereas Liam hadn't felt as though he had a home in a very long time. Although, in truth, the inn had a warmth about it now that managed to draw him in and make him want to stay, when for years he'd barely been able to come home without itching to get away again as soon as he could.

Just then, Mrs. Higgins, the inn's head chef, stepped out of the kitchen and pulled him in for a hug. "Liam! Well, aren't you a sight for sore eyes? I heard you were back but didn't get a chance to feast my eyes on you yesterday. Stand still and let me get a good look at you." Mrs. Higgins grinned at him, her eyes twinkling. "I can see that you're still the heartbreaker you always were."

Knowing better than to argue with the woman who used to change his diapers when he was a baby, he let her bring him into the kitchen, where he grabbed a piece of perfectly crisp bacon. "Are there any of your delicious scones left?"

She nodded to a tray beside her. "I just pulled a

new batch fresh from the oven. How many, sweetie?"

Only Mrs. Higgins would call him *sweetie*. And, strangely, it was okay when she did it. Because she was one of those very rare people who was just as nice as she seemed. No hidden shadows. No secrets.

"How about four?"

She raised her eyebrows. "Got a big appetite today, do you?"

"I'd like to take some out for Christie too."

Her expression softened. "Such a wonderful person, isn't she? And so good with the guests. Although I've always thought there's a little bit of wicked inside her to get out." Before he could reply to her offhand comments, she said, "Let me just add a pot of tea. It's a new maple tea that she's been experimenting with for the festival." She handed him the tray. "Her idea to launch the event is a smart one for this town, no question about it." She patted his hand. "With Wesley gone, I'm so glad you're here to help Christie take care of everything. Lord knows her load is heavy enough."

When he carried the tray out to Christie, she looked up in surprise as he placed the scones and tea in front of her. "Mrs. Higgins said these were your favorite." He had a feeling that if she knew it had been his idea, she might refuse them.

"They are. Thank you." As she picked one up, she seemed wary of him. Given the way he'd grilled her the previous night, he couldn't blame her.

Still, though jumping right back into it with her this morning wasn't the wisest choice, he needed her to know something. "My secretary found Wesley's letter."

"I knew he had to have contacted you," she said, clearly relieved to hear it. "Did he tell you anything about his whereabouts?"

"No." Damn it. "Just what he'd said in his note to my parents."

"I'm sorry. I know you were hoping for clues. We all were."

Liam felt a pang of guilt at what he wasn't telling her—that Wesley had, in fact, said more. *It's my fault. Treat Christie kindly—she deserves it.* Of course he wanted to be kind to her—but he also wanted answers as to where his brother had gone.

But since she clearly wasn't yet ready to tell him, he asked instead, "How have things been going here at the inn with him gone?"

She poured two cups of tea and handed him one. It smelled surprisingly good, like being out in the thick sugar bush behind the inn.

"Good. Busy, but good."

"Mrs. Higgins mentioned a maple festival?"

Christie's face lit up. "It's going to be wonderful." She handed him a well-designed flyer. "Three days of nonstop maple syrup, maple cookies, maple candies." She lifted her cup. "Even tea. I've found some incredible vendors over the past few weeks. I really think people are going to love being able to tap the maple trees themselves. I had someone come out and do a demonstration for me a few weeks ago, and it was really fun." She pointed to a spreadsheet in front of her. "Just a few more details to iron out and the festival should be smooth sailing in two weeks."

Liam scanned the flyer. "How are you managing to run the inn by yourself and put on this festival at the same time? Especially with Wesley gone?"

"Honestly, it hasn't been easy. But I've been pulling it all off so far." She gave him a little smile that made his heart do funny things inside his chest. "Besides, who needs sleep? I figure I can do a little reverse hibernation after the snow thaws and the festival has passed."

"What are you going to do if a ball drops?"

She was about to take a bite of her scone when his question registered. Holding it halfway to her mouth, she said, "Excuse me?"

"It's great that you've been managing to pull everything off so far. But what's going to happen when you have a problem with one of your festival suppliers and you're needed to deal with an emergency at the inn?"

Her face paled. He felt a little bad about poking

holes in her plans, but spotting problems—and solving them before they happened—was a big part of his career success.

"I suppose I'll have to deal with those issues if they come," she finally said. "And hope that they don't."

"I disagree," he said with a shake of his head. "You should hire someone to deal with the festival and focus on your job at the inn."

She dropped the scone back on the plate. "The festival is mine. I'm not hiring someone else to take it over for me when it's the first thing besides running the inn that I've ever felt really proud of."

He couldn't believe the way she continually spilled her innermost thoughts and feelings. He would never—ever—admit to anyone the kinds of things she did. How could anyone be this devoid of pretense? But that didn't change the situation she was currently in—one where it was far too easy for her to be pulled in a half-dozen different directions.

Which was why he had to say, "I'm afraid I don't see how the situation can continue for much longer. I saw the way you ran around taking care of everything yesterday at the wedding, and I can also see how much energy it takes to run the inn. I'd hate for this business to suffer because you're focused on some festival."

"First of all, Wesley trusted me with the inn while he was gone. I would never let any part of it suffer."

Last night he'd seen the same fight in her when he'd relentlessly gone after her about his brother. "Second, it's not just *some festival*. The Tapping of the Maples Festival is going to do great things for this town and the inn. And third, considering *Wesley* is the owner of the inn, I'm going to ask you to respect his wishes and let me run it as I always have."

Liam knew why Wesley hadn't told her the full truth. He'd asked Wesley to keep his involvement in the inn quiet. Just another half lie to add to all the others.

It looked like it was time for one secret less.

"Actually, Wesley and I own the inn together. All these months, you've been working for both of us."

CHAPTER SEVEN

Christie felt her eyes widen at the news. She narrowed them again as she glared at Wesley's far-too-attractive brother. It was just one surprise after another around here, wasn't it?

"Why didn't Wesley tell me you own the inn with him?"

"I never planned on coming back to run it," Liam said, "so it wasn't relevant."

Last night, he'd told her he'd sold his business in Boston and that he was looking for something new to work on. Could running the inn be what he meant? Because she wasn't at all sure that she could work with a man like him bossing her around.

"No, I suppose it wasn't relevant to *you*," she said, not bothering to keep the sarcasm from her voice. "Only to your employees, who have no idea you've been Wesley's silent partner all these years."

A muscle began jumping in his jaw, and she waited for him to defend himself, to point out that Wesley was just as much at fault for not telling her the truth. Or, possibly, to apologize for keeping her and everyone else in the dark.

Instead, he simply said, "Now that the situation has changed, I'll need you to show me everything about running the inn."

She couldn't stop her eyes from widening again at the thought of having to spend big chunks of time in close quarters with Liam.

Just then, a couple came down the stairs carrying a baby. "I hope we didn't keep anyone up last night," the woman said. "Janie has some trouble sleeping out of her usual crib." Her husband was trying to manage all of their bags and the car seat and bottles on his own, but he was clearly having a difficult time.

Christie was incredibly glad for a reason to move away from Liam. "Don't worry about a thing. Your room was in the corner, and I'm sure no one heard her crying. If it would help, I'd love to hold Janie for a moment while you get your things packed up and into the car."

"Oh, that would be wonderful. Thank you!"

Christie's heart squeezed as she looked down at the baby's big blue eyes and sweet little mouth. "Hey there, pretty girl. I hear you're quite the traveler." When the baby started to fuss, Christie made funny faces to get her giggling, then told her mother, "The two of us will be just fine until you have your hands free again."

When the phone behind the counter rang, Christie shifted the baby to her right hip and picked up the line.

"Absolutely," she said to the caller, "we'd love to be a part of your wedding plans in July. I'm a little bit tied up now, could I call you back in a few—" She paused, listened. "Oh, I see. You need to do it right this second?" She looked over at Liam, who was the only one in the room without his hands currently full, and a devil landed on her shoulder. Before she could stop herself, she said, "I'd be more than happy to book it all with you right now. Could I put you on hold for ten seconds and then we'll get started?"

When they agreed, she put the phone down, walked over to her new surprise boss, and handed him the baby. "Keep her entertained for a few minutes, would you?"

Liam looked utterly, supremely uncomfortable. But, amazingly, the little girl snuggled in closer to him, her soft blond hair falling across his upper arm as she gave him an adoring coo. Christie almost snorted at how quickly he had the baby caught up in his spell.

By the time she got off the phone with another summer wedding booked, the couple and their baby were gone. But Liam remained.

She'd never pushed at a boss like that, had never deliberately gone and done something she knew would get her in trouble. But, for some crazy reason, he'd brought that out in her. A little bit of the daredevil. It hadn't been on any kind of grand scale, but frankly, she was more than a little surprised to realize it was there at all.

And, even crazier, instead of apologizing for it, she let another devil jump onto her other shoulder. "I've decided how we should start your training."

He raised an eyebrow. "How?"

"By cleaning the bathrooms."

⋆ ⋆ ⋆

Liam didn't like *cute*. He never had.

He wanted the people he worked with—men and women both—to be direct. To the point. But never, ever cute. So why, then, was he constantly wanting to grin around this woman?

Liam hadn't shadowed anyone since his first college internship at a venture house. But given that he was considering an offer to acquire several more lakefront inns throughout the Northeast, hands-on was the way to go. He'd need to understand every single part of the business in order to have a true sense of whether he could run it at peak profitability. Starting with the bathrooms.

"Sounds good to me."

"It does?" She looked more than a little thwarted

by his easy agreement. Had she been hoping to get to him?

This time, he was the one letting a grin loose before he knew it was coming—or could stop it.

"I didn't think I'd ever see it," she said, so softly he almost didn't hear.

He shouldn't want to move closer. But it seemed that some things were uncontrollable, his reaction to her most of all. "What didn't you think you'd see?"

"Your smile."

As thrown off his game as he'd ever been, he told her, "People don't say things like that."

"I have no edit button," she agreed as embarrassment shot across her face. "I obviously need one."

Right then, a woman who was probably in her early twenties came in. "Sorry I'm a few minutes late. Last night's snow made it harder than I thought to get into town."

Christie introduced him to Alice, but as she stepped away from the front desk, her cheeks were still pink as she met his eyes. "Looks like you and I are free to head upstairs."

Hating the way the light had gone out of her eyes, he said, "I spoke out of turn just now, Christie."

She simply shrugged, trying to act like it was no big deal. But he could tell that it was, when she said the one thing guaranteed to make sure he paid for the way he'd just spoken to her.

"I'll let you tackle the toilets."

* * *

"No one is ever going to complain about our standards of cleanliness," he told her a while later. "That's for sure."

Liam's face hadn't been this close to the porcelain since his early teenage drinking days. And though he worked out daily, he hadn't done this kind of awkward physical work in a very long time either. The truth was, he rarely even had to make his own bed. Either his housekeeper took care of it, or he was in a hotel with service.

One thing was certain: He'd be leaving way bigger tips in the future.

Christie didn't respond, but from her profile as she wiped down the bathtub, he could see a small smile was finally back on her face. Her natural beauty was radiant enough that even with her hair pulled back into a ponytail and a smear of soap across her left cheek, he couldn't take his eyes off her.

Being down on his knees on one of the inn's bathroom floors should have been as strange as it got in Liam's world. But it was far stranger to realize that the inside of his chest felt off-kilter too. As though muscles that had rarely been worked were trying to move again.

She looked over her shoulder at what he'd done. "You're really good at that, you know. Thank you for giving it your all."

She held out a hand to help him up off his knees, and before he could think better of it, he took it and stood. But he didn't immediately let her go. How could he when the touch of her skin sent electric sparks of heat shooting through him—and her lips had opened into a tempting *O* of surprise?

Maybe if he'd had any control whatsoever around her, he would have dropped her hand and gotten the hell out of the too-small bathroom. Instead, he found himself reaching out with his free hand to brush away the bubbles on her cheek.

He didn't just hear her swift intake of breath; he felt it reverberate through her jaw to his hand. All he could think was how soft her skin was.

And how badly he wanted to touch her again.

"You had some soap on your face." His explanation sounded strangled. He wouldn't have recognized the voice as his own if he hadn't felt it vibrate in his throat.

"Thank you for cleaning it off."

Her breathy words did crazy stuff to his insides, had him thinking even crazier things. Like would her lips be as soft as her skin? And would they taste like the first ray of sunlight in spring?

Liam had lived a perfectly controlled life for nearly twenty years. But in less than twenty-four hours, Christie Hayden was destroying that control. Without even trying.

Abruptly, she took a step back. "Lunch. We missed lunch." Her cheeks were far more flushed than they'd been before they touched. She covered them with her hands as if she could somehow hide her reaction from him. "I'll go see what Mrs. Higgins can whip up for us."

She turned and fled the room. But Liam stayed exactly where he was.

His reaction to her was unacceptable. She was not only his brother's ex-fiancée, she was also his employee. Liam had never mixed business with pleasure. He wouldn't start now. Not only did he need Christie to keep running the inn during Wesley's absence, but working closely with her was the best way to learn the hotel business top to bottom. And he needed more experiential data in hand before making any acquisition decisions for the other inns he was considering.

Leaning on the sink, he stared at himself in the mirror he'd cleaned with his own two hands. Coming back to Summer Lake had never been easy. He'd prepared himself for dealing with his family. With his mother, especially.

If only he'd known that the real person he should have prepared himself for was Christie. For her sweet smiles. For her breathtaking beauty. For her surprising strength. And for her charm that masqueraded as guileless honesty.

In the end, that was the most dangerous thing of all about her. He could protect himself from everything else, even the attraction that sparked between them like a live wire. But the seeming purity of her responses, the way she spoke every thought and feeling aloud regardless of whether it helped or hurt her…

Liam hadn't believed there was a woman alive who possessed those qualities.

But despite how sweet Christie seemed, he couldn't let himself forget that she still hadn't come completely clean with him about Wesley.

CHAPTER EIGHT

With renewed determination to find out what he needed to know about his brother—and not let attraction derail him again—Liam headed downstairs to the kitchen and slid into a seat across the table from Christie. She was sitting by a small window that looked out on the lake, and there were two bowls of soup on the table. It was a clear, bright day, and the layers of ice on the surface of the lake had begun to melt beneath the sun's warmth. For all the power of winter's cold and ice, it could hold out only so long against the growing heat of spring.

"I've spoken with Wesley's other friends," he said in a low voice. "None of them know where he is."

She blinked up at him in obvious surprise at his sudden shift back to his brother, then said, "He obviously doesn't want to be found." A whole host of emotions flitted across her face. Regret. Frustration. And finally, resignation. "I don't know all of his reasons for what he did. But what I do know, I can't tell you. I'm sorry."

"If he's in trouble," Liam said, "I want to help him. I need to help him."

She closed her eyes tightly for a moment, then reopened them with a shake of her head. "He made me promise not to tell anyone his reasons."

Liam leaned in closer to say, "He couldn't have meant me. I'm his brother."

"I'm really sorry, Liam." Regret seemed to hang on her every word. "But he told me he needed time. I'm trying to give it to him."

Though he wasn't at all satisfied with her response, he asked, "Why did you come here, Christie?" He told himself he simply wanted to know because he was on a fact-finding mission about his brother.

She didn't answer for a long moment. Finally, she said, "I was ready for a change."

There was nothing quite like hearing his own words from last night come back at him—and knowing them for the nonsense they were. If he was going to get any more out of her, it was obvious that he was going to have to give a little more of himself first.

"Fair is fair," he said softly. "Last night, you wanted to know why I sold my business. After fifteen years of launching new companies for other people, I started to feel like I've learned everything there is to know about venture capital. I'm ready for a new challenge. I want my own business. That's why I bought the inn with

Wesley. Because I knew it wouldn't be long before I'd be here learning the business, top to bottom." And maybe, even though the entire idea was nuts, he'd started to wonder if he'd bought the inn because he wanted a reason to come back home one day.

"Thank you for telling me that."

Even when they were at odds with each other, she was polite. Sweet. "It's going to be your turn to answer my question soon, but we should eat first." He didn't like that she hadn't had so much as a sip of soup yet. He buttered a big piece of bread and slid it over to her. "I've never had such good bread anywhere. Mrs. Higgins puts even the Parisian bakers to shame."

She stared at him for a long moment. Almost as if she wasn't used to having a man look out for her this way—simple things like making sure she didn't skip meals. Finally, she reached for it and took a small bite. "Tell me about Paris while we eat."

It was clear that neither of them had forgotten she owed him an answer to his question about why she'd come to Summer Lake. But first, he wanted her to replenish some of those calories she'd burned off while cleaning the inn's bedrooms like the Energizer Bunny.

"The architecture is amazing. Every time I go back, I'm surprised all over again by just how much visual stimulation there is." He'd never been asked to put his feelings about Paris into words before, and he found that he was discovering his feelings at the same time as he was sharing them with Christie. "Throughout Europe, history is all around you, every moment of every day. Past and present, they all come together with perfect fluidity, from the ancient stone walls of the Louvre to the postmodern pyramid in the middle of its courtyard."

Her eyes lit with interest. And, if he wasn't mistaken, with longing. "I've read so many books about Paris that sometimes I feel like I've been there. I've dreamed about walking along the Seine, about standing in the middle of Notre Dame Cathedral looking up at the stained glass, and then going for coffee at Les Deux Magots to try to hear echoes of the great writers in the walls." She cocked her head as she looked at him. "Summer Lake must seem so small compared to everywhere you've been."

"It's certainly small," he agreed, "but this part of the world is nice too."

"Even compared to Paris? Or Rome?"

"There are so many beautiful places that if you tried to rank them, you'd go a little crazy."

He could see the stars in her eyes as she tried to imagine all that beauty. It was obvious how badly she wanted to travel and see the world. So, then, why hadn't she? He knew plenty of people who could barely scrape together the money for plane fare, but that didn't stop them from traveling.

More questions were on the tip of his tongue, but upstairs in the bathroom, he'd been schooling himself on how to proceed from here on out. *Keep your distance. Don't get any closer.* Which meant keeping personal questions that had nothing to do with Wesley's disappearance to himself.

She put down her spoon and used a piece of bread to wipe her bowl clean before popping it into her mouth. When she looked up again, her cheeks turned that lovely shade of pink he was liking far too much for either of their sakes. She quickly chewed and swallowed. "I usually have much better table manners than this. Wesley and I have known each other for so long that we're pretty informal with each other. I guess I forgot for a moment that you and I have only just met."

Something inside his chest grew warm at the knowledge that she was comfortable with him. "Actually, I think you're on to something." He grabbed the heel off the loaf and broke it in half, using it to clean his bowl just as she had.

They ate in silence for a few minutes before she said, "You asked me at the beginning of lunch why I came to Summer Lake, and I don't want you to think I make it a habit not to answer direct questions. The quick and dirty answer is that I needed a fresh start."

"There are a lot of places you could have started over, rather than at an inn in the middle of the Adirondacks."

"Sometimes it's good to go where no one knows anything about you."

"You knew Wesley," he reminded her.

"He'd told me about Summer Lake for years and swore that if I ever came to visit, I wouldn't want to leave. Maybe that's what took me so long to finally come here. Maybe I was afraid to fall in love with someplace I couldn't easily pick up and run from."

There she went again, saying things that most people wouldn't dare say out loud. Heck, most people wouldn't even admit something like that to themselves—that they always ran. That they were afraid.

There were so many questions he still wanted to ask. But he knew better, knew that learning more about her would only draw him more deeply toward her. And he couldn't let that happen. Couldn't let himself fall for her.

"Alice needs to head home soon." She pushed her chair back and cleared their empty plates from the table to put them in the commercial dishwasher. "I should probably check on the front desk, make sure nothing has come up that she needs me to deal with before she leaves. Unless you want to look over my shoulder at the front desk, I'm sure you have more important things to take care of this afternoon."

He got the picture. She wanted to get rid of him for a little while. And the truth was, he needed a break too. From her smile, from her fresh scent, from the way he wanted to run his fingers over the strands of hair that had escaped her ponytail to see if they felt as silky as they looked.

"You've taught me a lot today." Despite his need to remain on guard with her, he couldn't deny that she was very good at her job. "Thank you."

Instead of accepting his compliment, she gave him a guilty look. "Something tells me you already knew how to clean a toilet. And the truth is, I might have been a little bit upset with you earlier. I shouldn't have wasted so much of your time with cleaning the rooms."

"I appreciate you telling me that, but you didn't waste a single second of my time. I need to learn this inn from the ground up, and that's what you were showing me. Most people wouldn't have the guts to hand me rubber gloves and a scrubber."

He could easily read the surprise on her face as she flushed and said, "Okay then, let me know if you need anything else today. Otherwise, I'll see you tomorrow. And this time, you have my solemn vow that I won't ask you to get on your knees with a scrub brush."

But as she walked away, Liam found himself having the dangerous thought that it would be more than worth it if she did, if only so he could spend more time with her.

CHAPTER NINE

There shouldn't have been anything exciting about bumping into each other as they made beds and vacuumed floors, but even doing completely mundane tasks with Liam got Christie's heart moving too fast.

Especially since she was still reeling from that one beautiful, heart-stopping smile that he'd given her at the registration desk earlier that morning.

She still couldn't believe how good he'd been about doing whatever she tasked him with. He hadn't once acted too important for cleaning bathrooms or dusting. Even Wesley complained about cleaning rooms on days when they were short-staffed. But Liam had simply gotten to work and done a heck of a job. Maybe even a better job than she, given how distracted she'd been by his nearness.

But the craziest thing of all was not so much that she could feel herself falling under his spell—it was that moment in the guest room when he'd seemed just as captivated by her. As though brushing soap off her cheek had been only an excuse to touch her.

On her way to the front desk, Christie caught sight of herself in a hall mirror. Her eyes were bright, her cheeks were flushed, and her hair looked like she'd been driving in a convertible with the top down all afternoon.

She must be crazy to think Liam was attracted to her, she thought as she pulled out her hair band and tried to quickly finger-comb her hair. She didn't have to see pictures of the women he dated to guess his type. Polished. Highly educated. Perfect.

Not that it mattered, she reminded herself. Because even if he was attracted to her, and even if Wesley's disappearance hadn't been hanging awkwardly between them, she still wouldn't allow herself to go near him with a ten-foot pole.

Once upon a time, Liam's mysteriousness, and the hints of pain in his eyes, would have had her giving herself over to him, like a modern-day beauty to the beast, turning herself inside out to save him—and win his love. Only, all the while, she'd inevitably end up losing herself more and more. Until the day he decided he was done with her.

Christie knew all about losing, about trying to rebuild herself into something whole again. A look back into her relationship file told a clear-cut story. One handsome, dangerously mysterious man after another. Wesley had been the only deviation in the pattern, but that was only because she'd been trying to swing as far as she could in the opposite direction.

She absolutely refused to fall into the old trap again, couldn't repeat the same cycle she knew by heart. Especially not when one Kane brother had already left her in the lurch.

For once in her life, she was going to be strong and smart rather than letting her contrary heart lead the way. She was going to save her emotions for a man who was capable of returning them.

"Sorry I've been gone all day, Alice," she said as she approached the desk.

"Don't worry about it," Alice said, and then, "Hey, did you do something to your hair? Or are you wearing different makeup?"

"No. Why?"

Alice studied her a little more closely. "Maybe it's just that your cheeks are flushed from cleaning rooms. It's practically a workout the way you do it."

Oh God, she hoped Alice wouldn't put two and two together and realize what—who—was actually responsible for her flushed cheeks. She could only imagine the gossip in town if people thought she was already drooling over her ex-fiancé's older brother…

"You know what?" Christie said as she grabbed her down coat. "We're pretty low on fire logs. If you don't need me at the front desk, I'll head out and bring some in before you go for the day."

"It's really cold out there," Alice said, "and we probably have enough logs to last the next couple of days."

But Christie had already shoved her feet into her snow boots and was heading outside. The crisp, cold air shocked the breath out of her for a moment. But instead of turning around and heading back into the warmth of the inn, she was glad for the way the cold woke her up.

Because she couldn't daydream about impossible happily-ever-afters—or the most beautiful smile she'd ever seen—in this kind of weather.

* * *

Liam was surprised to find his father at home, lifting a heavy sander out of his truck instead of off working one of his construction jobs around the lake. "I've got the other side, Dad."

Neither of them said anything more until they'd carried the sander into the house and up the stairs to his parents' bedroom. Most of the furniture had been taken out. Only the bed frame and mattresses were propped against the wall.

After they put down the sander, his father said, "I could use an extra hand with the bed too, if you don't mind."

When Liam was a kid, he and Wesley had played hide-and-seek in the huge king sleigh bed. His father had made the head- and footboards out of a birch tree he'd cut down himself. Growing up, Liam had thought his father was the biggest, strongest man in the world. Taking in his father's gray hair and slightly gnarled knuckles, he wondered when that had changed. He hadn't spent much time with his father since leaving for college. Suddenly, Liam realized it was one of the things he regretted most.

"I'm happy to help," Liam told him.

Moving the heavy frame was a two-man job. No question about it, he thought when his muscles complained at the weight, he had spent too much time behind a computer these past years. As a boy growing up in Summer Lake, he'd always been outside. Boston had plenty of nice spots, but nothing compared to his hometown.

"Couldn't have done that without you," his father said after they'd cleared out the room. "I've been meaning to refinish these floors for a long time. Figured since work is a little slow right now, it would give me a chance to finally get your mother off my back. You know how she's been wanting me to redo these floors since you were in high school."

Liam was about to suggest they head down to the kitchen to discuss Wesley's possible whereabouts when his mother called up the stairs, "Liam? Henry? Are you up there?"

Liam thought he saw his father's shoulders tense and his mouth tighten at the corners. That made two of them.

Susan was standing in front of them before either man could reply. "Oh good, I'm glad you're here, honey," she said to him, and then to his father, "I hope you didn't scratch any of the walls getting that bed frame out."

"We were careful, Susan," Henry replied in a flat voice.

Odd. Liam had never heard his father respond to his mother like that. What was going on here? First, Wesley disappeared. And now, his father was practically standing up to his mother. If Liam added in the way Christie kept getting under his skin, it was starting to feel like the earth was shifting on its axis.

His mother raised her eyebrows at Henry's curt reply before reaching out and putting a hand on Liam's arm. "When I saw your car, I was hoping you were here to tell us that you've heard from Wesley."

Regardless of how he felt about his mother, the hope in her eyes was difficult to see. Especially when he didn't have any good news for her. "He did send me a letter. Similar to the one he left you." He ran a hand through his hair, using the movement as an excuse to shift away from his mother's touch. "Unfortunately, he didn't say where he was going or for how long."

Susan's face fell. "How could he just leave us all? It isn't like Wesley to do something like that."

Without an answer for his clearly distraught mother, Liam could relay only the information he did have. "I've spoken with several of Wesley's friends, and none of them have heard from him either."

"I can't help but think that none of this would have happened if Christie hadn't come here. Obviously, things weren't good between them. Perhaps that's why he felt he had to leave."

An instinctive urge to defend Christie rose inside him. But his normally mild-mannered, quiet father beat him to it. "That's ridiculous, Susan. He adored Christie. Just like the rest of us do."

"Ridiculous? *Adored?*" His mother's color was high. "He was fine before they got engaged. Everything was just fine."

"No," his father countered, "everything was not *just fine*. And instead of blaming Christie for hurting your son, you need to open your eyes and give her credit for single-handedly holding things together at the inn."

Blinking rapidly in surprise, Susan turned to Liam for support. "Now that you're here, you can take over the inn for a while, can't you, honey?"

"I spent the morning working with her and can tell you firsthand that Christie is an excellent innkeeper. I have no intention of taking over for her or replacing her." Deciding to end the conversation—and this whole poorly thought-out visit—Liam turned toward the stairs. His father followed him, putting a hand on his arm before he could walk away.

"Thanks for the help, son. I'll be by the inn soon to see if you need me to return the favor and to catch up on what you've been up to." In a lower voice, he added, "I know this might sound strange, but unlike your mother, I'm not too worried about Wesley. Sometimes you need some distance to see things more clearly. Perhaps that's all this is for him—a chance to finally see things for what they are."

Too quickly, his mother was there again, following them down the stairs. "Don't go yet, honey. I've barely had a chance to talk to you since you've been back."

Even if Liam had wanted to stay, the workload at the inn was tremendous. "I've got to get back to see where I can pitch in."

Liam was almost all the way out to his car when his father called, "Your mother is sorry about her outburst. Please don't say anything to Christie about it."

* * *

"How dare you apologize for me!" Susan barely held in

her outburst until Liam was gone.

"Someone needed to apologize," Henry shot back. "You were completely out of line talking that way about Christie."

"Why are you speaking to me like this? I'm not the one who hurt Wesley so badly that he felt he had no choice but to leave town."

"Whatever drove him away, it wasn't Christie." Her husband's normally cheerful, relaxed expression had settled firmly into disgust. With her. "Couldn't you see how upset she was when she gave us the news that they'd called off their engagement—and that they never should have made the mistake of getting engaged at all? She has never been anything but honest with us and everyone else in this town. Wesley should have stayed to face the music with her."

How could he possibly talk that way about their son? Susan went back on the attack. "You should be worried about Wesley, not some girl we barely know. What if all along she was seducing him into giving her control of the inn?"

Henry's bark of laughter at the word *seduce* shocked her. "Seduce him? Are you kidding? There wasn't an ounce of spark between the two of them. You had to see that. If you ask me, not getting married was the best thing they could have done."

God, how she hated his talk of *sparks*. The sparks

used to burn so brightly for her and Henry. Where had those sparks gone? For so long, she'd held out hope that they would come back. But now that Wesley was gone, sniping and fighting had replaced the heavy silences between them.

Leaving her nearly all out of hope.

CHAPTER TEN

The next morning, Christie woke shivering. The heat was on, and she hadn't kicked off the covers, but her bedroom was strangely cold again.

She half expected to see her breath in the air as she reluctantly got out of bed. She'd left the doors open to the living room when she went to sleep, and the heat should have come into her bedroom. Instead, it was as if there was some kind of invisible barrier there keeping the warmth out…and holding the icy cold in.

Over the past nine months, when she'd heard stories about the inn being haunted, she'd discounted them as small-town folklore. The thing was, ever since moving into the newly redone top-floor suite, she'd started to wonder if they might possibly be true.

Of course, once she stepped into the shower and let the water warm her up the rest of the way, she had to laugh at herself. The inn wasn't haunted. She was just tired from staying up and working on details for the festival long after everyone at the inn was asleep. With another big day ahead of her—one in which she needed to be at her best so that she didn't fall any deeper under Liam's spell while she trained him on the inn's day-to-day routine—she forcefully brushed the remaining suspicions from her mind.

The past few weeks had been nuts. Between Sarah and Calvin's wedding and Liam's appearance, she felt like she'd been juggling half a dozen slick and slippery pins while balancing a plate on the tip of her nose.

Today, she vowed, was going to be better.

Not just better, she thought as she got out of the shower and wrapped a towel around herself. Today was going to be *great*. And the breathtakingly beautiful view out the window proved it. The sun was rising over the snow-dusted lake, yellows and golds and pinks radiating from the sky to the icy treetops on the mountains that surrounded Summer Lake.

For all that she longed to see the seven wonders and smell the salty scent of the ocean as it crashed on coasts all over the world, Summer Lake would always be a haven for her soul, for her dreams.

Liam being here and Wesley being gone didn't change that. This small town, her friends, her career as innkeeper—they were all important parts of her new life. She'd just have to hold out hope that one day she'd find the missing pieces: a husband who loved her as much as she loved him, and children to cuddle and play with and love the way her parents loved her.

Oh yes, it was going to be a fantastic day. She'd make sure of it. Any challenges that came her way, she'd face head on with a smile and courage. No matter what.

* * *

All morning long, while Liam worked in the small office behind the registration desk, Christie had been moving between the front desk and the dining room to oversee their guests' breakfasts and departures. She was cheerful, but not overly talkative. Interested without being intrusive. All in all, the perfect innkeeper.

He had to hand it to Wesley; his brother had done a great job hiring her to manage the inn. What she might have lacked in experience nine months ago, she'd certainly made up for with raw energy and sheer willingness to learn.

All night, he'd gone over the half-dozen good reasons to keep his distance. Foremost among them was that it was a small town, she was his brother's ex-fiancée, and he didn't mix business and pleasure. But Liam knew better than to think that any of these were strong enough to keep their attraction at bay.

In the end, the only barrier strong enough to do that was the fact that he despised secrets of any kind.

Christie's concern—and love—for his brother

shone through so clearly that Liam didn't doubt she was keeping the secret because she loved Wesley and not because it particularly served her. If anything, he could see the way his brother's secret weighed her down. But she'd kept it anyway, even though Liam had told her over and over that he needed to know. And in the end, that was what he couldn't allow himself to forget. Not when secrets had done so much to destroy his past.

"Christie." A man's low voice carried through to the back office. "You don't know how much I've missed seeing your pretty face."

"Mark?" She sounded utterly taken aback. "What are you doing here?"

"I came to see you, baby. It wasn't easy to find this little town after a snowstorm, but you're worth it."

"How is your wife?" Christie's voice held a sharp edge Liam hadn't heard before. But as she asked, "And your children?" he realized the edge was dulled with pain.

He didn't know yet who the man was to Christie. But the sure knowledge that he'd hurt her—and the way he'd called her *baby*—had Liam dropping the file he'd been reading and curling his hands into fists.

"That's what I came here to tell you," the guy said. "My wife and I are getting a divorce. I've been missing you so much, I couldn't wait any longer to come find you."

Liam reeled from the implications. Had Christie been seeing this man while he was married? His entire body tensed at the thought that she'd broken his one utterly unbreakable rule: Never get involved with someone who was married.

"I know you're probably still a little mad at me," the man continued in a cajoling voice. "But the truth is, I didn't realize until you were gone just how good you were for me. No one has ever taken care of me like you do." Liam could barely remain in his seat. Regardless of what Christie's relationship had been with this guy, Liam wanted to rush into the entry and ram his fist through Mark's face as he said, "Tell me how I can win you back."

But before Liam could jump to her defense, she said, "Do you really want to know?"

"I really do, baby."

"Go home. Tell your wife you're sorry you've been such a terrible husband and father and hug your kids. You don't want me. You only want what you can't have."

"Christie, I know you don't mean that."

Liam didn't like the edge that had crept into the man's tone. At last, he left the shadows. "Is there a problem?" He didn't waste much time looking at Mark, besides confirming that he was scum. Polished and well dressed, but scum nonetheless.

Clearly flustered and embarrassed as she realized that he'd overheard everything, she said, "I was just telling Mark that I needed to get back to work. Right away."

Her old lover's eyes moved between the two of them, narrowing before he returned his gaze to her. "When do you get off? I'll wait for you so that we can talk privately."

Before he could think about what he was doing, Liam put a protective hand on the small of her back. Though her warmth instantly permeated his hand, she stiffened at his touch, then shifted to the side so that she was just out of his reach.

He shouldn't have touched her so intimately, but he hadn't been able to stop himself. No matter who she'd slept with, or how wrong it had been, it was pure instinct to want to protect her. Which was why he remained standing at her side. If she needed him to bodily throw this guy out, he'd be more than happy to take care of it.

"My schedule is really busy right now," she said. "I can't—"

"I came all this way," Mark whined. "At least hear me out. Just let me take you somewhere private tonight to explain everything to you. To try to make you understand."

With a resigned look on her face, she said, "I have a meeting tonight, but I might be able to spare a few minutes this afternoon."

Mark looked triumphant as he said, "Tell me when and where, and I'll be there. Your terms this time."

"Four p.m. Follow the signs to the public dock. I'll meet you out there."

His eyes grew big. "Are you kidding? It's freezing out there. Can't we meet somewhere warmer?"

"I thought you said they were my terms this time?"

He did a quick double take, almost as though he didn't quite recognize the woman standing in front of him. Or her strength. "Okay," he said, putting his hands up. "You're right. I'll be there."

Christie held herself perfectly still until he left the inn. Only then did she let her breath go slowly, her shoulders dropping slightly from her battle-ready position.

Liam half expected her to make an excuse about what had just happened, to try to spin it into something it wasn't. But he should have known better. Because Christie not only didn't act like other people—she also didn't seem to know how to brush *awkward* under the rug like anyone else.

"I'm really sorry about that," she said softly. "I'm just glad no guests came in while he was here."

Twenty years ago, Liam had learned how quickly

things could change in fifteen short minutes. How his mother could go from being the person he loved and trusted most in the world to a virtual stranger. He'd vowed to keep himself far out of the path of any emotions that might put him back in that teenager's shoes again.

Since meeting Christie, however, pushing his feelings away had been a surprisingly difficult task. But he'd already made the mistake of touching her today. He couldn't afford any more mistakes. Especially given what he'd just learned—that she'd been the *other woman.*

What if one of Mark's kids had caught him with Christie? It would have scarred them for life.

A part of Liam wanted to lash out at her for making such a bad decision when it came to being with Mark, even if their relationship was in the past. But he forced himself to hold those words back and focus on business instead. "I've been reviewing the inn's files. I have a few questions for you."

She raised her eyebrows at his abrupt change of subject. "Is that something they teach you in business school? To act like nothing happened when we all know it just did?"

No one he worked with had ever been this bold, or this up front with him. But he knew better than to let himself get so riled up about whom she dated. "Your personal life is personal." The intense effort it was taking not to let himself get emotionally involved with her made his words hard. "And so is mine."

For a moment, he thought she might push back again. But then she simply nodded, one tight dip of her head, and said, "Which files do you have questions about?"

Though he'd gotten exactly what he'd said he wanted, he couldn't help but regret the distance between them as they pored over spreadsheets and files. Just as he couldn't help but say, when four o'clock approached, "I don't think you should meet Mark this afternoon."

Her eyes met his, no longer cool, but obviously irritated by his intrusion into her life. A personal life that he'd told her just hours ago he wanted nothing to do with—when now he was on the verge of playing the role of her bodyguard.

"Thank you for your concern," she said carefully, "but I can take care of myself."

Knowing he should back off, but finding it impossible, he tried again. "If something happened to you, Wesley would never forgive me."

"Ah. Yes. Wesley." Another flash of irritation crossed her face. "Well, he isn't here to stop me, is he?"

And clearly, as she grabbed both her coat and her bag of knitting for the group meeting that night, then practically slammed the door in Liam's face, he'd better not either.

* * *

"That guy from the inn is watching us, isn't he?" Mark said.

For a moment, she'd thought Liam was going to insist on coming out here with her. And even though she wouldn't have let him, she couldn't deny that a part of her hoped he *was* in fact watching over her, given that Mark's behavior was suddenly making her more than a little nervous.

"What Liam does is his own business," was all she said to her ex, however.

Liam had also said that her personal life was supposed to be hers alone. But even as he'd said it, she'd known that he was disgusted by the conversation he'd heard. And who wouldn't be? Mark had been married while they'd dated. Though she hadn't known it at the time, it still made her sick to her stomach to think about the part she'd played in the betrayal of his wife—no matter how unwitting.

"I don't like the way he looked at you," her ex said, as if he had any claim to her at all.

Christie stared at him in shock. Had she really been in love with him? Or had she just been in love with a fantasy of the perfect man? Because it was almost funny just how imperfect Mark had proved himself to be.

Maybe next time around, instead of searching for *perfect*, she should deliberately look for *imperfect* so that things could only get better, instead of worse. The thought had her mouth moving up into an unexpected smile.

"I've missed you so much," Mark said, brushing her cheek with the backs of his knuckles.

A year ago, she would have nuzzled into his caress, rather than flinching and pulling away. But things had changed.

She had changed.

"I need to get back to the inn. I just came out here to tell you that I'm not going to get back together with you. Ever."

Anger simmered in the eyes that she'd once looked to for approval. For what she'd thought was love. But he quickly banked it as he tried to give her a caring look. "I remember the way you cried when you found out about my wife. You can't have gotten over me that quickly."

"I cried because I was ashamed of what I'd done." How could he still not see that?

"Oh, baby, you weren't to blame for anything. Dating you on the side was the only way we could be together. But now we won't have to hide our love from anyone."

He was reaching for her again, but before he could touch her, she backed even farther away. Liam had been right about one thing—coming here to try to talk some sense into Mark had been a mistake.

"I don't love you. How could I, when you don't know what love really means?" The wind whipped up around them, and she pulled her coat more tightly around her.

"And you think you do?" Now that he knew he'd struck out with her once and for all, his laugh was harsh. And pitying. "Do you really think there's a man out there who is ever going to be able to live up to your fairy tale?"

She wished with all her heart that she'd never met him, never wasted two years of her life with him. "There's a big difference between lying about every single thing for two years and wanting a fairy tale." With the wind whipping her hair and clothes around her on the public dock, she let the anger drain away. The man standing before her simply wasn't worth it. "Good-bye, Mark. Good luck with your marriage."

* * *

Liam kept his eyes trained on Mark until he got into his car and sped away too fast on Summer Lake's icy roads. The whole time Christie had been out there with that scumbag, Liam hadn't been able to breathe properly.

He didn't realize his mother had come into the inn and was standing beside him, following his line of vision out the window, until she said, "Is everything all right, honey?"

Hell no, everything wasn't all right. He was thinking far too much, far too often, about Christie. *Wanting* her far too much, far too often.

"I was just thinking about the inn's staff," was an honest, if incomplete, answer.

He moved away from the window, and she walked with him over to the registration desk. Only a coward would pray for a guest to walk in asking for help right now. And, unfortunately, only a lucky coward would see that prayer answered.

"About what happened over at the house yesterday," she said. "You shouldn't have had to see your father and me behave like that. Henry is a little tense lately. But he really appreciated your help moving the heavy furniture out of the room."

Not wanting to get anywhere near the middle of their relationship, he said, "Glad I could help," and then, "How's his business going?"

"Good. More and more people are moving here from the city who want to build or remodel, although he's increasingly picky about which projects he'll take on."

"And your graphic design clients?"

"I'm still working for about as many as I did when you lived at home." She looked a little nervous. "Speaking of home, we were hoping you could come to dinner tonight. It's been so long since your father and I got to spend some quality time with you. We don't know anything about your life. How your job is going. If you're dating anyone."

"Sorry," he immediately said, "I need to work the desk tonight." A smart man wouldn't have let her crestfallen expression crawl beneath his armor. But ever since coming back to Summer Lake, Liam had been anything but smart, hadn't he? "Tomorrow night might work, though."

His mother's smile was so bright, so big, it completely transformed her face. And despite himself, Liam felt a part of his heart soften.

CHAPTER ELEVEN

The minute Christie walked into Lakeside Stitch and Knit, she breathed a sigh of relief. She desperately needed a refuge for a little while from the emotions swirling around inside of her. She was a late convert to knitting, but found it wonderfully calming.

Denise Bartow, Sarah's mother, was busy helping a customer, and as Christie ran her fingers down a display of soft yarn, she was glad for the chance to focus on something other than the Kane brothers.

Although the real truth was that Liam was the only Kane brother she was focusing on at the moment...

Lost in her forbidden desires, she accidentally knocked into a display. She was scrambling to catch the cashmere skeins before they hit the floor when Denise rushed over to help.

"Sorry." Christie picked up a stray ball that had rolled across the wood-plank floor. "I'm afraid I wasn't paying enough attention." Because she couldn't stop thinking about a man she shouldn't be thinking about at all.

Denise waved away her apology. "Sarah always tells me I try to fit too much in a small space. And she's right. But I love all the yarns so much I can't stand to keep them in boxes in the back."

Christie adored Sarah's mother. Denise's open smile made her long for her own mother, for the warmth of arms that had held her since she was a baby. And yet, hadn't she just told her mom not to come visit for a while?

The problem was, Christie's mother saw everything. With five daughters, she had to. And Christie didn't want her to see how close to the edge of disaster she was. She promised herself that as soon as she'd turned everything around—when the Tapping of the Maples Festival went off without a hitch, when Wesley finally returned, when Liam left the inn on another exotic trip to the other side of the world—she would invite her mother and father and sisters and their husbands for a wonderful Summer Lake weekend.

"We just got in the most wonderful new pattern book," Denise said, drawing her attention to the photographs and patterns in a coffee-table-sized book. "Look at these."

Christie's eyes widened at the knitted lingerie, beautifully soft nightgowns—even super-sexy bra and panty patterns that made her blush.

"I'd love to knit up something from the book as a

sample," Denise said, "but with Sarah away on her honeymoon, I'm backlogged enough as it is."

"I'll do it." The offer was out of Christie's mouth before she realized it.

"Would you really?" Denise looked positively gleeful at the prospect of some knitting help. "I just know this book will fly off the shelves if people can see the designs brought to life."

"The thing is, I—" Christie was unable to get the words out—how she was already overloaded and shouldn't have made such an offer. Denise had been so kind since day one. How could she let her down on one small favor? "I was looking for a new project anyway," she finally said. And it was true. She just hadn't planned to start something new while she had so much else going on. "I left my wallet at the inn, so I'll come back tomorrow with the money for the yarn and pattern book."

"Oh no, you're helping me out. Of course everything is on the house." This was exactly why Christie loved Summer Lake so much. She'd known Denise less than a year, but she was treated like family anyway. Somehow, she'd find the time to knit a sample for the store. "Why don't you have a seat while we wait for everyone else to get here? You can thumb through the book to decide which pattern you might like to tackle. Although," Denise said, flipping through to a picture of a knitted slip that was both sexy and sweet at the same time, "this is the one I keep going back to."

"It's beautiful," Christie murmured. She could easily see herself wearing it, could feel the softness of the yarn as it skimmed over her curves like a second skin.

Denise clapped her hands. "Great! I'll get you everything you need."

While Denise gathered the proper gauge needles and yarn for her, Christie set out wine glasses for the knitting group members. Women were coming in now, one and two at a time. Ten minutes of small talk later, most of the regulars had arrived.

Christie was glad to see them all, but made it a point to sit next to Jean, Wesley and Liam's grandmother. She usually went by her cottage once a week for tea, but she'd been so busy since Wesley's disappearance that she'd neglected something they both enjoyed.

"I'm sorry I haven't been over to see you more in the past few weeks," she said as she cast on her new project.

"Cashmere," Jean said softly as she reached across to stroke Christie's new yarn between her thumb and forefinger. "My favorite."

Christie knew that conversations with Jean didn't always go in a straight line. Some people found the gray-haired woman a bit eccentric because of this, but it was one of the many things that drew Christie to her. As far as she could tell, Jean lived her life according to her own rules and no one else's. After all, look at the construction business she'd built up and passed on to her son, who also worked closely with William Sullivan. For a woman who'd started her career back in the forties, Jean's business success was nothing short of extraordinary.

"I'm knitting up a sample from this book for the store," Christie told her.

Jean's eyes went from the book to Christie, and her eyes filled with a sudden gleam. "Yes. That should work out just right."

Hmm. Nothing should have been strange about that. And yet, it kind of was. "Could I ask you something, Jean? The old ghost stories about the inn...when did they start being told?"

"You've felt something, haven't you?"

Christie didn't want to come across like a crazy person, so she began her answer by saying, "I'm sure it's nothing, but my new bedroom in the old honeymoon suite is so cold sometimes, even when the other rooms are perfectly warm. And a couple of times, I could have sworn there was something else, some kind of energy in the room with me." She shook her head at her own foolishness. "Listen to me. Telling you I think my bedroom might be haunted." She smiled at the woman beside her. "Clearly, I've been working too hard."

But Jean didn't smile back. Instead, the hint of loss, of sorrow that Christie had always felt was hiding behind her green eyes, rose to the surface.

"I knew this would happen," Jean said. "I told Wesley not to refinish that room. There's a reason it was closed off for sixty years."

"Wesley never said anything to me about potential problems with it." Then again, there were plenty of things her friend hadn't talked to her about, weren't there?

Christie was just about to ask Jean what had happened sixty years ago, when Suzanne Sullivan burst through the door.

"Sorry I'm late! Roman had to throw a couple of balls of yarn at me to even make me look up from my computer screen."

"How is that hunky bodyguard of yours?" Helen wanted to know.

The other women nodded, all obviously interested in living vicariously through the beautiful computer genius. No doubt about it, Roman Huson was quite a man. Big. Strong. Gorgeous. And head over heels in love with Suzanne.

Since she and Suzanne had become friends over the past months, Christie had learned firsthand that although Suzanne and Roman were perfect together, it hadn't always been easy for them. Especially considering that Suzanne's brothers had hired Roman to be her bodyguard, even though they knew she didn't want one. From what Suzanne had told her, despite their unorthodox beginning, their growing love had been both undeniable and irresistible.

Christie smiled thinking about how grumpy Suzanne's oldest brother, Alec, could still be about his sister's new boyfriend. As far as Alec was concerned, no one was good enough for Suzanne. Thankfully, he was coming around to the idea that she had found real love with Roman—a man who had been Alec's trusted friend for years.

"Roman's good," Suzanne said with a blush as she took an open seat on the other side of Christie, then pulled her yarns and needles out of her bag.

Christie was glad to see her friend looking so happy. And yet her chest clenched, the way it had when she was with Sarah before her wedding. It wasn't jealousy, she swore it wasn't. She didn't need her own love in order to be happy that her friends had found theirs.

Suzanne broke into Christie's thoughts as she turned to her and said, "I want to knit Roman a sweater." She pointed to a pattern for an Aran sweater. "What do you think of this one? Am I out of my mind for even thinking of tackling it?"

"I'm no expert," Christie said, "but I honestly don't think you'll have any trouble with it." Suzanne had only just recently learned to knit, but with her brilliant computer brain on task, she'd picked it up with remarkable speed.

"Oh good. Because I can already picture Roman wearing it...and then me having the pleasure of stripping it off him."

"What's this about stripping clothes off your boyfriend?" Dorothy wanted to know, and everyone laughed at the even deeper flush that covered Suzanne's pretty face.

When she turned to ask Jean if she had any advice for Suzanne about how to best begin her new knitting project, Christie was surprised to realize Liam's grandmother had left the store.

Had her questions about the inn driven Jean away?

* * *

Liam could have left the inn's front desk after dinner, but he figured it was just as easy to look through the final contracts that would turn over his venture-capital business here as it would be in the back office or his upstairs suite.

And it meant he'd be certain that Christie got in safely tonight. Just because Summer Lake was a safe small town didn't mean exceptions didn't happen. Especially if there was an angry ex waiting in the wings for a woman that he thought should be his.

The inn's front door opened, and when Liam saw her come inside, relief swept through him. "Cold out there, isn't it?"

She jumped. "Oh! I didn't expect you to be out here still." With a frown, she said, "I should have told you that we don't usually man the front desk after everyone is seated for dinner, unless we know there's going to be a late arrival."

The soft sound of her words fluttered across his skin as he drank in her beauty. He gestured to his paperwork. "I was fine working here."

She was in the process of taking off her down coat when her fingers stilled on the zipper, and she lifted her gaze back to his. "Were you waiting up for me?"

"I had to make sure you got home okay."

The way she looked at him then—with an equal measure of surprise and pleasure—made something inside his chest squeeze tight. Something that felt like the heart he'd always been so careful to keep locked up.

"Thank you."

Her words were so soft that the only reason he knew they'd been there at all was because he couldn't take his eyes off her. The windblown silk of her hair.

The flush of color on her cheeks. And the lush lips that made him want, more than anything, to steal a kiss.

If only to know that her fire burned as hot and bright as it did in his imagination.

CHAPTER TWELVE

Christie was exhausted, but even taking a long, hot bath and knitting row after row of the soft cashmere slip couldn't make her eyes close, or her brain turn off. She hated the horrible things Mark had said. And yet, what really had her sleepless in Summer Lake was that despite knowing how hesitant she should be to let a man near her heart after that awful conversation with her ex, she couldn't stop thinking about Liam. And that one perfect smile he'd given her the previous day.

One smile shouldn't mean so much.

But it did.

Just as it had touched her that he'd waited up for her tonight, to make sure she got home safely on the frozen streets.

As the numbers on her bedside clock flipped over from twelve to one and then two, she figured she should make progress with her to-do list for the festival. It was only when she stabbed herself with her pen one too many times that she finally gave in and threw it down. Climbing up into her bed, she turned off the lamp on the bedside table and closed her eyes.

But she still couldn't sleep, darn it!

God forbid that she shouldn't be at the top of her game tomorrow around Liam. Lord only knew how he'd manage to take advantage of her weakness.

Maybe he'd steal a kiss.

No! She sat up in bed and turned the light back on. How could she sleep if that was the kind of nonsense her brain was going to spit out at her? She was most certainly not going to kiss Liam. Not tomorrow morning. Not ever.

Just as she was repeating the vow to herself, she heard an awful wailing sound. Her first impression was that she was listening to a broken heart come to life. But the practical part of her had her jumping out of bed to figure out where the sound was coming from. If one of her guests was in pain, she needed to help him or her.

But when she rushed out of the bedroom, the sound got softer. Frowning, she stopped and turned. Her earlier conversation with Jean playing around the corners of her mind, she took a few steps back toward the bedroom.

Yes, the wailing was definitely getting louder.

What on earth was going on here? A strange cold patch was something she could accept. But strange sounds?

This was *way* too weird.

It had to be an animal, probably caught up between the ceiling rafters and the shingles on the roof. She was just reaching for her jeans to put on over the camisole and silk shorts she'd worn to bed, when she heard a key in her lock.

The door flew open, and Liam rushed inside. "Christie, are you okay?"

She'd never seen him in jeans, let alone without a shirt. *Oh my.* The sight of all those muscles, along with his rumpled hair and the dark shadow of stubble on his face, did funny things to her. Sending a rush of heat through her and goose bumps all across her skin at the same time. Along with making her mouth water…

"I'm fine," she said in a voice that was far more breathless than she'd intended. But she wasn't sure he heard her, because instead of stopping in his tracks and apologizing for barging into her locked suite, he had one hand on her shoulder and the other running over her forehead, brushing back her hair as if he were looking for bruises.

"Liam, I'm okay," she said again.

At last, his eyes locked on hers, and he seemed to hear her. Abruptly, he dropped his hands and took a step back. "I heard noises." His voice sounded raw. As if he was still working to fight back his fear that something might have happened to her. "I thought someone was hurting you."

"It freaked me out at first too." Honestly, she still didn't feel quite steady. But she wasn't sure if that was because of the noises...or because of how good it felt when Liam touched her. "I was worried it was one of the guests, but then I realized the sound is loudest in my bedroom." She looked toward her bedroom door, and when she turned back to Liam, his eyes were darker and filled with something that made her feel warm all over.

Suddenly, she remembered he wasn't the only one who hadn't had time to pull on clothes. Frankly, it was lucky she'd been wearing any at all. Imagine if he'd come in and found her naked.

Although the truth was that even without being completely naked, she could still feel him notice her. Really *notice* her, in a way that made every part of her tingle with heightened awareness.

But before she could grab her robe, he was saying, "Stay in here while I check things out," and heading for her bedroom.

Of course she wasn't going to do that. This was not only her room, but she also managed the inn. If something was amiss, it was her job to figure out what it was, no matter how messy the situation.

Quickly moving to his side, while simultaneously trying to ignore the sexy images that began flooding her mind from nothing more than being with Liam in her bedroom, she said, "I was thinking it might be an animal stuck in the ceiling."

He didn't look particularly surprised that she hadn't stayed out of the way. "Maybe. Although there isn't much space up there between the roof and the ceiling." He looked around the room again. "Whatever it was, it certainly isn't making any noise now."

"It's almost like it knew you were here," she said, thinking out loud, "because that's right when it stopped." She looked down at the keys dangling from his fingers and added, "Which wasn't exactly the use I had in mind for the master set when I gave them to you yesterday."

"You know I respect your privacy, but I couldn't stand the thought that someone might be hurting you."

"I'm fine," she gently reminded him, putting her hand on his arm without thinking.

As heat seared her again, she knew she should move back, knew that touching him in the middle of the night when they were both barely dressed wasn't smart. But moving away from him suddenly felt like one of the hardest things she'd ever done.

Especially with the low rumble of his words—*I couldn't stand the thought that someone might be hurting you*—washing through her senses, making her powerfully aware of the attraction still coursing between them.

Desperately, she worked to remind herself that she knew exactly where tumbling into bed with Liam Kane would get her. Yes, there'd be pleasure. She wasn't naive enough to think there wouldn't be. But there would be infinitely more heartache.

Along with an immediate search for a new job. In a new town.

But with her brain—and heart—still stuck on imagining what his kiss would taste like, she was flustered enough to blurt out, "Is it hot in here, or is it just me?"

"I assumed you had the heat cranked on high."

"I do," she said with a shake of her head, "but it never works in this room. Usually, it's really cold, but only in the bedroom. When I mentioned it to your grandmother, she said this room had been closed off for sixty years. Did you know that?"

"I knew it hadn't been used in a while, but I didn't realize it was that long."

"Your grandmother would have been in her early twenties back then, right?"

As he nodded, he noticed her festival paperwork spread out across the foot of the bed, along with the slip she'd been knitting on top of the pattern book. "Were you still up working?"

"I couldn't sleep, so I figured I might as well take

care of a few things."

"Don't you have enough on your plate already?" He didn't wait for her to respond before saying, "You can't do it all. Not without things starting to fall apart here at the inn. With Wesley gone and while you're teaching me the ropes, wouldn't it be easier if you let the festival go for now?"

Hating that he thought she would ever intentionally do anything to damage the inn, she decided to call him on what was really behind his frustrated words. "This isn't about the festival. This isn't about the inn. This is about what happened this afternoon, isn't it?"

In an instant, she watched Liam shut himself down. "Don't try to turn my concern for your well-being and the inn's into something it isn't."

She should let it go. She should let *him* go. But she was too tired to even try to rein in her impulses. "I saw your reaction to my conversation with Mark."

She watched emotion flash across his face, before he deliberately shut the reaction down. "I shouldn't have been listening to your private conversation. And I shouldn't have barged in here tonight either."

Beyond frustrated, she all but yelled, "But you were! And you did!" And the truth was that she hadn't been able to get his judgmental expression out of her head all night. "Why don't *you* be honest with *me*, for once?"

His mouth was tight, his eyes narrowed as he finally picked up the gauntlet she'd thrown down in front of him. "You broke up a marriage."

"If I'd known he was married, I never would have—"

"You must have known."

She couldn't pretend that didn't hurt. "He didn't wear a ring, he had his own apartment, he was free on evenings and weekends. There were no pictures of a family, no strange phone calls he didn't want me to hear."

"There had to be signs," Liam insisted. "Signs you were ignoring. Times you couldn't call him. Places you couldn't meet him. But you chose to ignore all of them."

It would be so much easier to stay on the defensive, but his words were pricking at so many things she hadn't wanted to admit to herself that she couldn't. Had she been more concerned with the fantasy of happily-ever-after than what was really right in front of her? And if that was the case, then wasn't she guilty of ignoring the reality about Wesley too—that a platonic life with him would never have worked out either?

"I didn't mean to hurt anyone," she finally said. "And I'll never stop regretting the pain his wife and children must be in."

"You have no idea how bad it can be."

The pain in his voice struck her deep in her solar plexus. "Liam—"

He took a deliberate step away from her. Then another. "Sorry for barging in. I'll check the roof and the water pipes tomorrow to see if those are the issue."

Obviously, he wanted to get out of her bedroom. To get away from her. Trying to push away all the emotions that had bubbled up, she worked to focus on the business of the inn instead. "Thank you, but that's normally something I would oversee." Even though it meant adding one more thing to her already endless to-do list.

She thought he would argue with her, tell her again that she wasn't some kind of superhero. Instead, he simply said, "I know you can handle anything that comes your way, Christie. You've proved that to me in spades this week. But I want to help."

And then, before she could react either to his surprising compliment or to his offer to take some of the burden from her shoulders, like the ghost she was almost starting to believe lived in the walls of her bedroom, he was gone.

CHAPTER THIRTEEN

The next morning, Christie was headed for Jean Kane's cottage when she found her on the lakeshore skipping pebbles across a patch of water where the ice had melted.

What, Christie wondered, had kept Liam's grandmother so young in so many ways? In addition to the clear delight she was having by the lake, Jean's skin was incredible for a woman in her eighties. Yes, there were lines in it, but they were mostly around her eyes and mouth from smiling.

Jean waved a hand in greeting. "Grab a handful of pebbles and give it a try."

Christie picked up a pebble and tossed it into the lake, where it skidded off the nearby ice.

"Just takes a little practice," Jean said encouragingly.

Many dozens of throws later, when Christie finally managed her first good skip, she cheered out loud.

Jean grinned, then said, "Now that the wind is picking up, why don't you join me for a cup of tea in my cottage?"

"I'd love that." But before turning away from the lake, Christie took another deep breath, letting the clean, crisp air fill her up and push away her lingering tiredness. The Adirondacks were so lovely in all seasons. Having arrived the previous summer, it was a real thrill to experience her first spring in the small lakeside town. "It really is lovely here, isn't it?"

"I never wanted to live anywhere else," Jean said as they walked together toward the yellow-and-white cottage that sat just above the beach.

"That's exactly what I thought the first time I came to Summer Lake," Christie admitted.

A few moments later, they were in the tidy, bright cottage and Jean was fussing with her teapot and tray. Soon, they were having an elegant midmorning tea, complete with butter cookies imported from England.

"This is marvelous, Jean," Christie said as she sipped her Earl Grey and nibbled a cookie. An idea suddenly struck. "We should do a special tea once a week at the inn, for both guests and locals. And if it's successful, we could even open up a tearoom off to the side of the inn, serving teas from all over the world!"

"You remind me so much of myself when I was younger," Jean remarked. "My brain was always spinning, always creating something new and exciting, like the tea service that I'm sure would do very well at the inn. Speaking of which, how have you been managing without Wesley there to help you?"

Not wanting to say anything negative about Jean's grandson, Christie carefully replied, "My workload has certainly increased, but Liam has been really helpful, so I'm hoping to have a little more breathing room soon."

"What do you think of my eldest grandson?"

Christie worked like crazy not to blush. "Liam is very intelligent." And so sexy that it was nearly impossible to think about him without remembering his hands on her, or how much she'd longed for him to kiss her. More than once. "He seems so interested in everything around him."

"Yes," Jean agreed. "He definitely is. Especially when he's surprised by something beautiful, something precious."

A dozen questions crowded the tip of Christie's tongue. What had he been like as a child? Why hadn't he been back to the lake in so long? Had he been in a serious relationship? But if she asked any of them, Jean would surely know Christie was interested in him as more than simply her almost-brother-in-law.

Which was why she said instead, "Last night at the knitting group, when I asked you about the strange things I've been sensing in my bedroom at the inn, what did you mean when you said you knew it would happen?"

Jean didn't answer right away. She took her time finishing her cup of tea and then poured again for both of them. Christie reined in her impatience, knowing that Jean had always been a woman who lived by her own timetable.

Finally, she put down her teacup and began to tell Christie a story.

⋆ ⋆ ⋆

Summer Lake, 1945…

As the youngest daughter of one of the richest men on the lake, Jean Farrington grew up in one of the biggest houses there. Her whole life, she had been content to live in Summer Lake—although the past years had been bumpier than expected, what with the boys she'd grown up with going off to war. Not to mention all of the drama surrounding Olive and her forbidden—and doomed—love affair with Carlos last year. Thankfully, Olive had found a new, lasting love with Kent Thomas, and they were now happily married.

However, in the aftermath of Olive's affair, their father had all but dropped prison bars around his daughters, and Jean had to learn to live under a microscope. It had been horrible. Jean had always longed to learn as much as she could about the world around her. She enjoyed female pursuits just fine and was a decent knitter and seamstress, but knitting was never going to become her passion, as it was for Olive.

What she really loved was building things. Even as a little girl, she'd been happy to play for hours with blocks, and her teachers had always remarked on her remarkable aptitude for math and science. Still, she'd known instinctively that no one would ever approve of her picking up a hammer or saw, so she'd funneled her interest first into her dollhouses and, when she grew too old for those, into sketching first her father's house and then most of the other houses around the lake, big and small.

She especially liked the tiny cottages where happy families came to play in the summer. For years, she'd had a picture in her head of the cottage she was going to build for her own family. She could even see her babies playing on the sand, her sister coming over with her own children.

The only thing she couldn't see clearly was the man who would be her husband.

She knew all of the boys from school too well to imagine actually marrying one of them. And, of course, her father hadn't given her many chances to date anyone who didn't live in Summer Lake. Besides, with all the grilling he subjected her dates to, any boy who dared ask her out ended up sorely regretting ever looking her way.

Fortunately, in the spring following Olive's wedding, Jean found more freedom than she'd had in years. One crisp, clear day, she grabbed a sun hat with a knitted rose-colored sash around the brim, slung her bag over her shoulder, and headed out into the sunshine.

She walked for a long while, stopping now and again to skip a pebble or two. It was something a child would do, and she was supposed to have grown out of the habit a long time ago, but she couldn't see the point of giving up something that was so much fun.

She was planning to sketch one of the new houses being built about a mile down from her house. She loved watching the foundation go in and the studs go up for the walls. While she enjoyed seeing the finished product—cozy or grand, cute or historical—it was the internal workings of the building that truly captivated her.

Dorothy, a friend from school, called her name. After Jean slowly made her way over, Dorothy said, "Have I told you how much you remind me of a turtle?"

"Many, many times."

Jean just couldn't see the point of rushing anything. Perhaps it was because she was the youngest child. Olive had always been the one in a hurry. To walk, according to their parents, and certainly to fall in love.

Whereas Jean simply enjoyed the world around her. She loved the lake. Loved her family, her friends. Loved reading great books and roasting marshmallows by a bonfire on the beach.

The two girls headed into the diner and drank hot chocolate while they chatted. Suddenly, Dorothy's eyes grew big as she looked at something over Jean's shoulder. "Oh my. Now, *there's* a man."

Dorothy had a tendency to be boy crazy, so Jean didn't give much credence to her statement. She didn't bother to turn around and see whom she was talking about. She was pulling out a few pennies to leave as a tip when Dorothy grabbed her arm and hissed, "He's coming over here. Act natural."

Jean laughed out loud. Of course she was going to act natural. She didn't care one way or another about some strange man.

At least, until he said, "Excuse me, ladies, could I intrude on your conversation for a moment to ask a quick question?" His deep, rich voice sent thrill bumps popping up one by one across the surface of her skin.

When Dorothy chirped, "Sure!" in an overly bright voice, Jean knew it was up to her to act normal for both of them.

She slowly turned around on her stool at the counter. "How may we help you?"

It was fortunate that she finished her sentence before she lifted her eyes to the man's face.

He was beyond handsome.

She'd studied the human face and form for years, both in books and with pencil and sketchbook in hand. But she'd never seen a face that held such symmetry. Only the slight bump across the bridge of his nose broke up the perfection. At the same time, it was the imperfection that so well highlighted everything else.

Perhaps it was her father's lockdown during a formative period in her growth, or maybe it was just her natural personality, but Jean had never learned the art of disguising her reactions. Which meant that she simply stared wide-eyed at the stranger. It wasn't hard to do, considering his eyes had locked on hers as well. Despite being in a crowded diner, it felt like they were the only two people in the room.

And deep in her soul, she knew that the man she would marry was standing right in front of her.

At long last, he cleared his throat. "My name is Thomas Kane. I've come to Summer Lake from New York City to meet with a Mr. Farrington this afternoon. But I'm afraid his business office on Main Street is locked. Do you have any idea where I might find him?"

Smiling up into his light green eyes, she said, "He's my father."

* * *

Their courtship was short and oh-so-sweet. Thankfully, her father was overjoyed by Thomas's attentions to his younger daughter.

Jean was overjoyed by them too, even if she didn't understand why Thomas thought he needed to give her so many gifts, such expensive things that were so pretty and so fragile. She supposed she could simply have said thank you over and over again without truly speaking her mind, but that felt like lying. And Jean didn't believe in lies.

"I don't need so many pretty things," she told him one night when he sat across from her at another fancy restaurant, another beautifully wrapped box sitting on her empty dinner plate. She gave it back to him. "If this is who you think I am, then I'm not sure you know me very well at all."

His gaze was as intense as she'd ever seen it when he replied, "I know exactly who you are, Jean. You're a loving daughter. You'd do anything for your sister. You'd risk a piece of yourself before you'd ever let one of your friends be hurt. You have no idea that you're the center of so many lives, that you're the lynchpin that holds them all together." He paused, looking down at the box in his hand, before looking back up and saying, "Anyone who knows you, anyone who loves you, would never try to keep you in his life with stupid gifts." The sincerity, and passion, in his gaze kept her spellbound as he said, "He would know that once you loved, it was forever."

She was in his arms a heartbeat later, the word *forever* echoing on her lips as she kissed him.

* * *

Three weeks after they'd first met at the diner, he found her by the lake, sketching. He hadn't needed to say a word, hadn't needed to announce his presence for her focus to shatter. Any time he was near, she lost hold of anything but him, was literally unable to keep from smiling. And there was nothing more she loved than the look in his eyes when he smiled back, as if she was a perfect surprise, a gift he'd never expected would be given to him.

But although she reached out for him to join her on the sandy shore, neither his serious expression nor his position changed. "What is it, Thomas? Is something wrong?"

His gaze roved over her face. "What would a brilliant girl like you want with a man like me?"

She didn't have to think about her reason. It was obvious. And very simple. "I love you."

She put her hands over his, and he lifted them to his lips in a gesture that seemed almost desperate. Something was wrong, but she didn't know what it could possibly be.

And then, almost in slow motion, she watched him drop to one knee on the soft green grass that bordered the sand. "Marry me. Please. You're all I truly want in the world. Just you."

Later, after they'd gorged on kisses and whispered promises, Thomas met with her father to ask for her hand in marriage. Her father was as happy as she'd seen him since Olive's wedding day.

* * *

Their wedding day dawned sunny, with spring flowers all around the inn for the ceremony and reception. Olive, Dorothy, and several other women from the knitting group had just finished helping her with the finishing touches on her hair and makeup and had gone, so that she could have a few quiet moments alone with her thoughts, when there was a knock on the door.

"Jean." Thomas stepped inside and stared at her in awe. "You're breathtaking. The most beautiful woman in the world."

She knew she was pretty at best. But when she saw herself through his eyes, she believed what he'd said.

A teasing smile on her face, she moved toward him in her wedding gown. "Don't you know it's bad luck for the groom to see the bride before the ceremony?"

But he didn't tease her back. "My luck changed the

moment I set eyes on you."

His arms came around her then, and she barely had a chance to whisper, "Mine too," before he was kissing her with all the love in his heart...and she was kissing him back with just as much.

* * *

When she said, "I do," Jean realized that although she'd never felt incomplete, Thomas had completed her just the same. And oh, how she savored every moment of their wedding night in the penthouse suite at the inn, from the sweet kisses he ran all across her skin to his whispered words of love.

Her mother and then Olive had both pulled her aside to explain what was expected in the marriage bed. Of course, she'd read enough books over the years to have a pretty good idea already. And yet, nothing could have prepared her for Thomas. Not only the exquisite pleasure that he gave her, but also the depth of love in his eyes every time he looked at her.

When he finally stopped caressing and kissing her long enough for her to fall asleep in his arms, the last thing she heard over the beating of his heart beneath her ear was his low voice saying, "You'll have my heart forever."

Perfectly warm in the comfort of his arms, she fell into a dreamless sleep. She didn't need her old dreams anymore. She and Thomas would make new ones together.

But as the dark of night turned into dawn, the warmth leached out of the bed, out of the room. Out of Jean.

Because she awakened alone.

Thomas was gone.

* * *

Present day…

Christie's teacup clattered onto her saucer in shock at the unexpected twist in Jean's otherwise very romantic tale. But before Christie could even think about asking whether Thomas had come back, Jean said, "Storytelling always wears me out. Would you mind helping me clean this up?"

"Not at all," she said, reluctantly accepting that she'd heard all she was going to from Jean today.

But as she walked back to the inn, she couldn't help but wonder—if Jean and Thomas had celebrated their wedding night in the top-floor bedroom at the inn, could that be why it always felt so cold?

Because love hadn't only been made in that room. It had also been lost.

CHAPTER FOURTEEN

"Are you the person responsible for this Tapping of the Maples Festival?"

As soon as Christie saw Mr. Radin walk into the inn, a warning bell went off in her head. She'd never had anything against him until he'd stood up at that town hall meeting last fall and tried to tear Sarah apart for suggesting new condos might go up along the lakefront. He was entitled to his opinion, but it was the way he went after her friend that had been truly horrible. He'd actually invoked Sarah's late father's name, telling her that James would have been ashamed of what his daughter was doing to his beloved town.

Christie had always forgiven too quickly. More than once, being able to hold a grudge might have helped her steer clear of personal disaster. But she hadn't managed to forgive Mr. Radin for hurting her friend. And today, unfortunately, he was wearing the same angry expression as he had during the town hall meeting.

"Yes, that's me," she said in as polite a voice as she

could manage. "I'd be happy to answer any questions you might have about the festival."

He slapped down a thick folder. "You can't drill into Adirondack Park trees without the proper permissions. I've filed a halt petition with the Preservation Council."

Christie felt her mouth fall open, but at that moment she was powerless to close it. She stared at the papers, not wanting to touch them. "I checked everything out with the park's agency before I started putting the festival together."

"Then they didn't read the codes any better than you did. The Adirondack Park is preserved for a reason—so that people like you can't come here from the big city and destroy our trees. We don't need more buildings and machines and people ruining our land. You're no better than that friend of yours with her condos."

"How dare you make some sort of claim that I'm trying to destroy the forest." She was glad for the anger that shot through her, if only because of the energy it gave her to stand up to this bully. "You could have come and talked to me first, before filing this petition. You should have given me a chance to address your concerns before escalating things to such a high level." It had never occurred to her that someone would try to stop her from putting on a small festival.

"All that talk just gets in the way of what needs to be done. I believe in taking action first."

She had to bite her tongue to point out how well that had gone for him, given that he was alone, grumpy, with virtually no friends in a small town that thrived on interpersonal connections. "The festival is in two weeks, Mr. Radin. Vendors are in place. People have already made their plans to attend the festival and have booked rooms at the inn and all of the local B&Bs. Pulling the festival now would be a headache and a heartache for more than just me." She hated begging for things, but this was more important than her pride. "Please reconsider this petition. I'm not the only one who will benefit from this festival. It's not just going to be good for the inn. This entire community will reap the rewards of it. And I will personally make sure that none of the trees are harmed in the process."

Suddenly, he smiled, a smug expression with no warmth behind it. "The Preservation Council will make certain of that."

* * *

Across the lake, Susan and Henry were down on their hands and knees in opposite corners of their bedroom. He was sanding by hand, while she worked carefully to finish the already sanded planks with a paintbrush.

Though Susan had practically had to beg him to let

her help him with the bedroom floors, the truth was that she had never cared for work like this. Painstaking, patience-bending work had always been Henry's forte. Like his mother, Jean, he wasn't one to be rushed. Susan, on the other hand, liked seeing something go from idea to reality as quickly as possible.

Still, she wanted—needed—to be in the bedroom with him, on the floor with a paintbrush, listening to the steady scratch of sandpaper. She dearly hoped working together on something they both wanted would bring them closer together. That they'd lie in bed when it was done and know that they could still be a team.

Funny the things one didn't realize about someone when one was still in the first flush of new love. She'd loved how considerate he was, how seriously he thought about everything she asked him, rather than just giving her whatever answer she wanted to hear, like most men would. And if his mother had driven her a little crazy in those early years with the way she never seemed to answer a question directly, Susan had believed Henry was different. But more and more, she'd come to see just how similar they were. Wesley had the same easygoing patience. Only Liam needed change, needed a faster pace, the way Susan did—even if he didn't want to admit that they had those personality traits in common.

She was thrilled that he was coming to dinner tonight. No matter how strained things were between them, he was still her son, and she loved him dearly. Looking down at her watch, she saw that it was time to pull the cherry pie—his favorite—out of the oven.

Her back was stiff as she stood, and she stumbled slightly to her left. Before she could prevent it, a can at her heel tipped over and lacquer poured out all over the boards that Henry had worked so hard to sand to perfection.

She bent down to grab the can, but as she did so, she accidentally stepped into a puddle of goo. Slipping, she had only just hit the floor when her husband was there, running his hand down her arms, checking for places she might be hurt. And it felt so good to be touched by him.

"Does anything hurt?"

Just her pride. But she couldn't admit that, not even to her husband. Especially not to him, it seemed. "No. I don't think so." She started to get up, but his hands were firm, holding her right where she was. A thrill shot through her at the proof of his strength, something else she'd somehow forgotten.

"Stay put for a little while," he insisted. "Give your body a chance to recover from the fall." That was when he finally looked from her to the huge mess she'd created. "Well, that's something, isn't it?"

Though he hadn't outright blamed her for screwing up, she thought she could hear the resignation in his voice, as if letting her help had been a bad idea right from the start. "I didn't do it on purpose."

He didn't look at her, just shook his head. "I didn't say you did."

"But you were thinking it."

His chest filled with a deep breath, one that he let out before he said, "No, I wasn't. Although I thought I was pretty clear about closing the containers before you went anywhere."

She pushed out of his arms, getting to her feet as fast as she could in the sticky glop that covered her. "I should have known working together would be a bad idea."

He was up on his feet just as fast. "Don't try and turn this around on me." The moment where he'd put warm hands on her like he used to was clearly long gone. "You're the one who's been pushing me to do the floors. You're the one who demanded to help. If you'd just let me do it the way I planned, none of this would have happened."

"You know what?" Emotions roiled through her, making it impossible to think through her words before they spilled out. "We never should have started this. We never should have tried to pretty up the past and make it look new again. We can't sand down and refinish something that's fundamentally broken. We'll never be able to go back to the way it used to be."

* * *

For how many years had Henry tried to avoid this conversation? He had always loved Susan so much that he couldn't let himself imagine a life without her.

But more and more often, he had to wonder if he'd been wrong.

If only they hadn't started this renovation. For years he'd told her the same thing: that he didn't feel comfortable turning away paying business to spend the time working on his own home. But that had been only a superficial reason. In truth—and it was a truth he wasn't at all comfortable admitting to himself—he'd been worried about spending so many hours in the house with his wife when they seemed to manage best with only evenings and weekends together. And now that his fears had become reality, he didn't know what to say, what to do.

So when he smelled something burning, it was actually a relief to be able to rush down into the kitchen, where black smoke was pouring out of the oven.

"Oh no, my pie!" Susan tried to push past him to get to it.

He caught her arm before she could open the oven and burn herself.

"Let me go!"

She was talking about the oven and her burned pie, but he had to wonder if *Let me go* was what she'd really been saying to him all these years. Only he hadn't wanted to listen.

"I can't let you burn yourself." It didn't matter that he was angry with her, that she'd hurt him more deeply than ever before with what she'd just said in their bedroom. *We never should have tried to pretty up the past and make it look new again.* He simply couldn't stand the thought of Susan ever being hurt.

At last, she backed up out of the way of the oven door. Henry carefully opened it. Just as he'd expected, sizzling hot smoke billowed out of it. The pie was a black lump of coal on the middle rack. Susan was already opening windows, but he knew the smell would linger long after this afternoon.

Just as the words that had been laid between them would remain: *We'll never be able to go back to the way it used to be.*

"If I start working on another pie right now," she said, "I can probably get it made before Liam comes for dinner."

"I don't think dinner with Liam tonight is such a good idea." It wasn't fair to subject him to the tension between his parents.

But Susan was adamant. "He's our son, whom we

only rarely get the privilege of seeing. We can't let our problems get in the way of a chance to sit down with him for a few hours."

She was right. He'd missed Liam a great deal these past years and knew the likelihood of his leaving the lake again soon was high. "Then you'd better make the replacement pie. I'll go clean up upstairs and see if anything can be salvaged."

She winced at his words, even though he could have sworn he'd been talking about the floors and nothing else. But he'd never been comfortable telling lies. Which would account for the unease that had been building up inside him all this time.

Because hadn't he been lying to himself about his marriage for nearly twenty years?

"I'll put a bottle of paint thinner in the shower for you in case the lacquer doesn't wash right off." Despite his efforts to the contrary, his voice was strained, rough around the edges where emotion was tearing away at him.

"Henry..."

He wasn't used to hearing a plea in her voice, and that was what made him stop halfway out of the kitchen and turn around. Susan was the strongest person he knew. Even stronger than his mother. But now, for the first time in a very long time, she looked like she was about to break.

"I didn't—" She wiped away a tear falling down her cheek. "What I said upstairs, I didn't mean it." But they both knew she had. Because they'd been limping along half broken for too long.

Knowing he was going to regret it, but unable to stop himself, he said, "Do you know why I finally decided to refinish the floors?"

His wife—so lovely after thirty years that she was still turning heads—blinked at him from her post by the window. "Why?"

"Because I was hoping fixing the floors might fix us."

"Oh, Henry—"

He held up both hands to stop her. "But you're right. Shiny new floorboards aren't going to heal what's broken between us. Not when one little mistake means having to rip them up and throw them away."

"What are you saying?" Her mouth was trembling, and although there were no more tears rolling down her cheeks, her eyes were bright with them.

"I don't know yet." He felt the weight of every strained moment between them. "Let's just have dinner with Liam tonight and take it from there."

"Okay."

But it wasn't. And he wasn't sure anything would ever truly be okay again.

CHAPTER FIFTEEN

Christie was going to have to cancel the festival.

After reading through the petition start to finish and then again to make sure she hadn't missed anything, she had no choice but to face the truth. While the Adirondack Preservation Council hadn't yet made a judgment, at this point the petition was enough to put a halt to the proceedings until they'd reviewed all of the arguments for both sides. Unfortunately, the next formal review session wasn't for three weeks—one full week after the festival should have already taken place.

All these weeks, Christie had thought she was doing such a good job of holding it together, had been proud of how strong she was becoming.

Right now, she felt anything but strong.

"How's everything going so far today?" She jumped at the sound of Liam's voice. How long had he been standing there watching her try not to fall apart? "I didn't intend to be gone for so long," he continued, "but one meeting with my former business partners in Boston turned into six, the way it always used to."

Frustration with Mr. Radin and his stupid petition, with Wesley for leaving her to deal with everything alone—and with Liam for making her feel things she had no business feeling—had her throwing out an uncharacteristically sharp, "I'll tell you how everything's going. The festival is off."

Frowning, he set down a tray that held cookies and two cups of coffee, and she belatedly realized he must have been worried that she was working through her meals again.

"What are you talking about?" he asked. "Why would the festival be off?"

She slid the petition across the counter. "Courtesy of Mr. Radin."

"Isn't he the bored loner who likes to stir up trouble?"

She touched the tip of her nose with her index finger. "Bingo! He's filed a petition against my festival with the Adirondack Preservation Council." She pointed to the bound papers. "It's all right there in black and white."

His frown dug in deeper as he flipped through the pages. "This is nuts." He shifted his gaze back to her. "Aren't you going to fight it?"

She shrugged, all the fight from the previous night knocked out of her. "In order to fight the petition, I'd need to present my case at the next council meeting.

But that isn't for three weeks. And even if the meeting had been before the festival date, it would probably be a full-time job to comb through all of the rules and regulations in the hopes of convincing the council." She hated to admit this, but it had to be said. "You were right last night. I can do only so much."

"You didn't seem to think I was right." Though his words were blunt, his voice held no recrimination.

"Well, you were." She was barely managing to hold his gaze when all she wanted to do was run up the stairs, crawl into bed, and pull the covers over her head. But she had a job to do running the inn. She couldn't lose that too just because everything else had fallen apart. "Besides, I thought you'd be happy about the festival being off."

"I honestly don't know what to think right now."

He never lies. The thought hit her right between the eyes.

So many men had lied to her over the years—even Wesley, by withholding the truth of who he really was—that she'd given up hope of finding one who didn't.

"I don't like the way Radin went about this, Christie. He should have come to you first, been up front about his concerns, rather than weaseling in some loophole in the park's policies."

"That's what I told him."

"I'd like to have seen that." A smile almost raised the edges of his lips as he spoke, and she found herself actually holding her breath, she wanted to see it so badly. Today, more than ever.

When she realized she was staring, she quickly said, "In other news, William Sullivan said he knows a guy who could look at the pipes and roof. Unfortunately, he's away from town for the next week, but he'll squeeze us in as soon as he returns."

"Until then," Liam said, "why don't you move into another room?"

"I'm perfectly okay where I am. A few noises aren't going to bother me again." She couldn't let them when she needed to prove to Liam that she could hold it all together. Admitting that she was still more than a little freaked out by the ghostlike sounds in her bedroom definitely wasn't in the cards.

Of course, that was right when the front door blew open, and she was so on edge from both lack of sleep and heightened emotions that she jumped back—and tripped over a box of flyers for her festival.

Before she knew it, Liam was around the counter and his arms were around her, making sure she didn't knock her head on something sharp and hard. She knew she should step away and put at least a handful of feet between them. But his warmth—and his gentle touch—were irresistible.

"Thank you for catching me."

"I would never let you fall, Christie."

Suddenly, it all felt so inevitable, the kiss that was finally going to happen. A kiss that she didn't know why she'd even bothered to fight for so long. Especially when she could no longer deny just how much she wanted to taste him. Wanted to feel his strong muscles pressed against her. Wanted to give in to her own innate sensuality that he'd brought out in her from the first moment she'd set eyes on him, despite all the barriers that lay between them.

This was what was really between them. This heat. This attraction. This need that was pumping through her, head to toe, inside and out.

His eyes grew even darker as he leaned in, his lips barely a breath away from hers.

The phone rang, loud and jarring enough for them to have no excuse not to break apart.

She picked it up with a shaking hand—and with the palpable loss of his touch, his kiss, aching inside of her. "Summer Lake Inn."

Was that her voice, all breathy and disappointed at losing out on a kiss she'd wanted so badly—but knew better than to take? In any case, hearing Liam's mother's voice should have broken the spell that had been weaving itself around them.

But even speaking to Susan couldn't knock sense

into Christie as she said, "Sure, he's right here." She held out the phone, and when Liam's fingertips brushed against her knuckles as he took it from her, her entire body jumped with renewed awareness.

"Yes, I'll be there for dinner at six with a bottle of your favorite wine from Napa Valley," Liam said to his mother. To the untrained ear, his voice sounded perfectly pleasant, but Christie noted how still he'd become. As though he had to be prepared for disaster every second around Susan. "Okay, see you soon."

He put the phone down and asked Christie, "Will Alice be here at five to take over the front desk?" When she nodded, he said, "Good. Because I'd like you to come to dinner at my parents'."

"Me?" She couldn't hide her shock. "Why would you want me to come with you?"

"First, because it's the only way I can guarantee that you'll actually eat something rather than work through your next meal."

His obvious concern for her well-being made her throat feel tight. Men, in her experience, rarely took care of her. She had always been the one to take care of them.

"Second, because I think you could use something to take your mind off the festival. And third—" He paused for a moment before finishing. "Because I'd really appreciate not having to sit across the table from them by myself."

God, she thought as she couldn't stop herself from nodding. She was such a sucker.

A sucker for the desire she saw in his eyes.

A sucker for the pain inside him that she couldn't help but want to heal.

And most of all, a sucker for the breathless hope that one day he'd let down his walls and give her a smile that was full of real joy, true happiness.

Because despite knowing better, despite trying to stay strong, she was already falling for Liam Kane. Harder than she could ever remember falling before.

CHAPTER SIXTEEN

"You're beautiful."

Christie's heart, which was already beating too fast, jumped so hard behind her breastbone that she was afraid Liam would see the front of her dress thumping to its rhythm. This wasn't a date, so it didn't matter what she looked like. Still, she'd tried on one outfit after another upstairs and even put the blow dryer and her makeup bag through their paces.

Worried that her voice would give away how nervous she was, she simply smiled her thanks. That silence lasted through the drive to his parents' house and was broken only when they got to the front door.

"Thank you for being here with me tonight," he said in a low voice. "Doing this alone would have been—" He shook his head. "Hard. Really hard."

"You're welcome," she said softly, wanting to reach out to take his hand and give it a squeeze. If he were any of her other friends, she would have. Only, she wasn't sure what they were—if *friends* was the right word for what was beginning to happen between them. "Just kick me under the table when you're ready to go, okay?"

She was rewarded with one of his rare smiles—and she actually lost her breath.

The door suddenly opened. "Liam, what are you doing standing out here in the cold?" His mother registered Christie's presence a moment later. "Christie?" Susan shot a confused glance at her son.

Liam's father was far more welcoming. "Christie, what a nice surprise. I'm so glad you could join us tonight. Come in, you two."

Christie managed a smile for Henry as she let him take her coat. She could feel Liam's eyes on her, could practically hear him worrying that he'd brought her into the lion's den. But these weren't her parents. They were his. And clearly he had problems with them, big enough that he'd needed her as a buffer. She shot him an encouraging smile along with the silent message not to worry about her.

But his frown only deepened as he looked around the kitchen. "Is something on fire in here?" There was a distinct odor of smoke, but everything in the house looked okay.

"Susan burned the first pie she made," his father explained.

Susan shot Henry a furious glance. "I didn't hear the timer. It was an accident."

"I wasn't implying anything else," Henry said. But his tone seemed to say otherwise.

Christie had never seen Susan and Henry act lovey-dovey with each other. But she'd also never seen them like this, sniping and going out of their way not to touch as they moved around the kitchen getting her and Liam drinks.

A short while later, they sat down to a delicious-looking meal. The problem was, Christie wasn't sure she'd be able to eat much. And not just because Henry and Susan were so clearly at odds—but because sitting so close to Liam at the small dining table, with his thigh pressed against hers, was twisting her insides up in knots.

Susan immediately asked Liam, "How is your business doing, honey?"

"I sold it." His parents were both clearly stunned by the news.

"Why would you sell your business?" his mother asked, obviously concerned. "You're so good at venture capital."

Henry didn't give Liam a chance to answer. "Maybe he was ready to move on, Susan."

Christie swore she saw moisture dampen the other woman's eyes at the words *move on*.

"I'm toying with a few other ideas," Liam said into the chilly air that hung between his parents. "And for the time being, Christie has been showing me the ropes at the inn."

"It's so nice of you to help out your brother with his inn while he's away, Liam," Susan said once she'd recovered herself.

Almost choking on her food, Christie turned to look at Liam. *Don't they know you're co-owner?* When he shook his head at her silent question, she gave him a look he couldn't misinterpret. *They're your parents. You should tell them.*

Surprisingly, a moment later, he put down his fork. "When Wesley decided to buy the inn, I made an investment in it, as well. I actually own half of it."

Susan's face creased into a humongous smile. "That's the best news I've heard in a very long time, honey. I hope this means you're going to be staying in town with all of us from now on."

"We'll see." Liam's response was the most non-committal answer possible.

Christie tried to ignore the pang in the center of her chest at just how low the odds of his staying were. It was yet another good reason not to let herself fall for him.

If only *good reasons* had any sway over her foolish heart.

At last, however, Henry seemed to be in agreement with his wife. "I agree, that's great news, son. As for whatever you do next, we're behind you every step of the way." But then, Liam's father cleared his throat, looking a little nervous. "If you've got any free time coming up, with what looks to be our last snowstorm of the year behind us, I was thinking about doing some hiking. I'd love it if you could join me."

Henry was a very sweet man. And yet Liam didn't exactly jump at the offer to spend time together. "I'll have to see how my schedule looks."

What, Christie wondered, could Liam possibly have against his father?

Obviously working to swallow his disappointment, Henry turned to her. "How's the festival coming along?"

She should have expected the question. After all, she'd been talking incessantly about it for months. "It was coming along fine, but—"

When she paused to figure out how to best explain things, Liam said, "We're currently dealing with some Adirondack Park regulations surrounding whether public tapping of the maples is allowed under the preservation rules."

Christie lost sight of everything but the *we* at the beginning of Liam's sentence. How many times had he told her to give the festival to someone else? But now he'd just said *we*, as though they were a team.

Obviously upset on her behalf, Henry said, "I'm

sorry to hear this when you've worked so hard on the festival, Christie."

"Wesley said everything was going well," Susan put in. "Before he left, in any case. And, honestly, while I'm sorry to have to be so blunt—" She pinned Christie with a hard look. "I still don't understand what happened between the two of you. Someone doesn't just pack up and leave the way he did. Did something else happen that you haven't told any of us?"

With each word out of Susan's mouth, Christie could feel her face growing hotter and hotter. How could she possibly continue to keep Wesley's secret under such direct scrutiny? Especially when she knew how worried her own mother would be if she just up and disappeared one day, leaving nothing behind but a note.

But before she could say a word, Liam said, "What happened between them is between them. It's none of our business."

Christie didn't even come close to masking her surprise. Not only had Liam stood up for her again, but it sounded like he was actually defending her right to keep his brother's secret.

"He's my son," Susan protested. "He's your brother. Don't you care what's happening to him?"

"Of course I do." Liam pushed back his chair and reached for Christie's hand to help her up too. "But I didn't ask Christie to join us for dinner tonight so that you could harass her and make accusations."

Christie realized she had to make a choice. To stay with the Kanes. Or to go with Liam. The Kanes lived permanently in town, and disappointing them would have long-term ramifications. Whereas Liam was planning to stay for only a little while.

Which was why it made no sense to choose Liam. But she couldn't have made any other choice.

It wasn't just the little sweet things he did so unconsciously, like always bringing her something to eat. It wasn't just how he'd rushed into her room in the middle of the night because he'd been worried about her. It wasn't just the way he looked at her, with more heat than she'd ever known before. It was also how he'd defended her in front of his mother.

"Liam. Christie." Henry's pleading voice had them stopping their departure from the kitchen. "Please stay for dessert. Your mother went to all the trouble of baking a second cherry pie after the first burned."

Leaving would be easier. So much easier than staying. But she also knew deep in her heart that if Liam left like this, it would only make things worse between him and his mother.

Christie put her hand on his arm. "I do love cherry pie."

Everyone held their breath. For so long that Christie was half expecting one of them to turn blue and pass out.

Finally, Liam said, "Can the inn survive without you for a little longer?"

She wanted to pull him down for a kiss. Because he was a good son. And family meant everything to her. "Absolutely." She turned to Susan. "Any chance you have vanilla ice cream?"

The relief in the other woman's eyes nearly brought tears to Christie's own. "I wouldn't serve warm cherry pie without it."

The next twenty minutes were entirely made of small talk about the town, the weather, and pro baseball prospects. When their plates were finally cleared of pie and ice cream, they said their good-byes.

As they walked out to the car, Liam said, "I thought that went well."

His deadpan comment was completely unexpected—and just what she needed to unravel the tension that had been coiling up tighter and tighter inside. For the first time in far too long, Christie laughed freely.

All because of Liam.

* * *

"Did you see that?" Susan was standing at the kitchen sink trying to wash dishes, but her hands were shaking so hard a plate knocked into the porcelain and almost broke.

As steam rose up from the sink, Henry rushed over to shut off the water. "You're going to burn yourself!"

But Susan felt numb. Too numb to notice a little hot water. "There's something going on between them." She turned away from the sink and looked at her husband. "Didn't you see it?"

"See what?" There was annoyance in his voice. He never used to talk to her like that. Even though she'd likely deserved it many, many times before now.

"The way Liam looked at Christie at dinner." Her voice was shaking now just as much as her hands were.

"He likes her. Everyone likes her."

"Are you blind?" Her words were sharp. "He could hardly take his eyes off her. And she blushed every time he spoke to her."

"Fine. So maybe they like each other as more than just friends. What business is it of yours?"

She whirled from the sink, water and suds flying all over the kitchen floor. "She has already driven away one of my sons. I'm not going to let her drive away another. I'm not going to let her ruin their lives one by one."

"Whatever Wesley's reasons were for leaving, that sweet girl couldn't have driven him away."

"Stop saying how sweet she is!" She was yelling

now, long past the point of being rational.

"Damn it, she is sweet. You say I'm the blind one. Now it's time for you to open your eyes. Can't you see that a woman like Christie is exactly what Liam needs?"

"You don't think I know what my own son needs?"

"No."

"And you do?"

"Yes, I damn well do. He needs a woman who will love him no matter what. Regardless of how hard things get. He deserves a woman he can love with his whole heart. A woman he isn't afraid to share anything with."

Oh God, he wasn't talking about Liam and Christie anymore. He was talking about the two of them. About what they used to have. About who they used to be.

Until she stupidly went and ruined everything, in one weak and horrible moment that she'd regret for the rest of her life.

"Henry—" She needed to tell him. She should have told him twenty years ago, right after she'd screwed up. She shouldn't have held it all inside. Because instead of the years making her betrayal seem less bad—every single year, every week, every hour had magnified her mistake a thousand times over.

But before she could tell him anything at all, he

said, "Stay out of it, Susan. Whatever is going on with Liam and Christie, let it be. If they've got something growing between them, it's their business and no one else's."

She knew he was right. She could feel it deep inside her torn-up heart. But fear had her saying, "She was Wesley's fiancée."

"If Wesley and Christie were meant to be together, they would be married right now. You read his letter. He didn't want the marriage any more than she did."

"But what will people think?"

"If Liam and Christie end up together, I hope people will think they're a beautiful couple. I hope they'll look at the two of them and see love. Real love. I hope that all anyone will want is what's best for them."

With that, he got back to work loading the dishwasher, and she was so tired, so weak—so scared—all she could do was sit on a kitchen chair and watch him work.

How had she ever forgotten what a beautiful man her husband was? Thirty years after she'd met him, he was still muscular, with broad shoulders, and strong arms and legs. His brown hair was mostly gray now, but it looked great on him. She could see both of her sons in Henry: Liam's build, his large hands and serious eyes; Wesley's artistry, his ready smile, the way he could get along with absolutely anyone.

She wanted to say so many things to her husband, wanted to tell him how much she loved him, but she could see how angry he was with her. And how she'd only dug the hole between them deeper with her comments about Liam and Christie. There had been a time when they could have talked about the women their sons were interested in without fighting about it. But not anymore.

He closed the dishwasher. "Will the sander keep you up?"

"You're not coming to bed?"

"There's a lot of work to do still on the floors."

Just yesterday, he might have asked her to come upstairs and help him. But she'd had her chance. And now she couldn't stand the thought of begging. Of being turned down. Of knowing for sure that he didn't want her.

She forced herself to keep what was left of her pride intact. At least until she left the kitchen. "Don't worry about me. I'll put my earplugs in."

She went through the motions of getting ready for bed in the guest room, where they were sleeping while they worked on the master bedroom. She lay down on the bed, curling up on her side with her arms around her knees.

Even with her earplugs in, she could feel the vibrations from the sander moving through her and was glad that they would keep her awake until Henry came to bed. Until she could put her arms around him and show she was sorry without actually having to say the words.

But even after the vibrations stopped, he never came.

And she had never been able to sleep without him beside her.

CHAPTER SEVENTEEN

Back at the inn, Liam walked Christie upstairs. The laughter had gone a long way to relaxing her, but standing with him in front of her door made her feel as skittish as a teenage girl on her first date. Even though no one in their right mind could have called that tense dinner with Liam's parents a date.

"Thank you, again, for going with me tonight," he said. "I'm really sorry I put you through that."

Wanting to say something to make him feel better, but knowing she didn't have the words, she couldn't stop herself from reaching up to cup her palm over his jaw instead. More than ever, she needed to be closer to him. Needed to touch him. Needed him to know that despite how difficult the night had been, she would do it all over again if he asked. And when he turned his jaw into her hand, actually letting her give him comfort, her heart melted even further.

He'd needed her once already tonight, as a buffer between him and his parents, and she'd given in to that need. Now, just steps away from her bedroom, she knew he needed her again. Only this time, it wasn't because he had a difficult relationship with his mother.

No, tonight he needed her for all the same reasons she needed him. Heat. Sparks. Undeniable attraction.

They were less than five seconds from a kiss, and her heart was fluttering like mad. But then he abruptly took a step—a large one—away from her, so that they were both backed up against opposing walls in the hallway.

Neither of them said anything for a long moment, one where the sexual tension was palpable between them. Finally, he said, "Don't be afraid to wake me up if you hear more noises tonight."

Disappointment flared so strongly that her, "Sure," came out sounding more like a croak than a word. Groping blindly for the doorknob, she somehow got her key inside and said good night.

* * *

The next morning, after tossing and turning most of the night—and wondering if Liam was doing the same thing—Christie decided to go see Jean again. Maybe today she'd be able to get more of the story.

She walked through the maple forest on her way to Jean's cabin. Christie had never seen anything like it before coming here. In the fall, the display of colors had been nothing short of mind-blowing. She hadn't expected the budding leaves of spring to even come close to matching that beauty, but she'd been wrong. Because as their bare branches reached out all around her, above her head, into the blue sky, she was overwhelmed by beauty. Growing up in Connecticut, she'd loved being outside, to go to the park or swim at the local pool, but being outside at Summer Lake was different. As though she was part of nature, rather than just being witness to it.

Four months ago, as fall had begun to give way to winter, she'd conceived of the Tapping of the Maples Festival on a walk through this forest. She'd felt as though she could take root like one of the seedlings between the large trees, that the mature growth would shelter her from storms and let through enough light for her to grow and stretch and become strong. Sap had been leaking from the trees, even then, and she'd reached out to brush some onto the tip of her finger. The pure maple syrup had tasted like magic. Like happiness. And she'd wanted to share that joy, that sweetness.

She still did. But now, with the petition...

She sighed and leaned against one of the maples, pressing her palm flat against it. Maybe there was a reason for all of this. For Wesley leaving and Liam appearing and Mr. Radin trying to stop her festival. What was it people always said? That when one door closed, a window opened? That sometimes the best things in life sprang from the most difficult?

She'd always been optimistic. Some might say blindly so, given her track record with jobs and men. But these past weeks were certainly doing their best to test that optimism.

"Good morning."

She nearly jumped out of her boots at the shock of finding Jean at her side. More than once Christie had thought the woman was as silent as a ghost. Just like her grandson, in fact.

"You really remind me of Liam," she told Jean. "You're both really good at sneaking up on people." When Jean laughed with obvious delight, Christie did the same. "And you both make me laugh at the most unexpected times."

"Liam makes you laugh, does he?" Jean raised an eyebrow. "Well, then. That's certainly something, isn't it?"

Christie didn't know how to respond. Instead, she said, "I haven't been able to stop thinking about what you told me yesterday. About your husband, Thomas. And how he disappeared just like Wesley."

"Well, there were quite a few differences. You and Wesley were never going to get married, for one."

"How did you know that? He didn't say anything to you before he left, did he?"

"Oh, honey, he didn't have to. Anyone with any sense knew it."

"Why didn't somebody tell me, then?"

"Some things you need to figure out for yourself," Jean said as they slowly headed through the trees toward her cottage. "Just like I needed to figure things out for myself way back when."

* * *

1945...

For three days, and two more long and lonely nights, Jean told no one that Thomas was gone. Everyone assumed they were simply having a perfect honeymoon when they didn't even come out of their rooms for meals.

She picked up the food left outside the door three times a day and flushed most of it down the toilet so that no one would know there was only one person in the honeymoon suite. She stared out the window for hours, keeping watch for him, even though she'd know the second he was back, would feel it deep in her soul.

Every day the room grew colder. And every night, as she dozed in the chair by the window, she dreamed she heard crying coming from the walls and woke up with tears on her cheeks.

When the sun rose on the fourth day, she held her

head high as she carried her suitcase downstairs, then turned in her room key at the front desk. She knew people had long thought of her older sister, Olive, as the strong one. But Jean had hidden reserves of strength she'd never had to tap into.

Until now.

"I need to leave my things here for now," she told the innkeeper, a lovely young girl who was new to town.

"Of course. Will your husband be back for them later?"

Jean simply said, "Thank you," before turning and heading for the door.

She walked the mile to her father's house along the beach, but she saw little of the beauty around her, barely noticed the sun beating down on her back.

Olive, who was visiting their parents, saw her first. "Did you walk from the inn? Where's Thomas?" Her sister stepped closer. "Have you been crying?"

Jean put her fingers to her cheek and wiped the moisture away. "I need to speak with Father."

"He's in the middle of a meeting with—"

But Jean was already moving past her sister, heading for the study. She'd thought the next time she walked through these doors, her husband would be beside her. Where was he? Was he hurt? She prayed he was okay.

"Father." She'd been told her voice had a lyrical quality, that she might have been a professional singer if she'd had any interest in it. Today it was flat as she stepped into the room. "I need to speak with you."

Three middle-aged men stood up quickly, their eyebrows rising as they took in her sleepless, tear-stained face. Smoke from their pipes swirled and curled up to the ceiling.

"Gentlemen, this is my daughter, Mrs. Thomas Kane." Still gracious despite her interruption, he said, "I'm in the middle of a meeting, honey. I'll come find you later."

She shook her head. "I need to speak with you right away." After three days in the inn's honeymoon suite, waiting and praying and hoping for the miracle of Thomas's reappearance, she'd decided that if her husband was, in fact, in trouble, she needed her father's help now, not later.

"If you'll excuse me, gentlemen, I'll be back shortly." She could tell her father was upset with her by the hard set of his jaw, the tight way he was holding his shoulders. He waited until they were out of earshot. "You embarrassed me back there."

"Thomas is gone."

Shock stopped him in his tracks. "What do you mean, gone?"

"I woke up the morning after our wedding and he

had disappeared."

"He disappeared three days ago?" When she nodded, he all but yelled, "Why on earth did you take so long to tell me this?"

"I was waiting. Waiting for him to come back."

She looked up to see myriad emotions cross her father's face. Empathy for her, disappointment, confusion. And, finally, anger.

"I gave him my money." With her father's help, Thomas had planned to start a new business in town. "Have you checked the account?" he asked.

"No." She hadn't thought about money. But now, she did. And she suddenly knew what her father would find when he went to speak with the bank manager. But there was relief there too. Because if Thomas had disappeared with her father's money, then it was less likely that he was hurt, wasn't it?

"Wait here," he commanded.

She knew he was going into his office, that he was rescheduling his meeting. She stood perfectly still, not moving a muscle as the three men filed out of the study to the front door.

"Come with me, Jean." He wasn't calling her *honey* anymore.

Thirty minutes later, all was confirmed. Thomas had come into the bank the morning after their wedding and withdrawn all of the funds but one hundred dollars.

Jean silently followed her father out of the bank and down to the public dock next to the inn. On this cool spring day, despite the bright sunshine, they were the only two people out on the lakeshore.

"You should have known better." His words were uttered through gritted teeth. All of them had been taken in by Thomas. Her father's pride would never live that down.

"We don't know why he took the money," she said, instinctively defending her husband.

"He took it because he's a crook."

But Jean could have never fallen in love with a bad man. "What if he isn't? What if he's in trouble? What if he needs our help?"

"That money he stole from me is the last help he'll ever get," her father vowed. "He was a con man. You were his target. The perfect, innocent little target."

Only, though Jean's heart was aching, she couldn't believe that it had all been a lie. Yes, she could accept that perhaps Thomas might have come into their lives as a con man. And, yes, she might have been his target. But by the time they had their wedding night, she knew with absolute certainty that their love had been real. Which meant there had to be another reason he'd left.

"We will have the marriage annulled right away,"

her father decreed.

She'd never talked back to her father. Never really stood up to him. But something had happened to her between that first kiss with Thomas and saying *I do*, between the love they'd made in the inn's honeymoon suite and waking up alone in an ice-cold room.

"The marriage was consummated, Father." He blinked in shock at her plain speech. "Thomas will always be my husband, even if he never comes back to me."

Her father's face twisted with disgust. "Listen to me, and listen close. From this moment forward, your new husband died in an unfortunate car accident. You will move back into our house and grieve him for an appropriate period of time. And then we will all forget this ever happened."

But six weeks later, she threw up her breakfast. And by the end of the week, her mother proclaimed it morning sickness.

Jean was pregnant with Thomas's baby.

CHAPTER EIGHTEEN

Christie was stunned to hear that the man Jean had loved with her whole heart and soul had conned her. That he'd left her pregnant. And alone.

Her tea had gone cold by the time she finally said, "That's why my bedroom is haunted, isn't it?"

Jean simply stood up to clear away the teapot and cups, neither confirming nor denying the ghost—or its cause.

But Christie knew.

She *knew*.

Her head spinning, she headed back to the inn. She was due to start her workday in an hour or so, but she wanted to go up to her bedroom first and look around. See if it looked different now that she knew for sure what had happened in that room to change everything.

Of course, now that she was waiting to feel the chill, to hear the horrible sounds, there was nothing.

Still, she found herself pulling a chair up to the window, the same window at which Jean had kept her vigil for three days, waiting and watching for Thomas to return. Despite all the signs to the contrary, Jean hadn't given up. Somehow, she had managed to survive—and push past—it all. Somehow, she had come out the other side able to skip rocks over the lake and laugh so freely in the maple forest.

Christie watched the cars move slowly along Main Street. She saw young mothers pushing their babies in strollers. Store owners unlocked their front doors and began the process of opening up for the day.

And suddenly, she knew that she couldn't give up either. She was going to fight the petition.

Her sense of purpose flooding back, Christie felt a million times better. How quickly she'd given up after hearing what Mr. Radin had to say. She'd thought she was changing, that she wasn't going to run scared anymore, but when put to the test, she'd crumbled like a dry ball of dirt in a child's fist.

Her excitement about the festival came rushing back as she compiled a list in her head of phone calls to make. She didn't know for sure if she could actually convince the Adirondack Preservation Council to give her festival another chance, but she sure as heck could give it everything she had.

* * *

Liam owed Christie. Big time.

She had thrown herself in front of an emotional bus

for him last night at his parents' house. One way or another, he was determined to give her back her festival.

He was also becoming an expert on the ins and outs of the Adirondack Preservation Council. He'd spent most of the previous night after returning from dinner at his parents' house scouring the Internet for information about park policy. And, more important, its loopholes.

His chief legal counsel hadn't been surprised to hear from him this morning—they'd been on the phone constantly during the past few weeks as he'd sold his company—but this time Frank was caught off guard by the assignment Liam had given him.

Sure, Liam knew Christie would be all right if the festival didn't happen. But what mattered far more was that her natural sparkle had almost been extinguished yesterday after Mr. Radin had trampled all over her plans.

Liam had never cared about a woman's *sparkle* before. But even the cynicism he'd wrapped around himself like armor for the past twenty years couldn't make him immune to the power of Christie's smile. Seeing it fall, and watching the sparks go out of her eyes, was nothing short of heartbreaking.

Heartbreaking enough to make him wonder if he might still have a heart, after all.

* * *

An hour later, Christie's renewed excitement was on the verge of fizzling out. She'd spent the past sixty minutes hitting one brick wall after another.

For some crazy reason, the one person she wanted to talk to about it was Liam. He hadn't wanted her to work on the festival, initially, but hadn't he used the word *we* last night? Maybe he would be willing to brainstorm some ideas with her. Because she really didn't want to give up this time.

She called his room, but there was no answer, so she went downstairs to look for him. Alice was checking out a guest when Christie asked, "Have you seen Liam?"

Alice nodded in the direction of the front porch. "He's outside on the phone."

Christie's heart did a funny little flip before diving toward her stomach. She and Liam hadn't kissed last night, but there was an attraction between them that she could no longer deny. And every time she saw him, every time they spoke, that awareness, that attraction grew stronger.

Liam wasn't on the porch, but she could hear his voice coming from the rose garden off to the side. In the summer and early fall, the rose-covered arbor was a favorite place for brides to marry their true loves. In the thaw of spring, the vines and stalks were still bare, but Christie found the garden to be lovely just the same, with its promise of new growth and beauty.

He was standing beneath the arbor, looking out at the lake, and the sight of him standing in the exact spot where so many grooms had stood before had her breath catching in her throat.

Her brain started playing tricks on her, changing the scene so that Liam wasn't wearing jeans and a button-down long-sleeved shirt anymore. He wasn't on the phone. It was no longer spring. Instead, she saw roses in full bloom all around him. He was wearing a tuxedo with a rose tucked into his lapel. And he was waiting for her to walk toward him in a beautiful, long white gown…looking at her with more love than she'd ever seen in anyone's eyes.

What was wrong with her brain? Why was it playing this trick on her—showing her a vision that seemed impossibly real? So real she could actually smell the roses in the air, when she knew darn well there wasn't a single flower petal in sight.

That was when a snippet of his conversation floated over to her.

"Will the entire council be there this afternoon?" After a short pause, he said, "Good, we'll be there at four o'clock." Hanging up, he turned around and found her standing there staring at him. "Christie." She swore his eyes lit up when he saw her. "I was just about to come look for you. We have a meeting with the Preservation Council this afternoon to present a counterpetition for your festival."

She was so grateful. Beyond grateful. But guilt was there too. Because now she knew for sure what she'd suspected from the start: Beneath Liam's walls, inside the barriers he'd erected all around himself, he was a good man. Truly good.

"I'm sorry for what I said yesterday. For saying I thought you'd be happy about the festival being off."

"You don't ever need to apologize for being honest, Christie. You were angry. I told you to pass off the festival to someone else more than once. You had every reason to assume I'd be happy about it. But honestly, I'd much rather wipe the smug smile off Radin's face."

* * *

Liam had made a lucrative career out of thinking things through—and never making mistakes. But somehow, Christie was changing everything.

Because he hadn't realized—nor had he wanted to accept—just how hard it would be for him to keep his focus on the job at hand when she was sitting so close in his car. Close enough for him to breathe in her sweet scent. Close enough that he could easily reach over and curl his fingers around hers as they cruised down a narrow back road on their way to the meeting.

"Tell me about growing up here, Liam."

He didn't like to think back on his childhood. And, perhaps, if she'd asked him another time, he wouldn't have told her anything at all, apart from generalizations. But he could tell she was nervous—something that affected him nearly as much as her fading smile. So he said, "Wesley and I used to sail every Saturday and Sunday during the summer races. Did he ever take you out in the *Flying Scott*?"

"Only once, but I'm afraid I'm not much of a sailor. After getting his instructions about the mast or the stern or whatever it is backward, it nearly hit him in the head and we ended up tipping over in the middle of the lake."

"You didn't go out and try again?"

"I should have. It just seemed easier not to, I guess. You know, that way Wesley could have a good sail without worrying about me."

Liam was on the verge of offering to take her sailing once the ice on the lake melted and the water warmed up. But since staying here until summer had never been in his plans, he said instead, "Our father taught us to sail. To this day, he's still one of the best sailors I've ever met. Thirty knots coming at him and he doesn't even blink. He just grins and hikes out into the wind."

"I like Henry a lot."

He could hear the affection in her voice. "He's a good man," he agreed, his words gruffer than he intended.

"Why don't you go hiking or fishing with him, Liam? He wants so badly to spend time with you."

He should have been upset that she was poking into his private life, but he found that he was simply glad to have helped her forget about their meeting for a few minutes. And, truthfully, a part of him liked knowing that she cared.

He took a deep breath and blew it out. "My relationship with my father is complicated."

"He loves you. That's not complicated."

He knew what was coming next. She was going to ask about his mother. Thank God the Preservation Council building had just come into view. "We're here."

* * *

Two hours later, Christie felt like a limp dishrag as she and Liam walked back to his car. "I had no idea it would be like that." She slumped on the leather seat beside him. On the drive out earlier that afternoon, she'd been nervous about being in the small car with him. Now, she was too tired for nerves.

"Meetings like that call for one thing," he told her.

"A short rope and a tall tree to hang it from?"

Another time she would have appreciated his low chuckle as he clarified, "A stiff drink."

She wasn't big on booze, but if ever there was a time for alcohol, this was it. The council had allowed them to say their piece. They had taken the documentation she and Liam had put together. They had asked a zillion questions.

And they'd promised nothing.

Zilch.

Nada.

Liam pulled into the kind of roadside dive she would never have had the guts to come to on her own, one with a dozen motorcycles parked outside.

"I've driven past here so many times," she said as they headed inside, "but never thought to stop. Have you been here before?"

Before he could answer, she heard someone call out, "Damned if I ever thought I'd see this day come again. Liam Kane live and in the flesh."

Liam nodded at the heavily tattooed man behind the bar. "Christie, meet Dick. We're in need of two of your specials."

Despite her shock that the two men knew each other—she'd assumed Liam lived solely in a world of suits—she couldn't help but smile back at the man who was grinning so widely at her. "It's nice to meet you, Dick."

"Nice to meet you too." His hands were deft as he quickly mixed up their drinks. "Good to see you back home, Liam. You've been missed."

Glasses in hand, they headed over to a small booth in the corner of the dark room. "He seems nice," she said.

"You like everyone, don't you?"

"Until I see a reason not to like them, yes."

"That trust is going to get you hurt, Christie."

She rolled her eyes. "That's so cynical."

"But true."

More frustrated now by what Liam was saying than she'd been for the two hours they'd done their song-and-dance for the council, she picked up her glass and took a huge gulp. Her eyes were watering when she put the drink down. "My God, what's in this?"

"Who knows?" he said with a shrug and another one of those almost-smiles. "No one's ever been able to get Dick to give up the recipe."

Maybe she should have been angry with Liam for poisoning her with this way-too-potent drink. Maybe she should have been crying over the fact that their one shot at convincing the council to let her have her festival looked to be a big goose egg. Instead, she found herself laughing over the way everything in her life had spun so totally out of control. It was either laugh or cry. And she was afraid that if she started crying, she might never stop.

"I'll be right back." Amazed by how unsteady she felt on her feet after drinking only a few ounces of Dick's concoction, she was back sixty seconds later. "Got it," she said, triumphantly holding out the recipe.

"Dick told you what he puts in his signature drink?" Liam asked incredulously.

"I asked nicely."

"Only you could make a man spill a secret he's been holding on to for decades."

She took another, smaller sip of the surprisingly delicious drink. "If you ask me, he was dying to have someone to tell, but everyone's been too afraid to ask him all these years." Bolder for the drink, she leaned across the table. "Now it's your turn to tell me a secret."

She wasn't expecting his expression to change so quickly from teasing to deadly serious. "Stopping here was a bad idea. I'm sure you want to get back to the inn."

He was already pushing his chair back when she put her hand over his to halt him. She wished she could be inside his head, wished she could understand what had caused this abrupt change in him when they were finally relaxing with each other. But since she couldn't read his mind, she said, "I thought we were having fun. What did I do wrong?"

His eyes were dark, his jaw jumping. She felt the air change, knew everything between them was on the verge of shifting, a split second before he said, "This, damn it."

And then his hands were in her hair, and his mouth was on hers, and he was kissing all of the air from her lungs.

She'd wanted this kiss for too long to do anything but reach right back for him and deepen the sweetest, most sinful kiss she'd ever tasted.

When he finally pulled away and she could figure out how to form words again, she whispered, "That was my secret too."

CHAPTER NINETEEN

Liam made sure there were no more kisses in the bar or during their drive back to the inn.

He should apologize to Christie for losing control like that, for taking something she hadn't offered. But how the hell could he ever be sorry about kissing her? She was softer, sweeter than any woman had ever been…and he wanted her more than he'd ever known it was possible to want anyone or anything.

Even though the way she'd flat-out asked him to tell her his secrets had cut straight to the core of him. Almost as if she knew things that she couldn't possibly know.

"Liam?"

She said his name as they were getting out of his car in the employee lot behind the inn. The moon was barely a sliver, and it was dark. So dark he should have been safe stealing another glance at her beauty in the car's lights without being caught out as a thief.

"Are you sorry you kissed me?"

He should have known she would ask him something like that, the exact question no one else would dare say aloud.

Liam tried to remind himself that she couldn't possibly be the open book she seemed to be—the same reminder he'd been repeating to himself for days. Only this time, with the taste of her kiss still on his lips, though she still hadn't come completely clean with him about Wesley, he just couldn't get himself to believe it.

He opened his mouth to say yes, they shouldn't have kissed. But the lie wouldn't come. "No, I'm not sorry. Are you?"

"How could I possibly regret that kiss?"

He should have had an answer for her. Should have been able to clearly, and definitively, lay out all the reasons they shouldn't get involved. But somehow, being with Christie felt inevitable. From that first moment he'd seen her at Sarah and Calvin's wedding, he'd been inexplicably drawn to her. And no matter how many times he tried to pull away, in the end he'd found he couldn't actually do it.

Not even when she moved closer, so close that he swore he could almost hear her heart beating as she said, "Would you please kiss me again?"

Sweet Lord. No one had ever asked him to kiss her like that. With such honest desire. No wonder his bartender friend had given up his drink recipe to her. Christie was irresistible.

And then she was putting her hands over his shoulders and tilting her mouth up to his—and even the strongest man in the world couldn't have stopped himself from kissing her again.

Her lips were soft, and she tasted like a mixture of the syrup in her drink and something that was uniquely Christie. One kiss wasn't nearly enough, so he kept going back for one more, and then another, and another after that.

How could anyone taste this good? How could anyone be this pure, this giving?

He couldn't keep his hands from gripping her tighter, from dragging her closer. Couldn't stop his heart from racing faster and faster as she made little sounds of pleasure, of joy, that shot right through to the center of him. And as she wound her arms tighter around him, she was everything he'd ever wanted, but had never let himself wish for.

In her kiss, there was more than just passion. She stirred up something so much bigger than desire inside of him—impossible hope and dreams for a future that he'd always believed could never be his.

Only, with every moment that passed, with every kiss Christie so willingly gave him, images of his brother touching her the same way grew larger, more insistent. Liam had never been a jealous lover. He'd never been possessive. But now, with nothing more than a few of Christie's kisses on his lips, all he could think was, *Mine.*

He dragged his mouth from hers. In the faint moonlight, he could see that her mouth was swollen from his kisses. He'd never wanted a woman this much, had never been on the verge of throwing her over his shoulder and carrying her upstairs to his bed. "Did my brother kiss you like this?"

Her eyes widened with shock. "Excuse me?"

He needed to stop, needed to take a step back and apologize for his jealous question. Instead, he did just the opposite. "Was this how he held you?" He ran his hands down from her shoulders to the rise of her hips.

She pushed against his chest. "You're acting like a child in a sandbox fighting over a prized toy."

He forced himself to release his hold on her. Damn it, he wasn't acting any better than her bastard ex-boyfriend had. But now that they were admitting the truth of their attraction to each other, he could no longer deny that visions of Christie and his brother together had been playing around the edges of his mind all week. Visions that had his stomach twisting.

"I'm going crazy thinking about the two of you," he admitted in a rough voice that he barely recognized as his own. Hell, he could hardly believe that he was standing in the parking lot of his inn pleading with a woman who used to be his brother's fiancée, begging her to tell him she wasn't thinking of anyone but him when they were making out.

"He never kissed me like that," she told him. "He barely even touched me."

Liam wanted so badly to believe her. But how could he when he knew firsthand that she was utterly irresistible? "That's impossible. How could he have been with you and not touched you?" He shouldn't have reached out for her again, shouldn't have let a strand of her hair thread through his fingers, but he had no self-control anymore. "How could any sane man possibly keep his hands off you?"

"I swear," she said in a raw whisper. "We barely even kissed in all the months we were together."

He should have been ecstatic to hear it—and he was—but in some crazy way, he was angry too, on Christie's behalf. "How could you have accepted that? Didn't you think you deserved to be with a man who wanted you? How long did you think you were going to be able to keep your desires buried?"

"Wesley was kind. I knew he loved me. Maybe not as a woman, but as a person. It was more than anyone else had ever given me. I thought that dating a married guy was my biggest mistake, but I managed to top that by almost marrying a gay man." She slapped her hand over her mouth. "*Oh no!* I promised him I wouldn't say anything. He told me he needed time." She looked horrifically guilty about the secret she'd let loose. "It was his secret to tell, not mine."

"Why didn't he tell me?" Liam was reeling from her revelation. "Why didn't he tell any of us, only you?"

"He said it would break your parents if he told them, though he wouldn't tell me why. As for why he didn't tell you—" She looked away, as if she didn't think he could handle hearing the truth.

"Christie." He put his finger on her chin to tip her face back up to his. "Be honest with me. You're the only one who always is."

He could hear, could feel her breath catch, before she finally said, "Maybe he didn't tell you because you make sure everyone is afraid of you. That they don't get close to you. Like how you barely say a word to your mother, even though she's so hurt every time you push her away. Your father too."

They were hard truths. Each and every one of them.

Because for all that he wanted to tell himself he hadn't known about Wesley, was that really true? Wasn't it more that Liam had been so caught up in his own life and career and doing anything he could to stay away from his parents? Hadn't he been so damn busy telling himself it was better for everyone if he stayed out of their business, that he hadn't had even a minute to spare for his brother? And even after returning to Summer Lake this week, hadn't he made sure not to get too close to anyone? He hadn't looked up any old friends. His mother had to beg him to come to dinner. His father was desperate to take an hour and go for a hike.

And all he'd done was work like hell to shut them out.

"I care about you, Liam." Christie's words were filled with the sweetness he craved, warmth that seeped deeper into his cells with every moment they spent together. "All week I've been trying to tell myself to stay away from you. But you're a good man."

"How could you think that when you're right about everything you just said?"

"Because you didn't have to help me today—you did it because it was the right thing to do. You didn't have to stay to pitch in at the inn. That wasn't your agreement with Wesley. But even though you don't really want to be at Summer Lake, you've stayed to help. And—" She paused, then swallowed hard before saying, "I want you. I can't seem to stop wanting you."

Just the way he couldn't stop wanting her. "If I were a good man," he said in a raw voice, "I would walk away from you so that you could find someone better."

She blinked up at him. "You're not going to walk

away right now?"

He answered her by sliding his arms around her and kissing her in a way he'd never kissed another woman. There was heat there, of course, but emotion trumped everything else. Emotion that stunned him in a way very few things ever had.

Liam had believed he would always be able to compartmentalize the physical from the emotional. He'd been so sure that no woman would ever change the core of who he was or what he believed to be true.

But with a handful of kisses, Christie was already breaking in. Breaking through. Breaking down. Everything he'd been so certain about. Everything he'd held on to for so long as the only way to move forward.

From the first moment at the inn, he hadn't been able to take his eyes off of her. And now that he knew just how sweet she tasted, now that he'd heard her sounds of pleasure, now that he'd felt the shiver of arousal move from her body to his—there was no way he could keep denying that he was in deep. Far deeper than he'd ever thought to be with anyone.

So when he finally lifted his mouth from hers, there was only one thing left to say. "How can I walk away from you?"

"You walked away from your family."

No one had ever called him out on his bad behavior like the one woman he couldn't stay away from no matter how hard he tried. "You're right. I walked away from all of them."

"Tell me why."

"People lie." He stroked her cheek, needing to touch her constantly, wanting to be as close to her as he could possibly be. "That's why I walked away. And that's why I can't lie to you. I can't tell you that everything is going to work out, that this kiss is going to turn into a happily ever after."

He didn't know what he expected her to do, but she didn't flinch. She didn't pull away. Instead, she simply said, "Tell me the truth, then."

"I don't want to hurt you."

"Good." Her mouth moved into a small smile. "I'm sick of being hurt."

If he were smart, he would stop right there and make sure he didn't say anything else that would drive her out of his arms. But, then, how could he possibly live with himself? "Christie, I'm trying to tell you that I can't promise you anything."

He was surprised by another one of her beautiful smiles, a bigger one this time. "Is this where I'm supposed to slap you and call you a cad for kissing me like you just did?"

This conversation wasn't going the way he thought it would. Any other woman would have pulled away and written him off. But not Christie. She surprised him at every turn. "You said it yourself," he forced himself to remind her. "You've been trying to convince yourself to stay away from me."

"Yup," she said, as blunt as he. "But I also can't seem to help myself where you're concerned."

It would be so easy just to stop talking and kiss her again. But he wouldn't be able to live with himself unless everything was laid out, clearly and on the table, so that neither of them could ignore the truth of the situation. "Your reasons for wanting to stay away from me couldn't have changed. Tell me what they are."

"Seriously? You want to hear why I should know better than to want you?"

It was the only way to ensure he didn't hurt her. Which was exactly why he needed to make himself say, "Here are mine: You were Wesley's fiancée. You work for me." He paused before giving her the most important reason of all. "And you deserve to be with a man who can give you everything you want."

She made a sound that was somewhere between disbelief and a laugh. "My reason is much simpler than that. You're the beast."

Whatever he'd expected, it wasn't that. "If it's so simple, then how come I'm not following?"

"You know, like the *Beauty and the Beast* fable. Not that I'm that much of a beauty—"

"You are."

"I'm giving a point to you for saying that," she said. "But in a nutshell, I've spent way too many years finding broken men and trying to heal them—only without the happily ever after."

There was so much in what she'd just said, but one question stood out from the rest: "You think I'm broken?"

She met his eyes head on in the moonlight. "Aren't you? You barely speak to your mother. Your father is desperate for a relationship with you. And your brother has been keeping a secret from all of you his whole life. Did I miss anything?"

"Sounds like you've got it just about covered. Which means," he forced himself to add, "this is right when you should be saying good-bye to me."

"I disagree," she countered. "You and I have just been completely honest with one another. In my book, that's cause for celebration." Instead of moving away, she put her arms around his neck. "So…what do *you* think we should do about all of this?"

A dozen heated visions flashed through his brain before he could make himself say, "Sleep on it, probably."

"I'm really hoping you're going to tell me you don't mean separately."

"You do know you're not supposed to say things like that out loud, don't you?"

"Only because you're always telling me so."

He shouldn't have broken out into laughter. But he'd never been able to help himself where Christie was concerned. And even though nothing had been settled between them, he couldn't help himself now either. Especially when she looked utterly delighted.

"It's even better than I thought it would be," she said.

No one had ever confused—or captivated him—this much. "What's better?"

"Your laughter. I've been wanting to hear it for so long."

His heart felt surprisingly full as he said, "Come here and give me a kiss good night before we go back to our *separate* rooms."

"See, what did I tell you?" she whispered as she raised herself up on her tippy-toes and held her mouth a breath away from his.

He told himself he was going to make sure this was the last kiss of the night even if it killed him to do the honorable thing. But he was so dizzy with the desire to taste her again that he could barely string words together. "What did you tell me, Christie?"

He felt her smile against his lips without needing to see it. "You *are* a good man."

And then she kissed him.

CHAPTER TWENTY

As Liam and Christie kissed in the moonlight, neither of them saw the lone figure standing in the shadows.

Susan had never spied on her kids before. She wasn't one of those overprotective parents who hovered and asked too many questions. And she certainly hadn't dropped by the inn tonight to try to catch Liam and Christie together. She'd simply come by to see if she could make peace with her son, knowing full well that she'd done nothing but drive him even farther away since he'd returned to Summer Lake.

While she knew that Liam and Christie weren't actually doing anything wrong—when she'd cooled down the previous night, she had to admit that Henry was right, and she should butt out of Liam's budding love life—she also knew they wouldn't appreciate her watching them. She desperately wanted to get back into her car and drive away, but if she so much as moved, she was certain they would hear her.

And she knew how it felt to be caught.

How, she wondered, as they finally made a move to go inside, could they not hear her heart beating when it had never sounded so loudly in her own ears? Especially now that she'd finally learned why Wesley had left: because he'd been afraid to tell them he had feelings for a man.

She and Henry had made their fair share of mistakes, but had they really done such an awful job as parents that he felt he couldn't trust them?

Unfortunately, Susan was afraid she already had her answer in the list Christie had given Liam of the reasons she should steer clear of dating him. A list he'd agreed was accurate: *You barely speak to your mother. Your father is desperate for a relationship with you. And your brother has been keeping a secret from all of you his whole life.*

Susan could no longer deny the painful truth: She had failed both of her sons.

When she finally deemed it safe to move without being seen, she ran to her car and quickly drove away. Henry was waiting on the porch when she got home.

"I was wondering where you went," he said, and then, "Are you crying?"

"I went to the inn to talk to Liam. But he and Christie—"

Frustration flew across Henry's face. "I don't want to hear it. Whatever they're doing is their business."

It was instinctive at this point for her ruff to go up at his tone. But where had her pride—and her mistakes—gotten her so far? So she forced herself to say, "You were right. Their relationship is their business."

Henry's eyes widened with surprise at her admission. "Then why are you crying?"

"Wesley is gay." Realizing what it sounded like, that she was crying over her son's sexual orientation, she quickly clarified, "I accidentally overheard Christie tell Liam why Wesley left. Our son swore Christie to secrecy because he thought the truth would *break* us."

"My God." Henry sat down hard on one of the porch rockers. "How could he have thought that?"

"I keep going back to what a wreck I was after James died." Her brother had passed away unexpectedly nearly twenty years ago from pneumonia. But the man they'd seen crying at her brother's funeral had clearly been more than a friend. He'd been her brother's partner. Only, her brother had never come out to her either. "Wesley must have mistakenly thought he had to marry Christie to make sure I didn't fall apart all over again."

"And when he couldn't do it, he ran," Henry confirmed thoughtfully.

"I've ruined so many things." Her legs were shaking, and she could feel them about to give way. But her husband was there before she could fall. Just like he always had been.

"You're freezing cold. We need to go inside and sit near the fire." She was grateful for his warmth, for the way he cared for her even when she didn't deserve it. And he was right. She was cold. But it was a cold that had hardly anything to do with the temperature.

Secrets were ripping her family apart. First, Liam had pulled away from her. And then, Wesley had run.

She needed to come clean about everything. Now. Tonight. Before the secrets ripped her husband away too.

But inside by the fire, as Henry held her and she reveled in his warmth and touch for the first time in far too long, the fear of actually losing him kept the truth of what she had done twenty years ago locked up tight inside her heart.

* * *

Christie had never been promiscuous. She wasn't a virgin, of course, but she never slept with anyone until they'd been dating for a while. Not because she was a tease, not because she was frigid, but because she'd never been able to let herself go physically without emotion tying her to someone.

Liam had left her at her door like the perfect gentleman. And though she knew they should let their ridiculously hot kisses settle a bit before they took the next step, it was taking every ounce of self-control she possessed not to grab her master key and unlock his door.

To offer herself to him.

On top of all that, her bedroom was suddenly frigid. Almost as though some unseen presence were trying to kick her out of it...or get her to invite Liam back in to see if his presence would warm it up again.

"I don't have the energy for you tonight," she found herself saying to the room at large.

Thump!

She should have known better than to issue a challenge like that. Because the sounds that started coming from the walls weren't the sad wails they'd been before—this time they sounded impatient.

Okay, say she was willing to believe that there was a ghost. Did this spirit expect her to solve its problems? More specifically, had this bedroom been waiting sixty years for true love to set it straight, after Jean's honeymoon had ended in such tragedy?

Christie snorted at the thought. "If you're waiting for my love life to turn things around for you," she said to her bedroom walls, "you're going to be in for a much longer wait."

Thump!

She could have sworn the wall was talking back to her, a loud banging akin to a foot stomping in frustration.

"Yes, I'm as frustrated about it as you are," she replied, even though this conversation was taking weird to a brand-new level. "If I were you, I'd look to one of the couples getting married at the inn. Trust me, you're bound to have better luck there. Besides, you've had decades to deal with this. Why now? Why me?"

As soon as she could get away from the front desk tomorrow, she was going to hunt down Jean and keep pouring tea until she got the rest of the story out of her. Maybe if Christie had some clues as to what had happened after Thomas left, then she could make whatever was going wrong in this bedroom stop.

Reaching into her bedside table, she pulled out earplugs and jammed them into her ears. But sixty seconds later, she knew it was pointless. The knocking had become even louder—a *thump, thump, thump* that was sure to make the headache that had been forming in the back of her head come to full fruition.

And then she realized it wasn't the walls knocking.

It was someone at the door.

* * *

Liam had tried to do the right thing. He'd intended to say good night to Christie with one final kiss. But then he heard those sounds coming from her bedroom, and how could he possibly have stayed away?

Now here he was, standing in front of her door again. He'd knocked once, then twice. The master keys were still on the coffee table in his room. He wouldn't barge in on her again, even if it meant catching another glimpse of her in her sexy pajamas.

Liam knew he should not only get the hell back to his room, but also do everything he could to keep things from going from complicated to ridiculously messy. If he didn't know better, he'd think there was some outside force pushing the two of them together. But he just couldn't believe in anything he couldn't see and touch.

Which brought him right back to where he was now. Standing in the hallway, dying to see her. Dying to kiss her again. Dying for even one more smile, if that was all he could get.

Finally, the door opened. "Hi."

Her beautiful smile had him smiling back. He simply couldn't help it. "Hi."

"You heard the sounds?"

"I did."

"Want to hear it close up?"

He knew what she was asking him. And it had nothing to do with the strange sounds. "More than you know."

"Oh, trust me," she said with another gorgeous smile, "I know."

"One day you're going to stop surprising me."

"I hope not," she replied. "You seem like a man who likes to be surprised."

She was wrong. He hated surprises. Or used to anyway. But there was something so incredibly engaging about the way he could never predict what she was going to say next. Or do, apparently, because a moment later, she was tugging him inside, locking the door behind him, then cupping his jaw and moving to her toes to kiss him.

She was so soft. So sweet. And so damned sexy, made more so by the lingering innocence that surrounded her. As if she was desperate for the chance to experience more pleasure than she'd ever had before. As if she thought that he could be the man to give her that pleasure, to find her sensual limits and push past them in all the best possible ways.

He tried to let her stay as the lead on their kiss, but he wanted her too much to follow through with that plan. Seconds later, he had his hands threaded through her hair so that he could tilt her head back and move his mouth from hers to the hollow beneath her chin.

"Listen," she said softly. He was so lost in the deliciously decadent task of learning the taste of her skin, it took him a few seconds to realize what she was saying. "The thumping stopped. I think our kissing is making the ghost happy."

He wasn't a man who kissed and laughed at the same time. But he couldn't contain it as he said, "Forget about the ghost. Kissing you makes *me* happy."

"I like making you happy," she said, before proving it with another sweet kiss.

But although he wanted nothing more than to pick her up and carry her into her bedroom, her words hit way too close to home. "I want you to be happy too. And maybe here, tonight, we can make each other happy. But not in the long run." Because he could never make the mistake of trusting anyone completely. Not even her.

She stroked her fingers down from his face to his shoulders and chest as though she couldn't resist touching him now that she finally had the chance. Through his T-shirt and jeans, he could feel the heat of her. He wanted to feel so much more, wanted to get so much closer, with nothing between them, but he couldn't let it happen with a lie. With deception.

He could practically see her mind working as her brows moved together and her eyes focused on an imaginary point. For all that it seemed she was just blurting things out all the time, she could be extremely thoughtful. She simply hated to hide the truth of her feelings from people. He'd never known anyone like her.

At last, she said, "It keeps occurring to me that a

smart woman would be playing games to try to keep your interest. But I've never had the heart for games."

"I don't either," he agreed. "But I'm worried about you getting hurt. And I would hate myself for causing your tears."

"Aren't you worried about yourself too?"

Though they'd agreed to tell each other the truth, he tried to be gentle as he said, "I'm not the one looking for someone to love me."

"Are you sure about that?"

Her whispered question made his chest clench. Clench so tightly, in fact, that he couldn't stop himself from pushing back just as hard as she was pushing him. "You were right in the parking lot. We aren't going to end up like one of those fairy tales. You're beautiful, and I want you more than I've ever wanted anyone, but your love isn't going to make me a new man."

Now she'd have to back down. Give up. She'd tell him to go. And even though it was the last thing he wanted, he'd make himself leave.

But she remained in his arms as she said, "You don't need to become a new man, Liam."

It killed him to have to hurt her feelings now so that he wouldn't crush them later. "Maybe not, but your love isn't going to turn the Kanes into one big, happy family either."

He watched for a flinch. Was certain that this time

she would.

Instead, her eyes flashed with determination—and something that looked, strangely, like humor. "And here I was thinking that sleeping with you tonight would do just that."

"Christie." Her name was a warning on his lips. He was trying to be careful with her, and she was bound and determined to foil him at every turn. Didn't she know that just the words *sleeping with you* were the proverbial straw that was going to break his vow to do right by her?

"Liam." She mimicked his warning tone well. "I know what you want me to say. That I'm going into tonight with my eyes wide open. That making love with you won't change anything. That I won't hold you to more than a few sinful hours between the sheets when morning comes. But I just don't have it in me to tell you the dozen different lies that I know you want to hear."

"I don't want you ever to lie to me," he insisted.

"Good, because here's the unvarnished truth: I can't promise you I'm not going to get hurt. And I definitely can't promise you I'm not going to fall head over heels in love with you, even if you never let yourself love me back. But I am absolutely certain that I want to make love with you tonight. Please, Liam, stay with me."

No other woman had ever talked to him like this. No one had ever had the courage to be so honest with her emotions. So up front about the mistakes she might make.

On a groan, he captured her mouth with his and lifted her into his arms. Seconds later, she was lying on her bed beneath him. He didn't ask for her pleasure, he stole it. But he knew that she was stealing just as much from him as she slicked her tongue over his.

Only, they weren't taking anything from each other tonight—they were giving each other exactly what they needed. Not just pleasure, not just the chance to let *wild* take free rein...but one perfect night to spin their attraction into something so much bigger than merely pleasure.

CHAPTER TWENTY-ONE

No one had ever kissed her like this, with such desire, with such heat, with so much need. And she needed him just as badly.

He was hard everywhere she was soft, and the things he knew how to do with his mouth to hers—*my God*. She could kiss him all night long and still not know how he did it. How he made every part of her come alive with nothing more than the brush of his lips over hers. How every cell in her body heated with need as he tangled his tongue with hers. How the nip of his teeth there, and then there, and then—*oh yes*—there, made her nearly shatter into a million breathless pieces.

She wrapped her legs around his waist and urged him to take anything—everything—he wanted from her. But instead of answering her body's plea, he lifted himself up on his forearms to stare down at her.

"You're so beautiful."

"Thank you."

"Thank you?" He ran his fingertip gently along her

hairline. Little tingles met his touch, and she almost whimpered at the pleasure of it. "I don't think you understand quite what I'm saying." His eyes were just as dark, just as unfathomable as ever. But his tone was richer, filled with a depth of emotion he'd never let her hear before.

"I do." Her voice sounded breathless. "You think I'm pretty."

His smile was tinged with heat. "You're so much more than pretty, Christie." He pressed a kiss to the spot on her forehead that he'd been lightly caressing. "Gorgeous. Stunning. Perfect. None of those words do you justice."

She'd expected heat, pleasure. She cared enough for Liam to find emotion in their kisses and caresses. But she hadn't thought there'd be such heartfelt words from a man who was so cautious with them.

He kissed her then, a kiss that echoed his words. A kiss that made her believe what he was saying was real.

"Something happens when you kiss me," she admitted. "I feel beautiful."

"Never doubt that you are, not for one single second."

She felt as though he was seeing all the way into her soul, into the hidden part where she'd tried to ignore the hurt from every man who had rejected her for not being exciting enough. For not being a risk taker, or knowing how to say the right thing at the right time. Even with Wesley—especially with Wesley—she'd lost sight of herself as a sensual woman.

One kiss at a time, Liam was giving that feminine power back to her.

She still had her robe on, and she wanted nothing more than to be naked beneath Liam, his powerful body pressing hers into the mattress. She reached for the sash, but before she could untie it, his hands were over hers, stopping her.

"Undressing you for the first time is a pleasure I don't want to miss."

She actually whimpered at the sensuality of his words. "Okay. But could you hurry?"

That smile she loved to see so much played around his mouth. "No."

She groaned with disappointment even as her body heated up with increased anticipation. "Pretty please?"

"So sweet." She watched his long, strong fingers slowly untie her sash. "And usually so good at getting what you want with that sweetness."

She was about to protest the *usually* when his fingertips grazed the bare skin of her belly. Words fled as she sucked in a breath, her muscles trembling beneath his touch.

"Such lovely skin." He shifted on the bed so that he could press a kiss to that bare patch. "And so beautifully sensitive."

Another kiss followed the first, but before she could thread her hands into his hair, he was moving away again, taking the lapels of her robe and sliding it off her shoulders.

With every inch of skin he uncovered, there was another kiss. Places that had never been sensitive before responded to his slightest touch, to the brush of his lips followed by his fingertips grazing the new spot he'd marked. Until finally, he slid the robe all the way off her arms.

He'd seen her in fairly skimpy pajamas before, but though there'd been attraction between them a week ago, it hadn't been this red hot. And neither of them had had any intention of acting on it. But oh, were they ever acting on it now as Liam slowly ran his fingertips down over the straps of her top.

"Just take it off, already!"

"All this time, I thought you were so patient," he said, a heated chuckle underlying his words.

"In case you didn't hear me earlier," she said in a far more petulant tone than she could believe was coming out of her mouth, "I said I want you." She waited until his gaze met hers. "Really, really, *really* want."

That won her a kiss, one that seared them both. With the few brain cells she had left, she tried to wriggle out of the rest of her clothes. But Liam's hands were there before she could.

"Not yet." He ran kisses over every inch of her newly bared skin, then said, "Lift your arms for me, sweetheart."

She was so bowled over by the endearment that she actually froze. Maybe she should have let it slip by, should have silently locked it away in her heart for cold winter nights, but how could she? "You called me sweetheart."

"Arms up," he said again, and as she did as he asked, she knew he was uncomfortable with what he'd just said. But she still needed him to know, "No one's ever said that to me before. I liked it. Say it again. Please."

For a long moment, she thought he might ignore her request. But then he lowered his mouth back to hers, and the word came against her lips so softly that she might not have heard it if she hadn't been able to feel it too.

"Sweetheart."

And when he kissed her again, Christie realized she wasn't in danger of falling anymore. Because despite every warning he'd given her—and despite every warning she'd given herself—she'd already gone and done it.

* * *

Liam wasn't a man who spouted poetry to the women he bedded. Sex had always been about taking care of physical needs. Sex had never been about laughter, or teasing. Definitely not about emotion.

And yet, Christie was drawing all three from him.

He knew what he should be doing, knew what was smart. Pulling away from her. Telling her he was sorry he'd come to her tonight. Saying this was a mistake.

The problem was, his brain was no longer in charge. Although, if that were the only problem, he might still have been able to dig into his self-control and leave before things went any further. Only, something else was leading tonight with Christie. Not simply a body that desired her.

But a heart he didn't have the first clue how to control.

How could he when what he saw in her eyes humbled him? Pleasure. Freedom. Joy. And so much emotion it made his chest clench with longing.

Longing to be worthy of her.

So when she reached for him again, he vowed to give her as much ecstasy, as much bliss, as she could bear. He kissed his way down her body, from her forehead, to her cheekbones, to the sensitive curve where her jaw met her neck. He tasted the hollow of her collarbone, then her shoulder and upper arm, then a spot on her inner elbow that made her shiver, then down to her hand so that he could kiss each fingertip one at a time. And then he did it all over again on her other side, leaving no part of her unearthed, untasted, unadorned.

Because every inch of her was a miracle. One that he'd never thought to deserve.

She was begging, pleading, by the time he found the swells of her breasts with his tongue. She arched into him, and it was an invitation he couldn't deny as he cupped her sweet flesh in his hand and took first one taut peak between his lips, and then the other. Over and over, until her hands were threaded in his hair. Until she was tugging him even closer. Until she was begging him again—to take more, to take everything.

He'd never wanted anyone this much, never knew desire could be so sharp, so overwhelming, so goddamned good. And still, his need for her continued to peak, to grow bigger and bigger with every kiss he ran down from her breasts to her rib cage and then her stomach. Her muscles quivered just beneath her skin as he devoured her, but she wasn't the only one shaking. He was too, his hands nowhere close to steady as he tried to memorize her every curve and hollow.

He wanted to go slowly, to wring every ounce of pleasure from her before morning, but when he gripped her hips and she lifted herself into his mouth, there was nothing in the world that could have stopped him from taking more.

She was so damned hot. So damned sweet. And so beautifully unashamed of her sensuality as she rocked against him to drive his tongue deeper against her sex, into her core.

Nothing had ever been this good before. Nothing had ever come anywhere close to being as beautiful as the scent, the sounds, the feel of Christie as her climax took her over. For the rest of his life, he'd be replaying the way she called out his name, her voice drenched not only with pleasure, but also with rich, heady emotion.

When she finally stilled beneath him, he ran kisses back up her body, over the curves that he wanted to keep exploring—in the water, on the beach, in the woods, in the shower, in his own bed. Anywhere and everywhere he could have her.

When he was finally levered back over her again, she cupped his jaw and kissed him. And kissed him. And kissed him. Until everything inside his brain had turned to mush, so that the next thing he knew she had reversed their positions and was lying on top of him.

"Now."

The one word fell from her lips like nectar, and he had to drink from her lips again as she made surprisingly short work of his clothes and putting on protection. And then, in one seamless move, she was taking all of him inside of her, right where he longed to be.

Wrapped up in Christie, in her sweetness, in her warmth. And in deeper, truer pleasure—and peace—than he'd ever thought possible, as their bodies moved together as one.

CHAPTER TWENTY-TWO

Many times throughout the early-morning hours, Liam had wanted to wake Christie and make love to her again. But he hadn't had the heart to disturb her when he knew how badly she needed the rest. And the truth was that it had been a revelation just how much he'd enjoyed holding her in the dark, feeling her breathe deeply and evenly against him as he finally let himself relax for a few hours. Only now that the sun was rising over the lake was she slowly waking in his arms.

Her hips were pressed to his front as they both lay on their sides. She was using one of his arms as a pillow behind her head, but his other hand was free. Free to roam slowly, gently, over her bare curves.

The little hitches he could hear in her breath as she came fully awake and arched so that her hips were pressed even closer to his, took him from aroused to desperate for her within seconds.

Thankfully, he wasn't the only one with no self-control, because when he slid his hand from her breasts down to the vee between her legs, she opened for him on a soft moan. She was so hot, so ready, so perfectly made for pleasure, that he'd only barely stroked over her sex when she was coming apart for him with a shudder and his name on her lips.

After putting on protection, he lowered his lips to the bare curve of her neck at the same time that he came into her. And just like the night before, as they moved together so that pleasure peaked, then jumped higher still as they found release together, it was as though they were made for each other.

Only for each other.

They lay panting in each other's arms when she said, "Good morning." Her first words of the day were husky. Lazy with fulfilled pleasure.

But he could hear the uncertainty in them too.

He couldn't give her the words she needed to push that uncertainty away, but he could kiss her again, just the two of them safe beneath the sheets even as the rest of the world waited outside her door. A world full of people who would eventually find out about the two of them, no matter how hard they tried to hide what was between them.

If he'd had any control around her, Liam would have felt confident in his ability to keep his feelings for Christie to himself. But given that he couldn't so much as look at her without wanting to touch her, kiss her—or keep from smiling whenever she was near—he knew there'd be talk. Questions.

This morning, the easiest thing would be to pull her back into his arms and make that flush of desire spread all the way across her skin. And it was tempting, so damned tempting, to do just that. But for all the pleasure it would bring, he'd learned long ago that the longer one waited to have a difficult conversation, the more difficult it was to have it. Until the day came when they could no longer talk at all.

That was why he forced himself to say, "I've never been with anyone from town before. But as soon as people see us together, there's no way we'll be able to hide our relationship." Because he was utterly incapable of pretending she hadn't rocked his world.

She reacted as though his statement were a bucket of icy water poured over them both—and he understood why. Reality had never been harder to face than after their night of perfect pleasure. Her muscles immediately went from loose to stiff, and she scooted from his arms, pulling the sheet over her naked skin.

Did she have any idea how tempting she looked sitting there, her silky hair tumbling across her shoulders, her mouth rosy from his kisses, her eyes big and so green there was no emerald that could outshine them?

"Liam?"

He shook his head, trying to clear it. "You're so

damned beautiful that I can't think straight." At her flustered expression, he moved closer, taking her hands and kissing them. "And I've screwed up every second with you since waking up."

He was glad to see a small smile work its way onto her lips. "Not *every* second."

Still holding her hands, he tugged her closer, close enough that the sheet slipped away from her curves. "I want to take you out. Tonight. On a real date."

"Why?"

If this conversation had been with any other woman, he'd be itching to get out of bed. To get on with the day. To get away from the woman's hopes. Her dreams. Instead, he was the one asking for more. And he was damn well going to make sure he got it.

"Because I like you." *So much. Too much.* Enough that she deserved a hell of a lot more from him than one night—and morning—of scorching sex.

Emotion flashed in her eyes as she murmured, "I like you too."

His chest clenched at the simple words. *Liking* each other was perfect. *Liking* her would be enough.

It had to be.

"So we'll like each other during the day and have hot sex at night?" she asked. "For as long as you're in town?"

Just as she'd said to him last night, she wasn't trying to hold him to anything more than physical attraction. So then, why did her words grate on him so badly? On his heart more than anywhere else, as he made himself nod and say, "Exactly."

She slid from the bed, pulling the sheet with her. "You're right, you know. People are going to have a field day talking about us. You're Wesley's brother and I'm his ex-fiancée." Her eyes, her expression, were clouding over more and more with each sentence. "It's a gossip gold mine for any town, but especially a small one like this."

"It's one of the reasons I tried to stay away from you," he told her. "But I couldn't." He held her gaze, wanting her to see the truth in his eyes. "I just couldn't."

She lifted a hand to his cheek and lightly stroked his jaw. "Well then, who cares what people think? Everyone is already talking about me. Might as well give them something fresh to gossip about."

She said it so easily, but he already knew how sensitive she was. The urge to protect her from being hurt throbbed inside of him. And the worst part of all was the sure knowledge that the people who were going to hurt her most of all weren't those who gossiped about her.

It was Liam himself, when he packed up and left again, the way he always had before.

But then she was lifting her mouth to his...and he could focus only on what he felt. Not just desire, but the kind of peace that he hadn't known for two decades.

Their kiss quickly spiraled into her legs around his waist, his hands on her hips, another blissfully sweet climb toward release. But then the phone rang, and she pulled back, her eyes dilated, her breathing uneven.

"You have to get it, don't you?"

"It could be Alice. Downstairs at reception."

A few moments later, she turned out to be right. "Thanks for letting me know. I'll be there." She hung up. "Your mother is waiting for me downstairs." Her voice dropped to a hush. "She'll know. She'll see me and know about you. About *us*. I know we just agreed not to hide our relationship, but I hadn't planned on telling your mother first."

"I'll come meet her with you."

She jumped out of his lap. "No! Whatever she wants, you'll only make it worse." As if she realized a beat too late what she'd said, she grimaced. "I just mean that because the two of you don't get along—" She pressed two fingers to her lips. "I'm going to shut up now and get in the shower so that I can meet your mother without looking like I've been having crazy sex all night long with her son." Her mouth quirked up on one side for a split second. "All morning too, I guess."

But Liam couldn't stand the thought of their night together ending so suddenly. Especially not if his mother was the reason for it.

He reached for Christie before she could lock herself in the bathroom. "Last night, this morning...they were perfect."

"Yes," she said with a smile, "they were."

"You never gave me an answer about tonight," he reminded her, lightly caressing the pulse point at her wrist, still dizzy with wanting her. Would there ever come a day when he'd have his fill of her sweetness, her smile, the silk of her hair between his fingertips? "Will you let me take you on a real date?"

She was silent for a moment before saying, "I like Thai food." She pulled out of his arms and was halfway into the bathroom when she turned back to him. "Although, just sex would be easier than you taking me out on a real date in front of the whole town, you know."

He'd already told her he wasn't going to fall in love with her. And they both knew he was leaving the lake as soon as Wesley came back and resolved things with everyone.

She was right that *just sex* should have been enough for him. But it wasn't.

Not even close.

CHAPTER TWENTY-THREE

"Good morning, Christie," Susan said in a bright voice. "I'm so glad you're finally up and about. I didn't wake you, did I? Or interrupt something important?"

"No," Christie said, "you didn't wake me." She fought the battle against blushing over the thought of precisely what Susan had interrupted...and lost. Fortunately, apart from a slightly questioning quirk of her eyebrows, Susan didn't seem particularly interested in Christie's too-hot cheeks.

"I had a thought about your festival this morning. And I think I know how we might be able to save it."

Utterly thrown off by Susan's very unexpected statement, Christie fumbled for time to settle herself down. "Would you like to sit in the dining room and have a cup of tea?"

They went into the sunlit room. "You really have done a lovely job with the inn," Susan said.

Hold on a minute. Was trying to help with the festival and complimenting her on the inn Susan's way of apologizing for her behavior at dinner?

Christie studied Liam's mother's face carefully before saying, "Thank you."

Susan held her gaze, and Christie was fairly certain she saw a silent *I'm sorry for the way I treated you* in her eyes, even though the words the other woman actually said were, "You're welcome."

Alice popped by to take their breakfast orders, and Christie was surprised to realize she was starving. Normally, sitting down with Liam's mother would have made her lose her appetite. Then again, she'd burned off a ton of calories having all that sex.

With Liam.

Her gaze flew to the other woman's face, and she couldn't stop her hands from covering her even hotter cheeks. Fortunately, Susan wasn't looking at her. She was gazing around at the room.

"There is so much history here. So much beauty everywhere you look. The first time I came to Summer Lake, I knew I wanted to stay forever."

Christie had never felt any real connection to Susan. Until now. The surprises just kept on coming. "It was the same for me," she said softly. "I saw the lake, the mountains, this inn, and I knew."

Susan turned her gaze back to Christie. "Have I ever told you how Henry and I met?"

Christie was glad that Alice came to them with the teapots and croissants right then. She needed more time to gather her composure. Perhaps if she'd had more sleep, she'd be better able to handle this strange conversation. Finally, she replied, "No, you haven't."

"We met right here. In this dining room. Henry was on a date with another woman." Susan chuckled, but Christie couldn't help but think there was some sadness behind it. "I didn't care, you know."

"Oh." Really, what was she supposed to say to that? Especially when she was sleeping with her ex-fiancé's brother. Talk about stones and glass houses.

"I've shocked you, haven't I?"

Christie wanted to say no. Anyone else would have, darn it. Instead, that truth serum that she drank at birth had the words, "A little bit," coming out instead.

"Well, you know how gorgeous my sons are, so—"

Christie swallowed her tea wrong and started coughing.

"Are you all right, honey?"

Honey? Had she gone to bed on one planet and woken up on another? One where Susan called her *honey*?

"I'm fine," Christie said, dabbing her watering eyes with the napkin as she tried to deal with the startling shift in Susan's behavior toward her. "Sorry. Go on."

"As I was saying, Henry was quite something when he was younger. He still is." Susan was silent for a moment. Pensive. Giving herself a little shake, she continued, "My family was renting a house across the lake for one week that summer. It was our last night here. I had one night to win him, so I pulled out all the stops, first in this restaurant and then later, at the Saturday night bonfire that all the kids were going to."

"You must have dazzled him."

She expected Susan to smile back at her. Instead, sorrow moved across the woman's face. "Once upon a time, I guess I did."

Christie wanted to say something to comfort her, but how could she? They weren't friends. And she had no idea what it was like to be married thirty years and hit a rough patch.

"In any case, we were talking about the festival, weren't we?" Susan said. "Do you know what the land around the inn was originally zoned for?" She didn't wait for Christie to answer. "Agriculture."

"Wait a minute," Christie said slowly. "I thought the inn was originally a tycoon's summer house."

"It was. He got rich from newspapers, but what he really dreamed of doing was farming." Susan gave her a wide smile. "I called a friend at the courthouse this morning and asked her to check their files. When the inn was turned into lodging, they added the commercial zoning. But they never took away the agricultural zoning."

"So, it's still a farm?"

"Technically, yes. And maple syrup comes from maple tree farms."

In her excitement, Christie couldn't stop herself from reaching out and squeezing Susan's hand. "Thank you for finding this." Now she and Liam could go back to the council with real firepower to ask them to pull the petition.

Liam walked into the room then, and Christie felt Susan's hand go still beneath hers. Slowly, Christie moved hers away.

"Liam, honey," his mother said. "Join us."

"Actually," Christie said, pushing back her chair, "I need to take over for Alice at the front desk. You can take my seat, Liam."

She was careful not to look at him, or touch him, knowing she was sure to give herself away. Liam might not be able to see that she was falling head over heels for him, but a woman would know it. His mother, especially. And Christie didn't think Susan would be at all happy about it.

Christie quickly said, "Thank you again, Susan," then left the room.

* * *

"What was Christie thanking you for?" And why had the woman whose bed he'd just left been holding his mother's hand? It was the last thing he'd expected to see.

"I think I've found a way around the festival petition."

Even though he'd been hot on the trail of loopholes, when his mother explained, he wasn't surprised by how smart her plan was. It was a stroke of luck, for sure, but one that might not have come about if not for Susan's knowledge of the Adirondack Park's history.

"It was nice of you to help her."

"I was thinking the same thing about you," she said softly. "You like her, don't you?"

"Everyone likes Christie. The guests. The locals. Even babies stop crying when she picks them up."

His mother's eyes softened. "I can't wait for the day I can hold your children." And then she shifted in her seat, looking more uncomfortable than usual. "I saw you kissing her last night."

Liam felt every muscle in his body go still. Just as he'd told Christie this morning, he hadn't been planning to hide their relationship. But he'd assumed it was their secret to tell. "How could you have seen us?"

"I came by the inn hoping to see you. To talk about—" She paused. "Things. I'd just got out of my car when I realized I wasn't alone in the parking lot."

"And you just stood there and watched us?"

"No."

"You said you saw us kiss."

"I did. But it wasn't like that, I swear to you, Liam."

He pushed back his chair to go, but she reached across the table and grabbed both of his hands. "Please, let me explain."

He'd heard enough of her explanations for one lifetime. He should have left, shouldn't have felt the least bit guilty about it. But she was his mother. And he couldn't walk out on her, no matter how badly he wanted to, especially with Christie's voice in his head.

You make sure everyone is afraid of you. That they don't get close to you. Like how you barely say a word to your mother, even though she's so hurt every time you push her away. Your father too.

"Go ahead," he finally said. "Explain."

"You and Christie were sharing such a private moment. And even though I have to admit I don't know how I feel about the two of you having a relationship—"

"It's none of your business."

"That's what I'm trying to say. I couldn't interrupt you, couldn't possibly have let you know I was there." Her gaze grew wistful. "I know what it's like to fall in love, Liam."

Fall in love?

No. She was wrong.

She had to be.

He'd come down here to talk to his mother about Wesley, not to discuss his first kiss with Christie. A kiss that had turned into a night—and a morning—of the most incredible lovemaking he'd ever known. With the sweetest woman he'd ever had the privilege of kissing. But he definitely hadn't planned on talking about *love.*

Pushing the word away, he suddenly realized what his mother's spying meant. "If you saw us kiss, then you heard about Wesley too, didn't you?"

She took a shaky breath. "My poor baby. I wish he didn't feel that he had to run."

"He didn't think any of us could handle the truth. And he's right, isn't he? Our family has never been able to handle the truth."

He'd said too much. He'd already stayed too long at Summer Lake, at the inn—and things were only going to get more complicated with his parents and Christie if he didn't shove off soon. Liam slid his hands free of his mother's grip. "There are a lot of people checking out this morning. I should see if they need more help at reception."

* * *

Susan's mouth was completely dry—so dry she could hardly swallow. She picked up her teacup, but her hands were shaking so hard that she could barely lift it from the saucer without spilling tea all over the table.

Liam had never spoken to her like that before. Never been quite so direct. *Our family has never been able to handle the truth.*

Fear and guilt rose up inside her in equal measure.

He hadn't given away her secret to Christie last night in the parking lot when the young woman had flat out asked him why he had such a fractured relationship with his mother. Susan should have felt safe, knowing that if he wouldn't tell Christie—the woman who clearly held his heart—he wouldn't tell anyone. But she didn't feel safe.

Not even close.

She'd come to the inn this morning to begin the process of making amends. Christie was easier to approach, of course, which was why Susan had started with her. They didn't have a long history, and the truth was, the young woman really was inherently likable.

There was no point in lying to herself anymore. Just as Henry had said, it had been clear right from the start that while Wesley and Christie obviously enjoyed each other's company a great deal, they were no love match. There were no sparks. Nothing that could possibly hold a family together through the ups and downs of life.

And Susan knew firsthand about those ups and downs. The thrill of saying *I do* beneath the rose arbor outside the inn. Discovering she was pregnant with each of her sons and then giving birth to them, two years apart. The joy she'd felt when she held each of her children for the very first time, when she'd looked into their eyes and known only love, a love so intense that she'd been stunned by the force of it.

But the flip side to all that joy had come when she'd lost her brother, and grief had propelled her into making a terrible mistake with a virtual stranger—and then another, even bigger one, with her son.

For two decades, she'd survived the fear, the guilt, but this morning she was suffocating under the weight of both.

Perhaps Christie would allow her to make amends for her chilly behavior over the past months, especially if her suggestion for saving the festival actually made a difference. But would Liam ever forgive her for making him carry the burden of her secret all these years?

And then there was Henry. Her husband had held her for the first time in a long time last night by the fire.

But she'd felt him warring with himself the entire time.

CHAPTER TWENTY-FOUR

Henry was glad he lived close enough to Jean to help out when she needed it. Sure, she could have fixed her own kitchen sink—could have done it twice as fast as he could in her heyday, as a matter of fact—but working with his hands always helped settle him. And he'd been twisted up in knots for what felt like forever.

"How is Susan doing?" his mother asked as she brought him a glass of lemonade.

He took a long drink, then said, "She's worried about Wesley."

"Has there been any word from him?"

"No." And now that Henry had more of an idea about why Wesley had left, he actually understood why his son had done it. Summer Lake was a wonderful town. Small, nurturing, comfortable, and not at all prejudiced or bigoted. But sometimes, a man needed to figure out some things for himself, away from the people who were so sure they already knew who he was.

Lord knew, there had been plenty of times when

Henry wouldn't have minded disappearing himself.

The one person he'd never had to hide from, fortunately, was his own mother. Jean Kane wasn't a woman who pushed. Since he appreciated the care his mother had always taken with him, he wanted to set her mind at ease about Wesley. "He'll come back when he's ready." Henry would let his son tell his grandmother his own truth at his own pace.

"Yes, I expect he will," his mother agreed. "This is home. For all of us."

Her comment had him asking, "Has Liam said anything to you about staying in Summer Lake?"

"Announcements aren't his style." She laughed. "Then again, neither is falling in love, and he's doing a grand job of that."

Henry almost dropped the wrench he was holding. "He's in love?"

"Liam looks at Christie the way you once looked at Susan."

Henry felt the muscles in his body tighten, one by one, until he was so stiff he couldn't move without fearing that shards would crack off. He and his mother never spoke about his marriage. Not once in thirty years had Jean broached the subject of his relationship with Susan. The two women had never been fast friends, but he'd accepted that they were different. One slow, one fast. One quiet, one loud. Both had a place in his life. In his heart.

It was none of his mother's business, and yet as he moved away from the sink to pick up a smaller wrench from his toolbox, Henry felt he had to say, "I still look at Susan that way."

"You used to call her Susie. For years, you never used her formal name. She was always your Susie."

His Susie.

He'd awakened this morning telling himself that everything was going to be okay. Wesley would come back when he was ready. Liam was home, for a little while at least. And Henry and his wife had shared a bed again. Maybe they hadn't really touched, except by mistake, but at least they'd both been in the same place at the same time.

Susie. Susan. They were just names.

But were they really?

Had his marriage finally passed the point of no return? After all these years of trying to act like nothing was wrong, now that the door to unrest was open, did he have a prayer of getting it closed again? Or was there no way back? Did Wesley have it right? Was leaving the only option?

"The truth is never easy to hear, is it?" He wasn't even pretending to work on the sink now.

"No," his mother said, her look at once intense and yet hazy. "Which is why I've never told you the full truth about your father." She nodded as if she'd just concluded a battle inside her own head. "But I think it's finally time."

* * *

1945…

If not for her pregnancy, perhaps Jean would have remained in her parents' house. It was certainly the easier path, to simply live the life she had before.

But loving Thomas had changed everything.

Most young women in her position would have been frightened. Jean wasn't naive enough not to be scared. Of course having a child would be a big adjustment. A huge one. It wasn't even that her husband's memory would now live on, whether or not he ever came back to her.

Having a baby of her own simply meant that now all of the love in her heart would have a place to flow. She loved her parents. Her sisters. Her friends.

But this love was already different.

Different, even, from the love she'd felt for Thomas.

What she'd felt for her husband had been pure. Deep and real. But neither of them had truly depended on each other, and she would find her feet without him. She would have to.

This child would look to her for its health. Its happiness. Jean would be there to give her baby all of that and more.

In the end, the one hundred dollars left in the bank account was all it took. She found a cottage where she could keep an eye on a toddler, with a beach where a growing child could run and play and learn to swim. Her parents tried to fight her decision, but the girl who everyone had always assumed was happy to follow the lead of others had turned into a woman who finally knew just what she wanted.

A home of her own. And a career with which she could not only support her child and herself—but that would also feed her mind.

Those first months, most of the carpenters in town weren't sure whether they were supposed to help her out to please her powerful father, or shun her to make sure she failed and had to move back home. She cobbled together a workforce of soldiers coming back from the war, and Jean got in there with them whenever she could, wielding a hammer until her stomach grew too big.

Other women watched her, women she'd known her whole life, and while some of them were aghast at what she was doing, many more of them told her that working for the war effort had given them a taste of something they wanted more of. Those evenings with her sister as they knitted blankets and caps and booties for her baby sowed the seeds for Lakeside Stitch and Knit. The two Farrington girls were the last the town would have expected to get their hands dirty with work. But they were more like their successful, driven father than even he wanted to see.

It had been a struggle to get her construction business off the ground. But bigger than the struggle had been the joy of it.

She would miss Thomas forever. No other man could possibly replace him. But when her water broke and the midwife made it to her cottage just in time to greet quiet little Henry, Jean was happier than she'd ever known was possible.

One year went by, then two, and she had a chubby, laughing toddler to chase down the beach.

That was when the letter came, with the ticket to New York City.

A dozen different thoughts and emotions coursed through her. She was thrilled to know that Thomas's hands had touched this ticket, to know that he wanted to see her again. She was surprised that he'd reached out to her like this. And yet at the same time, it was inevitable, because nothing had ever really been finished—the door had never been closed. She was nervous—terrified, actually—about seeing him again. About all the ways her life had changed, and all the ways she knew his life must have changed too.

But she never once thought about not getting on that train.

She never once considered not going to him.

She had to see him.

Because this time, she was going to be the one to make the decision about the door opening up again...or closing forever.

* * *

He was waiting for her at the station. His hat was pulled down low, and he was thinner, so much thinner, than he'd been before.

"Jean."

She wanted to run into his arms. But she knew somehow that keeping this distance was important. Vitally important. So she simply said, "Thomas."

"You must be hungry after the train trip. I know a place just around the corner. A place we can talk."

"Yes," she said softly. "I would like to talk."

Walking beside the man she loved so deeply, without touching him, without kissing him, was the most difficult thing she'd ever done. Far more difficult than telling her father that her husband had disappeared. Worlds harder than giving birth or raising a baby on her own.

With a table between them, coffee steaming from

cracked white mugs, he simply sat and looked. She did the same, drinking him in.

Finally, he spoke. "Falling in love with you was never the plan."

To keep herself from reaching out to touch him, Jean curled her hand around the mug, barely aware that it was scalding her skin. "My father supposed that was the case."

"He was right. Money was what I was after. You were my target. I should have been pleased by how easy you were to woo, how quickly you agreed to marry me."

Just as she should have been going cold at her husband's frank admission about why he'd pursued her. But there were many different truths, weren't there? And only one had ever been important to her.

"I loved you right from that first moment," she told him honestly, knowing there was no sense in pride here in this diner, sitting across from the man she still loved with all of her heart.

She watched his breath catch in his throat at her words, remembered the taste, the scent of his skin on their wedding night. The one sweet night that had given them Henry.

"One day," he said in a hoarse voice, "I realized I wasn't simply saying what I thought you wanted to hear. I was telling you the truth. I loved you. I wanted a life with you."

She hadn't needed him to bring her here to say that. She had never doubted his love for her. Well, maybe in the dark of night there had been a time or two when doubts had crept in. But sitting here, across a Formica-topped table, surrounded by rough-looking strangers, she would never doubt it again. "And now you want me to know why you left."

"God, yes." His grip on his own coffee cup was so tight that his knuckles showed white through his tanned skin. "I've barely slept since that night."

She waited silently for him to gather the strength to share the truth with her. Some things, she'd learned since leaving her parents' house and striking out on her own, took time. Making a baby. Teasing out a smile from a toddler's tears. Building a business.

And most of all, speaking the truth.

"If I had been working for myself," he said, "I would have stopped. I would have given up my previous life for you. So many bad decisions led me to you, Jean. So how can I regret everything in my past? I pulled myself up out of the gutter by working for the wrong kind of people. As soon as I fell in love with you, I wanted to pull out of the deal I'd made." He closed his eyes. "But I couldn't. Not when it would have put your life, your family's lives, in danger." His hands were shaking now, little drips of coffee spilling out across his fingers, running down to make puddles on the tabletop. "I had to take the money. I had to leave, even though I knew that when I left I could never come back. I could never risk your life just because I selfishly wanted your love for my own."

She'd been planning to tell him all along. Now it was finally time. "You have a son."

His mug of coffee tipped, would have spilled, but Jean caught it before it could turn over. Her fingers brushed his, and she let them go still over his hand.

Their eyes locked. Held.

"Henry is two and full of energy. He looks like you." She pulled her hand back to reach into her pocket, then handed him the photo.

"My God." Tears were streaming down his face. "He's beautiful." His eyes lifted from the picture. "So are you."

She could taste her own tears on her lips as she smiled back at him. And she could see, as clearly as she'd ever seen anything, that her husband wanted desperately to start a new life with her and his son.

She would have risked herself for his love in a heartbeat. To be with him. But she could never risk her own son.

Not even for the only love she'd ever know as a woman.

"I will never regret my love for you, Thomas." And

then she pushed back her chair and made herself say, "Good-bye."

⋆ ⋆ ⋆

Present day...

"My mother gave me a New York City paper the following year," Jean said softly. "Your father had passed away."

Henry was stunned by everything his mother had just told him. He knew he'd have to ask her to repeat it. Another day, when it wasn't all such a big shock.

"I never really understood what it was to have a father or lose one," he said. Not until he'd become one himself. Not until he'd realized that the very last thing he ever wanted to do was fail his children. And then anger, that previously rare emotion that he'd been feeling more and more lately, flooded in again. "The people he worked for stole everything from us!"

"Well," his mother said slowly, as was her way, "not everything. I still had you. You had me. There were siblings and cousins and grandparents and Susan and Liam and Wesley." She looked out the window, and her eyes lit up. "Speaking of Liam, he's here now."

As soon as Henry's son stepped inside, Jean gave him a hug. "What a lovely surprise."

Liam's eyes were warm as he looked down at his

grandmother. "Sorry I haven't been over sooner."

She waved away his apology. "You never need to worry about me."

Liam looked over her shoulder. "Dad, I didn't know you'd be here."

"Just helping fix the kitchen sink."

Jean walked over and took the wrench from his grip. "I've got it. Why don't you two go take some father-son time together."

Knowing it was an order, rather than a suggestion, Henry stood. But before he left, he pulled his mother into a hug, holding her more tightly than he ever had before.

"Thank you for telling me," he said for her ears only.

"I know we can't go back and fix the past," she said, "but I haven't given up hope that we have the power to fix the things that are broken now."

His mother had been everything to him as a child, and she was still the best person he knew, along with his sons. She'd had no choice but to give up her true love. But she was right that he did have a choice about his own. Susan—*his Susie*—was still there. It was simply the love they needed help to find.

But first, he'd start with doing his damned level best to fix things with his eldest son.

* * *

Liam and his father were climbing a steep, rocky section on their way to Echo Cliff. Rather than walking single file up a narrow trail, they were side by side, using their hands and feet to get up the rocks. The snow had melted almost all the way to the top by now, and icy water was streaming down the trail.

They'd been hiking in silence for quite a while, but although Henry was one of the most easygoing people Liam had ever known, it didn't feel like a comfortable silence.

How could it be when there was so much unsaid between them?

Liam had been close to his father until his teens, and he knew Christie was right, that his father wanted to be closer to him again. But had she guessed just how badly Liam also wanted to be closer to his father again?

Deciding it was time to break the silence, at least where he could, Liam said, "I'm glad you were free for a hike today. Even if I'm pretty sure Grandma threw us both out of her cottage a little while ago."

"She definitely did." A smile landed on his father's face while they shared a moment of appreciation for the quietly indomitable Jean Kane. His smile fell away as he cleared his throat. "Your mother told me why Wesley left."

Frustration bit at Liam. "He should have talked to me. I'm his brother. He should have known he could trust me. With anything."

"You're not responsible for his pain, for his secrets." Henry's voice was ragged. "If anyone should have seen his turmoil, should have guessed what he needed to get off his chest, it was me. His father. You and Wesley have always been the most important people in the world to me. You know that, don't you?"

For all the distance he'd put between them these past years, Liam did know it. "You've been a great dad."

He could practically see his father's brain working, knew the question that had to be coming next: *So then why did you pull away from me so long ago?*

Needing to do something, anything, to head that question off at the pass, Liam said, "You must also know that Christie and I are seeing each other." He left off *while I'm in town*, because he didn't want his father to think that Christie was in any way cheapened by agreeing to a short-term affair with him.

"I'm glad," Henry said. "Christie is a truly lovely woman."

Liam realized he hadn't expected anything less from his father than complete and immediate support. His father had always been there for him.

It was Liam who had turned away because he'd felt

he had no other choice.

As the hill grew steeper, the rocks became more slippery. Much like the way their conversation was going.

"Not everyone is going to take the news of us dating as well as you," Liam told his father between breaths.

Henry nodded. "True. But Christie is worth surviving a little gossip for, isn't she?"

Of course she was. "I'm not worried about myself. I'm worried about her. I don't want her to be hurt. By anyone."

His father smiled then, his whole heart behind it. "You're in love with her."

Liam went still on the rocks. He'd been stunned when his mother had mentioned love—and this double whammy from his father wasn't any easier to swallow. "I like her."

Like was an emotion he could recognize. *Like* was an emotion he could accept. *Like* would never cause anyone to cry. *Like* would never tear anyone apart.

When his father didn't reply, Liam reminded him, "I've only known her a week." Less than that, actually, if he counted up the days.

"I knew your mother for one night," Henry said. "That was all it took."

This was exactly the kind of conversation Liam

shouldn't be having with his father. Not when it rode far too close to the secret that he'd been keeping for twenty years. Still, he couldn't stop himself from saying, "Love at first sight doesn't always work."

The words were barely out of his mouth when his father began to slip on the rocks he was standing on. Liam quickly scrambled across to grab him before he fell.

"Thanks, son."

But as they hiked the rest of the way in silence, Liam knew his father didn't have anything to thank him for. Not one damn thing.

CHAPTER TWENTY-FIVE

Christie was working hard on her knitting sample for the store when someone knocked on her door at six p.m. In the middle of a complicated section of the pattern, she called, "Come in."

When she finally looked up, Liam's dark good looks took her breath away just as they always did. But it was more than her lungs that were affected. Her heart was too. Hoping. Wishing. Longing.

For something he'd already told her, flat out, that he couldn't give.

But then when his eyes moved over her, the pleasure reflected in them had warmth filling her. No man had ever looked at her like this, as though she was so beautiful he could hardly believe his eyes.

His gaze moved to the yarn in her hands. "I never asked what you're making." His voice was a little husky, reminding her of the way he'd sounded when they were making love and he'd called her *sweetheart*.

A flush moved across her cheeks. "Something from a new book Lakeside Stitch and Knit recently got in.

With Sarah still away on her honeymoon, Denise needed an extra pair of hands."

He picked up the soft pink cashmere. Watching his large hands gently stroke the delicate fibers, the same hands that had brought her more pleasure that she'd known was even possible, she practically shook with wanting him.

"Is it a dress?"

"Not exactly." She tried to take a breath, but it got all caught up in her throat. "It's a book of lingerie. This is going to be a slip. To wear under a dress."

He lifted his gaze from the yarn. "Will you wear it for me when you're done with it? No dress. Just the slip."

On the verge of melting into a puddle on the carpet, she couldn't speak. All she could do was nod. And then he was kissing her—thank God, because she'd never needed a kiss more. Dropping the needles, she wrapped her arms around his broad shoulders and pulled him closer.

But the sound of the needles hitting the floor had him pulling back from her. "Dinner," he said, as if to remind them both of their original plan. "I'm taking you to dinner."

"I have food in the fridge." She knew she sounded desperate, but she wanted him too much to care.

She saw in his eyes just how tempted he was by the

thought of staying in tonight, of canceling their dinner reservations and making a meal out of each other instead. But he still said, "You deserve more than just sex, Christie. So much more."

He was right. Only, dinner wasn't what she was after.

Love. That was what she really deserved.

But since all Liam was offering tonight was a nice meal out—and then mind-blowing sex afterward—she wasn't going to say no. She simply couldn't.

Thirty minutes later, they were in Wishing Lake, a pretty town that she hadn't had a chance to explore on her rare days off. It was a perfect Adirondack night. The sky was clear, the wind was still, and the air was sweet. She couldn't have set the stage any better for a romantic dinner…even if that romance was only ever meant to be temporary.

"This is a real treat," she told him as they settled into their seats and the wine was poured. "I love Summer Lake, but sometimes it feels like I never get a chance to leave town."

"The Adirondacks are definitely full of hidden jewels."

The way he'd phrased it had her asking, "Is that why we're at this lake? Are we hiding too?"

"I told you I'm not going to hide our relationship, Christie, and I meant it. I just thought it would be nice if our first date was for the two of us."

"You're right. If we'd gone to one of the restaurants in town, every eye would have been on us." Still, she couldn't help but feel that despite what he said, he might not actually be all that thrilled about being seen with her.

Her non-poker face must have given her away, because he said, "Tomorrow morning, how about we walk down Main Street holding hands?"

A surprised laugh left her throat. Did he have any idea how sweet he really was? "I don't know if we need to be quite that blatant. But thank you for offering."

"Once Wesley returns, once he isn't afraid to share who he is with the people who've known him his whole life, no one will think twice about you having dated both of us."

"I suppose you're right." Although, who knew when Wesley was actually going to come back? Not to mention when Liam would leave... "I meant to tell you last night about the man Wesley was with. But I got distracted."

Liam reached for her hand, his thumb stroking the inside of her palm in just the way to make her shiver with need. "Last night was about you and me. No one else."

Considering he had told her again and again that he wasn't right for her, that he wasn't going to stick around in the long term, he was surprisingly possessive about their time together. She shouldn't like it, should remember the lessons she'd learned from all her failed relationships, should make sure he understood that she wasn't his to possess.

But with Liam, she couldn't help but like it. Because she couldn't help but want to belong to him.

Just as she couldn't help but want him to belong to her too.

She needed to take a sip of her wine—a really big gulp, actually—before she could refocus her thoughts on what she'd been about to say. "John is someone Wesley and I have both known for a long time. He's a very nice person."

Liam's fingers stilled on the stem of his wine glass, and she could see his mind working. Processing. Considering. "Do you have John's phone number? Odds are, that's where Wesley is."

Christie knew Liam's heart was in the right place. He loved his brother. No one could doubt that for a second. But…

"Of course I'll give you John's number. And I know how deeply you care for Wesley. But please—" She paused, had to repeat it. "*Please* respect your brother's wishes. He asked us not to contact him. He told us he'd come back when he's ready."

"Wesley needs to know that I'm there for him.

That we all are. We always have been."

"Deep in his heart, he knows that," she promised him. "And when he's less confused and overwhelmed, he'll remember the love that's waiting here for him."

"How can you be so sure?"

"Because when Wesley and I called off the wedding, my family wanted so badly to protect me, to come and take me away from it all. But what I really needed was to figure things out for myself for once. I needed to do it away from the familiar comfort of people who would swoop in and take care of everything for me. I just needed to figure out how to love myself all by myself, for the first time. I needed to know that I was strong in my own right. That I'd been right when I saw Summer Lake for the first time and knew it was where I was meant to be."

⋆ ⋆ ⋆

So many times over the past week, Liam had wanted to get to know Christie better. Each time, however, he'd forced himself to push his personal questions away, if only to keep them from getting too close. But last night he'd been unable to resist his fascination with her body—and now he couldn't see how it made sense anymore to keep fighting his fascination with the rest of her.

"You long to travel, to see the world," he said.

When she nodded, he asked, "What if it turns out that Paris or Rome or Egypt is really where you're meant to be?"

"I suppose the best answer I can give is that I hope I get the chance one day to see if that's the case."

"Why haven't you, Christie? I see the way you are with the inn's guests. You're not afraid of meeting new people. In fact, you thrive on it. And if money is an issue, I'm sure you know there are plenty of ways to travel cheap."

She lifted her eyes to his, and he hated seeing the defeat in them. "I'm afraid to fly."

Even as she confessed her secret to him, he knew he should let her be. Should stop pressing her. But it wasn't enough to know the taste of her skin, or the way flecks of gold appeared in her green eyes when she was crying out her pleasure in his arms.

He needed to know everything.

"Why?" he asked.

She shook her head. "I don't know."

"There has to be a reason."

Budding anger replaced the defeat in her eyes. He didn't like knowing he'd made her angry, but he was glad to see the resignation disappear. "Don't you think that if I knew the reason, I would get past it, get on an airplane, and go somewhere?"

"Maybe." He knew he was putting his opinions in

where he shouldn't, but he couldn't stop himself. "Or maybe it's easier to stay stuck right where you are."

Her eyes flashed. "Says the man who clearly found it easier to leave than to stay and make things work."

He should have seen that coming. Her brain was not only incredibly quick, her heart was also dead on target. Every single time. "I had my reasons for leaving," he told her, leaving it at that, the way he always had before.

She stared at him for a long moment. "You and I slept together last night."

"Yes, I know," he replied, unable to keep from smiling now, despite the intensity of their conversation. "I was there, loving every second of it."

"We're probably going to sleep together tonight."

His grin grew even bigger. "I hope so."

"Me too." She paused again. "Here's the thing, though. I know you're not promising me love. You were really clear on that. But whatever it is that we're doing, for however long we're doing it, there has to be a foundation of honesty between us. I know this is our first official date, and on any normal first date, I'd be on my best behavior. But we're doing things a little backward." She paused, picked up her wine, and drank. "Wait a second." She took another large gulp. "Okay. Here goes." She pinned him with a serious gaze. One he couldn't escape. "Why did you leave Summer Lake,

Liam? Especially when I can see how much you love it here. I can tell that of all the places you've been and seen, *this* is really your home."

He'd known that if he let himself get close to her, this question would come. But that didn't mean he was any better prepared for it. "Something happened with my mother."

"What did she do? What happened that hurt you both so much?"

He had never been so tempted to give away his mother's secret. But he couldn't bear to pass his burden on to Christie. Wouldn't put her in the position of having to face his father, or Wesley, with the knowledge of what his mother had done. "Right after Wesley left," he said softly, "when I asked if you knew the reason why, you told me you wished you could tell me. But you couldn't."

She shook her head, clearly remorseful over the decision she'd made. "You love him so much. I should have told you earlier."

"No, I can see why you didn't. Wesley had your trust. It's like that. I don't want to keep you in the dark, but this isn't my secret to tell."

"Neither was Wesley's, but I ended up telling you."

That was when he realized she didn't yet know what Susan had seen. "My mother was there. In the parking lot last night."

"She was...in the parking lot?" She looked horrified.

"Yes."

"When we were—" She scrunched her eyes shut for a moment. "—kissing?"

"She heard our discussion about Wesley too."

"Oh no." Her words were barely more than a breath. "What have I done?"

"None of this is your fault."

"But how can Wesley possibly see it that way? He asked me not to tell anyone why he left. And here I've ended up telling everyone."

Liam loved his brother, but the urge to defend her was strong. "He has absolutely no reason to be angry with you. He should never have asked you to keep his secret."

"But your mother asked you to keep hers, didn't she? And you've kept it. All these years."

He didn't know what to say to that, not when a slide show of painful visions from twenty years ago immediately began playing inside his head. Only when he felt Christie's hand cover his did he remember where they were and shut the memories down.

"I'm sorry," she said softly. "We both know I should think before I speak."

He hated the way she took the blame for his problems. He couldn't give her love, but he could work like hell to give her confidence. To fly. To travel. And to believe in herself as much as he believed in her. "You're perfect just the way you are."

He'd never kissed anyone in public before, had always been put off by displays of affection in inappropriate places. But tonight, he didn't care what was appropriate and what wasn't.

His mouth found hers soft and waiting for his kiss.

⋆ ⋆ ⋆

"I was planning to take you to *my* bed tonight," he said a couple of hours later, when they were back at the inn, and they were alternately kissing and stripping off each other's clothes inside her bedroom.

"Mine was closer."

After the heavy discussion that led off dinner, they'd settled into telling each other stories, each trying to make the other laugh harder. Liam had wild tales of mischievous elephants in India; Christie countered with things that had happened with guests at the inn—true comedy-of-error stories.

"My bedroom is only warm when you're here with me," Christie murmured into the crook of his neck as he lifted her and carried her to the bed.

He laid her down on the covers and moved over her, making her sizzle all over, inside and out. "Go figure."

She giggled against his mouth as he gave her soft, teasing kisses. And oh-so-potent as he ran them down her body—they were delicious drops of heat, of desire, of something that felt like reverence. And she felt exactly the same way as she ran her hands over him, as she kissed his jaw, his shoulder, his chest.

She shuddered as he found every last one of her sensitive spots, and she lost hold of everything but the intense, soul-deep pleasure only Liam could give her. And yet, even as he moved inside of her and she took all of him, it still wasn't enough.

I love you was right there on her lips, wanting so badly to be said.

But while he might have let his walls down with her for one night, that didn't mean they were going to stay down forever. Especially when everything he'd been struggling with for so long at Summer Lake—all the secrets and problems with his family—were still right here.

Reaching the beautiful peak of pleasure, they jumped off together. But though she made herself swallow back the three little words, that didn't make them any less true. Any less real. Or any less powerful within her heart.

CHAPTER TWENTY-SIX

The next morning, Christie woke when Liam kissed her on the forehead, then headed into the bathroom and turned on the shower.

Feeling a million times more rested than she had in weeks, she figured it had to be because sleeping in Liam's arms made the bed better than any had ever been. But when she looked at the clock, she supposed it could also have something to do with the fact that she'd slept a couple of hours longer than usual. After all the tossing and turning she'd done since calling off her wedding and Wesley's leaving, she had really needed the rest.

She looked toward the shower. Boy, oh boy, was it tempting to join him. But with only thirty minutes until she was needed downstairs at the front desk, she couldn't miss her window to make a couple of very important phone calls.

She got up and put on her robe, then called Catherine at the town hall to ask her to take a quick look at the zoning maps for the property. Catherine confirmed what Susan had said about the agricultural zoning. Her next call was to the Adirondack Preservation Council.

"This is Christie Hayden. I was in to see you last week, but I've just learned something really important about the inn's zoning, and I was hoping to bring the new information to you today." She was smiling as she said, "Noon? Yes, I can be there by then."

With bells on.

She had only just hung up when Liam walked out of her bathroom with a towel wrapped around his waist…at which point she completely lost the thread of her thoughts as she took in his tanned skin, his muscles, and the heat in his dark eyes.

"Good shower?"

"Lonely shower."

The breath she was about to take caught somewhere in her windpipe. "I wanted to join you," she found herself admitting.

"Why didn't you?" he asked as he brushed a lock of her hair from her cheek and his touch sizzled through her.

Because I already want you too much. Because you're like a drug I can't get enough of. Because even though I know you're going to break my heart, when I'm with you, I forget all about the fall that's coming.

But she refused to ruin the time they had together by foolishly pushing for things he'd already told her he couldn't give, so she shook the thought out of her head. "I needed to make a couple of calls. My friend Catherine in the county clerk's office confirmed what your mother told me about the agricultural zoning. And I was hoping you could cover for me here for a few hours, because I've arranged to meet with the Adirondack Preservation Council at noon today."

"Of course I can cover for you." He grinned as he added, "Give 'em hell."

He kissed her again, and she was on the verge of forgetting all about the zoning maps and the council meeting, when he said, "I've got an inn to run. And you've got a festival to save."

From shower to dressing, to heading out to the clerk's office so that she could pick up copies of the zoning maps, to driving along the winding Adirondack roads to the Preservation Council building, Christie was pretty sure she didn't stop smiling the entire time.

"Ms. Hayden," the woman at the front desk said when she walked inside. "They're all expecting you. Are you ready to go in?"

Previously, when Christie had been standing in this light-filled entry, she'd been shaking with nerves. She'd been unsure of so many things—her feelings for Liam, along with her chances at persuading the council to let her festival go forward. And even though not very many days, hours, had passed—so much had changed.

One sweet kiss with Liam at a roadside dive had turned into so much more.

Liam's mother had approached her almost as a friend, or at least as an ally of sorts.

And Christie had decided to stop giving up.

Christie loved Summer Lake's community. Susan's suggestion to look into the zoning was wonderful. And, of course, Liam's support for her festival touched her deeply. But some things a woman had to take care of on her own.

This festival was her idea. Ultimately, it was up to her to fight the final battle. If she succeeded, if she failed—it was finally time to find out what she was made of.

From here on out, if she wanted something, she was going for it. Because she'd finally learned that the worst anyone could say was no. And for the first time in her life, she was banking on *yes*.

"Yes," she told the receptionist. "I'm ready."

* * *

"The festival is back on!"

Christie had been bursting to tell someone her good news. She'd assumed Liam would be the first person she'd tell, but just as she was getting out of the car, she saw Susan in the inn's parking lot.

"I'm so glad," Susan said with a wide smile.

"Your suggestion about the zoning was brilliant," Christie said.

"More like helpful. You're the brilliant one for coming up with the festival in the first place. I don't know why no one thought of it before now, actually. Maybe it takes someone with a fresh eye on the town to see something new. By the way," Susan added, "your flyers and posters look great, but if you need any help in the future, please don't hesitate to ask."

Susan would have been her first choice for the design, but she hadn't thought she'd get a yes. "I'd love to work together, but I'm pretty sure we can't afford your graphic design skills."

"Nonsense," Susan said with a wave of her hand. "I do pro bono work for local events all the time. Besides, my sons own the inn, and the festival directly benefits their business. Of course I want to help them in any way I can. In fact, you're just what Liam needs."

"I am?" Christie could hardly believe what she was hearing.

"Yes, you are."

Tears pricked at Christie's eyes. It was a day of miracles. First the thumbs-up on her festival from the council, and then the same from a woman she'd never thought even liked her. "I care deeply for both of your sons." More than anything else, she needed Susan to know that. "Wesley will always be one of my closest friends, and Liam is..."

"Very special," Susan said softly. "Congratulations, again, on your good news," she said, then got into her car and drove away.

Christie felt more than a little dazed when she headed into the inn. But Liam took one look at her and knew.

"You did it," he said. And then he swung her up into his arms and kissed her, right there in front of everyone.

Liam had joked about walking down Main Street holding her hand, but even though she knew their relationship would last only until he left town again, this felt like so much more than that.

CHAPTER TWENTY-SEVEN

The next few days were a blur of keeping the inn running while taking care of all the final festival details during the day—and making love with Liam into the late hours of the night.

Christie was equal parts exhilarated and exhausted. Plenty of people had seen her with Liam at the town hall looking at records, or picking up last-second produce at the market for the inn, or grabbing coffee. She'd seen people's confused glances, the way they were obviously trying to tell themselves there couldn't possibly be anything going on between Christie and Liam. And then he would put his hand on the small of her back, or lean in to kiss her forehead, and the *nothing going on* illusion would shatter.

"You do it on purpose," she said to him after he'd stroked her hair as they waited in line for coffee at the Moose Café.

"What's that?" His tone was full of innocence as they walked down the sidewalk, but she saw the wicked truth in his dark eyes.

"You touch me. Kiss me."

"Those are two of my favorite things. I can't help myself." He backed up his words with a light stroke of his thumb across her lower lip, and then his mouth on hers, right in the middle of Main Street.

"You like shocking them all, don't you?"

He pulled back at that. "It's not about shocking them. I'm proud of you. Proud to be with you."

"I know you are," she said, trying to stop herself from adding, "At least for now," and failing. When his mouth tightened, she regretted the words as much as she'd thought she would. "You were clear from the start about what you can give. About how long you're planning to stay in town. It's just sometimes," she said, barely above a whisper, "I find myself wanting more."

She knew how important honesty was to him, but she'd just told a lie. Straight to his face. Because she didn't want more *sometimes*.

She wanted more *all the time*.

She knew she had his respect. She knew he appreciated her. That she made him laugh when few others could. And all of that was great, amazing even.

But she wanted his love.

She'd hoped she could go into this relationship knowing the score, understanding what was possible and what wasn't, and come out on the other side having had a taste of something sweet and lovely. But

Liam had known better right from the start, hadn't he? He'd predicted her broken heart. And then he'd kissed her…and those predictions hadn't seemed to matter as long as he was close.

They got into his car, where the air was tense as he drove, filled with her longing and his reticence. He hadn't told her where they were going, just that he had a surprise for her. She assumed it had something to do with the festival. They were driving through the heavily forested part of Route 10 when the trees suddenly cleared and he pulled into a narrow gravel driveway.

"Where are we?"

"My property."

She shifted in her seat in surprise. "I didn't know you own land on the lake."

"I bought it a few years ago."

She should have guessed, knowing how much he loved Summer Lake, that he'd always planned on coming back here one day. For all the problems he had with his family, how could he resist? And despite the earlier awkwardness, hope moved through her that maybe, just maybe, he'd make that full-time move sooner rather than later. If he stayed in town, and they continued to date, it wasn't completely impossible that he could fall in love with her one day, was it?

Knowing her heart was running away with her

brain again—in a tremendously foolish direction, no less—she was just on the verge of vowing not to let it happen when she saw the most unexpected thing in the world in front of them.

"You have a *plane*?"

The first hint of a smile came back to his lips. "A floatplane."

She swallowed hard, felt the air begin to press and squeeze out of her lungs. "Your plane takes off and lands on the water?" Her stomach started cramping at nothing more than the thought of it. This was far worse than even her worst fear. At least normal planes landed on solid ground. She had a vision of the float tips digging in, the plane somersaulting—

"Now that the ice on the lake has melted, I was able to have it delivered." Liam's hand was gentle on her chin as he turned her face to his. "Come up in it with me, Christie. I want to take you flying."

"I—" Her mouth was dry, so dry her tongue stuck to the roof of it. She closed her eyes, whispered, "I can't."

"Sweetheart. Look at me." She made herself open her eyes, tried not to see the plane in front of them, floating there at the end of his dock, taunting her. "You are strong. Determined. Something like getting into a floatplane shouldn't break someone as full of resolve as you."

"It will."

"It won't. I know it won't."

"How can you know that?"

"Do you trust me?" he asked her.

Of course she did. More than she should. With everything, including her heart. Still, she could barely get the word out. "Yes."

"We'll just climb in," he said in a gentle voice. "Get used to the feel of the seat, the belts, the way the world looks from a front-row seat."

"You make it sound so easy."

"It will be."

And then he leaned over and kissed her, softly at first, but the passion that burned between them was never far from the surface. Like magic, her nerves, her fears, all started to melt away as their tongues danced. She reached for him, threaded her hands into his dark hair, and then she was on his lap and lost to everything but how much she wanted him.

Before she realized it, he'd opened the car door and she was standing on the sand in his arms. He took her hand in his.

"How am I supposed to think straight after a kiss like that?"

"You're not."

"You tricked me."

He didn't look the least bit guilty as he maneuvered

them across the sand and toward the dock. "I did." And then, just that fast, he had her sitting in the passenger seat of the small plane. "See? It's not scary at all."

Even though she didn't want to believe him, he was right. The console had a lot of buttons and switches and gauges, but she supposed it wasn't all that different from sitting in his expensive car.

And yet, she still didn't think she could go up in it.

"All day long," he said in that deep voice that always melted her insides, "I can hardly wait to make love with you each night. Do you know why?"

Oh God. No one had ever spoken to her like this. She couldn't get her mouth to form the word *why*, but Liam didn't let that stop him.

"Because I've never seen anything as beautiful in all my life as you are when you let go in my arms. And ever since we met, I've seen how much you love learning new things. How you love adventure. Even fighting for the festival with you has been fun." His gaze was full of more emotion than she'd ever thought to see. "Maybe it's just me being selfish. But I want to see the wonder in your eyes when you see the lake from the clouds for the first time."

If this wasn't love, she wasn't sure she knew what love was. She took a deep breath. And said, "Go."

He didn't wait another second, didn't give her time to change her mind. He fired up the engine, and they started to glide across the water. She let out a little squeak as he pulled back on the yoke and they climbed into the sky.

Just as her lungs were shutting down again, he reminded her, "One breath at a time. Just one, Christie. Just give me one."

She could do that, couldn't she? Just one breath. And then another when she was done with that first one. She wanted to pinch her eyes shut, wanted to pretend she was anywhere but in an airplane—but the dark blue of the water, the light blue of the sky, the faint wisps of clouds, the dark greens of the forest, were all starting to make their way into her brain. Snippets of beauty came at her like a flashing video screen, one after the other, so magnificent that she could still hardly breathe.

And that was when it hit her: She was up in the clouds in a tiny plane...and she wasn't dying.

Instead, she was more alive than she'd ever been before.

"Thank you." She hadn't realized she was crying until she said the two little words. Trying to take it all in—the magnificence of the lake and mountains and sky—her words were blurry with her tears of joy. "It's even more incredible than I imagined." Turning to face him, she saw that he was looking at her with such tenderness, such wonder, her heart actually skipped a beat. "No one has ever cared this much about me," she told him as they flew through the sky. "No one has ever made me face my fears like you just did."

She was stunned that he understood her so well, that he knew she'd not only survive the flight, but would also relish it completely.

No one had ever had so much faith in her. She'd trusted him with her embarrassing secret—that she was too much of a wimp to get on a plane—and instead of turning it against her, instead of finding her weak, he'd found a way to help her get through it. His tactic might have been unorthodox—no one had ever kissed her fears into submission before—but it had worked.

She wanted so badly to do the same for him, wanted him to know that she had faith in him too—and that he could trust her with his pain. Trust her to help him work through it...and finally let go of it.

"Are you scared now?" he asked.

She took a breath. "Yes."

He frowned, clearly not expecting that to be her answer. "You are?"

"I am." She smiled at him. "But it's a good kind of scared. I'm scared that I've wasted too much time. I'm scared that there are too many beautiful things out there for me to fit into one lifetime." She gathered up all of her courage to say one more thing. "And I'm scared about what I'm feeling for you."

CHAPTER TWENTY-EIGHT

Christie held her breath during the landing, but it was just as smooth as the takeoff. She was spoiled by having Liam as her personal pilot, because she trusted him in a way she'd never trusted anyone else.

Now, as he helped her out of the plane, his hands on either side of her waist, she tried to read his reaction to her confession. But too soon, they had to move away from each other to secure his plane to the dock.

Once that was done, he said, "Mrs. Higgins packed a hamper of food for us. It's in the trunk."

Her heart thumped inside her chest while they went to get it and then spread a blanket over the sand and sat down. But neither of them reached for the food.

"Thank you for flying with me." His voice resonated with the same emotion she'd seen in his eyes during the flight.

She had to reach over and take his hand in both of hers. Because after the gift he'd just given her—after the wonder he'd just shown her—she couldn't live with her earlier lie that she wanted more only *some-times*.

"I never expected you to come into my life," she said softly. "All those years I knew Wesley and he told me about his amazing older brother, I never realized just what you would mean to me one day." A thousand times more frightened than she had ever been of flying, Christie had to force herself to look Liam in the eye. "I've fallen for you. All the way." She sucked in a shaky breath. "I know you warned me not to, but you made it impossible to keep my heart to myself."

"Christie."

She squeezed his hand. "No. Please. I didn't just say all of that because I thought it would get you to say it back to me. I just—" She brought his hand to her lips, pressed a kiss to it. "You've become my best friend, Liam. And I need to tell my best friend that I've fallen in love."

* * *

Women had claimed to love Liam many times, but never like this. No one had ever bared her true soul to him. No one had ever put her heart in his palm and given him the chance to crush it so easily. So completely.

And he'd never thought his heart could feel so full, never knew just one word—*love*—could be so beautiful or mean so much.

Unbidden, a flash came of what it would be like to have Christie by his side from this moment forward. As his wife, in his arms every night. As his business partner, running lakefront inns across the Northeast together. As the mother of their children. She'd be warm and loving and a fierce protector—and proponent—for all of them.

He brushed away the tears that fell down her cheek. No one had ever meant as much to him as this beautiful woman sitting beside him. And he hated hurting her. Hated it with every fiber of his being.

"All my life," he said in a voice made raw with the deep emotions only Christie had ever been able to draw from him, "I've looked at things I wanted from every angle, and only when it made sense would I go out and get them. But the way I've wanted you has never made sense. Not when you'd been in a relationship with my brother. Not when you wouldn't tell me why he left or where he was. Not with you working for me. Not when I know you're looking for something I can't give you. But in the end, all that has ever mattered is how much I want to be with you."

"And you've got me."

"No, sweetheart. You're so much more, so much bigger than any one man could possibly hold on to."

"How can you call me sweetheart in one breath

and tell me not to love you in the next? You want to love me, don't you, Liam?"

More than anything I've ever wanted in my life.

But he still couldn't say the words.

And when she said, "I taught you how to make the inn's beds. Maybe I could teach you how to love me too," his heart actually twisted inside his chest at the hope he heard.

At the hope he would give anything to share.

He kissed her then, had to kiss her because she was so sweet and so honest in every single moment. Even the ones where she could be hurt the most. Especially those.

If he couldn't give her the love she deserved, he owed her an explanation at least, promises and secrets be damned. "When I was fourteen years old, I found my mother in bed with someone. Not my father."

Christie didn't gasp. She didn't exclaim. She simply held his hands over her heart.

"I should have been in physics class, but I'd forgotten my football helmet and had aced the quiz the day before, so the teacher let me skip out for a few minutes."

He'd never said these words aloud to anyone. All these years, he'd thought it was because he had to keep his mother's secret. But now, he finally realized that the reason for his silence went far deeper.

A part of him had hoped that if he never said the words aloud, somehow his silence could help erase the past.

"She probably thought there wouldn't be anyone home for hours. I didn't find them actually having sex, but she was wearing her robe and telling him what they had just done was a mistake. That they couldn't tell anyone what had happened. That she hadn't been thinking straight. She told him to put his clothes on and leave. That was when she walked into the hall and saw me."

He'd never forget the look on his mother's face. She'd been crying; he could see that, and he could see the self-hatred, the guilt already ravaging her face at what she'd just done. As soon as she spotted Liam, all of that had been replaced by fear.

"She stood in the hallway, her hand over her mouth, her face white. That was when he walked out and saw me too. He was an architect my father worked with sometimes. It was pretty much a joke in town that he'd screw anything in a skirt. He still lives a couple of towns over. He's married now. Has kids of his own." Liam had to clear his throat. "She told him to go. To get the hell out, and then she came to me, begging me, pleading with me not to tell my father what I'd seen."

"How could she?" Christie was clearly shocked.

He'd asked himself this question a million times.

"My father loved her so much. She was everything to him. I don't know how she could have cheated on him."

"No, I'm not asking about her relationship with your father." Christie's voice broke. "I want to know how any mother could possibly ask her child to do something like that. To keep such a horrible secret."

"She had no other choice."

"She damn well did!"

It was instinct to pull her onto his lap, to put his arms around her, to try and soothe her by stroking a hand down her back.

Her eyes were glassy with unshed tears—tears for him. "Has she ever tried to talk to you about it?"

"No." The one word came out sharp. Hard.

When she reached up to touch his face, her hand was blessedly soft and cool. "Have you ever told anyone before now?"

He shook his head. "But after my accident, everyone had to know that something bad had happened in our family." Even after all these years, it was far too easy to be right back there, standing in the kitchen while his mom wept tears of pure terror that his father would learn of her betrayal. "I couldn't listen to her begging anymore. Couldn't stand to look at her and see that fear. So I grabbed the car keys to get the hell out of there. I didn't have my license yet, but I shouldn't have been driving anyway. I think I hit the tree on purpose, as though somehow I could punish her by crashing her car. Instead, the car got fixed and I ended up with this scar on my face." He moved Christie's fingers over it, made her trace the slightly jagged skin under his cheekbone. "You've never said anything to me about it."

"I never see it." She gently, lovingly stroked his face. She pressed a kiss to his lips, then said, "And I wouldn't want to love someone again either, if that had been me. If I had been through what you've been through all these years." She leaned closer, pressed another kiss to his scar. "Are you ever going to talk to her about it?"

"No."

"Never?"

"Christie." He heard the warning in his voice, knew it had no place in a scene where she'd just told him so sweetly that she loved him. But none of that could stop him from saying, "Promise me you won't say a word about it. Not to her. Not to anyone."

She stared at him, time stretching out between them on the beach, the sun moving down behind the tops of the tall trees.

Her whispered, "I promise," floated away from them and out across the lake.

CHAPTER TWENTY-NINE

That night, the moment Christie opened the door to Lakeside Stitch and Knit, Sarah surprised her with a huge hug. "You look so tanned and gorgeous," she told Sarah when they pulled apart. "And happy."

Her friend's grin could have lit up the yarn shop all by itself. "I am. So, so, *so* happy." Sarah leaned in close to whisper, "You've got to tell me—is Liam as good a kisser as it looks like he'd be?"

"He—" She flushed as she licked her lips. "I—"

"Well, that's a *hell yeah* if I've ever heard one!" Sarah exclaimed. "I've staked out a quiet corner so that you can tell me *everything*."

Christie said hello to everyone in the knitting group, then grabbed a glass of wine and sat beside Sarah in the only private spot in the crowded group of knitters. As Christie pulled out her knitting, they all—thankfully—turned back to their gossip and laughter.

"Oooh," Sarah said as she reached out to slide the yarn of the almost finished slip between her fingers. "This is *so* sexy. Mom told me you were working on the pattern for the shop. But I think you should keep it."

"I couldn't." Christie shouldn't hate the thought of parting with the cashmere slip. After all, she'd known all along that she was making it to hang in the store as a sample next to the pattern book. Still, she hadn't forgotten the way Liam had looked at it—and her—when he said, *Will you wear it for me when you're done with it? No dress. Just the slip.*

"We both know you want to," Sarah said with a wicked glint in her eyes. "Now, just to make sure I've got it all straight, I got married on Saturday, and then you and Liam started kissing on..."

"Thursday." She'd never forget their first kiss...or any of the kisses that had come after. "But we should talk about your honeymoon."

"Later. So you kissed on Thursday, and then you..." She scanned Christie's face for clues. "That same night, huh?"

All Christie could do was nod. And say, "I love him."

Sarah reached for her hand. "You would never have slept with him if you didn't." Christie tried to blink back the rush of moisture in her eyes as Sarah added, "And I know that Wesley is going to be happy for you. For both of you."

Only a true friend would understand, without being told, just how much hearing that meant to Christie. More than anything, she wanted to confide in Sarah, to ask for advice on how to help Liam.

Keeping Wesley's secret had been hard, but at least she knew that he would eventually resolve his situation. Liam, however, would always be broken, as long as he held on to his mother's secret. As long as he carried the burden of keeping his parents' marriage together on his strong shoulders. And he would never really trust a woman, never really let himself love anyone, until the day came when he could let go of the secret.

But she'd promised him she'd never speak of it to anyone. So she simply said, "He can't love me back. Even before that first kiss, he warned me. But I would have loved him anyway."

She waited for her friend to tell her to run. To get the heck out of a relationship that wasn't going anywhere. But Sarah's expression was one of complete understanding.

"Even if Calvin couldn't have loved me back, I've never been able to stop myself from loving him." Sarah instinctively put her hands over her slightly rounded stomach. "I wouldn't want to, even if we never got to have our forever together." With that, she gently put the needles back in Christie's hands. "I really think you should finish this tonight."

"I'm not sure my head is in the right place. I'd hate to mess it up right at the end."

"How about this—while you work on those final rows, I'll tell you all about the Bahamas."

Sarah knew how much Christie longed to travel, that she could listen to travel stories all night long. And as her friend began her delicious tales about sun and sand and tropical adventure, Christie made one stitch and then another, until she finally realized she had relaxed for the first time in hours.

A short while later, she bound off the last stitch and looked up to find Sarah smiling at her. "It's beautiful."

Christie ran her hands over the delicate web of fiber. "It really is."

But a moment later, when a voice called out, "Susan, it's so nice to see you," Christie felt her entire body go tense. She steeled herself to stay calm as she looked over at Liam's mother, who had just walked into the store.

Sarah's gaze went from Christie to Susan. "Christie? Are you okay?"

She shook her head, tried to say something, but no words would come out.

"Come help me with some boxes in the back room." Sarah tugged her to her feet. Once they were away from the group, she asked, "Did something happen between you and Susan? Did she say something to you about dating Liam?"

"No." Thank God that was the honest answer. "But I still need to leave."

Seconds later, she slipped out the back door into the rain that had just started to come down and ran across the street. Back to the inn.

Back to Liam.

* * *

Susan wasn't a huge knitter, but she'd come to the Monday night knitting group enough over the years to know that there was usually comfort to be found there.

All day, she'd felt as though her skin was too tight, as though something inside of her was about to explode. To burst into a thousand little, messy pieces.

It didn't make sense. Apart from Wesley's continued absence, things were actually better than they'd been in a while. She and Henry were both making an effort to be kinder to each other, to appreciate each other. The night before, they'd even gone out to sit on the end of their dock to watch the stars. His hand had moved across to hold hers. And she'd let him.

What's more, Christie was bringing her closer to her son. Now that she was involved with the Tapping of the Maples Festival, Susan had a reason to go by the inn at least once a day. It was such a pleasure to see so much of Liam. They weren't saying anything important, but she hoped that would come eventually.

So then why did she have such a deep premonition of doom? And why did her secret—her lies—feel like it was looming bigger than ever?

Susan let Helen and Dorothy, two women she'd always thought were a hoot, settle her onto the couch with fat needles and thick, soft green yarn that reminded her of the budding leaves on the trees.

"We haven't seen you in months," Dorothy said. "Since the end of summer, isn't that right?"

Susan knew Christie was here every Monday night, and that had been part of the reason she hadn't been in since last fall. But she figured there was no longer a reason to stay away. "Henry and I have been fixing up our house," she said by way of explanation.

Helen raised her eyebrows. "Working on the house with my late husband made me want to take a hammer to his head. My hat is off to you, Susan."

It should have made her feel better to know that most husbands and wives didn't get along all of the time. It should have pleased her to note that people saw a loving partnership when they looked at her marriage. Instead, she felt as though it was just one more lie added to all of the others she'd been telling for so long.

She looked around the store. "Isn't Christie usually here on Monday nights?"

Sarah handed her a glass of wine. "She just finished her project and decided to leave early."

"I'm sorry I missed her." Trying to push away the dark, heavy feeling inside her chest, Susan asked Sarah, "How was your honeymoon? You're positively glowing."

Susan smiled in all the right places, making appropriate comments when necessary, and even knitted a few rows of a simple baby blanket pattern Helen got her started on. Unfortunately, coming to Lakeside Stitch and Knit tonight didn't make her feel any better. On the contrary, she felt more tense—and scared—than ever before.

Caught between her love for the husband she couldn't bear to lose and her love for the son with whom she would never have a real, loving relationship if she didn't confess, Susan felt as though her heart were tearing to pieces. And she was afraid that no amount of trying to knit the threads back together would ever make it whole again.

CHAPTER THIRTY

Christie hadn't planned to wear the slip tonight. But when she finally got back to her suite, stripped off her wet clothes and hung them to dry in the bathroom, the pull was too strong to resist. She'd just try the slip on this once to find out what it felt like against her skin, and then she'd put it away.

In any case, she needed to calm down before going to Liam tonight. Seeing his mother had yanked up all of her anger, all of her fury at what he'd been through over the years. Because of what Susan had made him promise. For all that he tried to act like he wasn't tapped into his emotions, she knew he was. So if he pulled her into his arms tonight and looked at her with those dark, heated eyes while she was so out of control, she was afraid of what he'd see.

Not only the desire to strike out at his mother on his behalf.

But also the love that she couldn't control.

He already knew she loved him, but since he couldn't love her back, she knew better than to smother him with it.

With trembling fingers, she picked up the cashmere slip and put it over her arms and head. The knitted fabric was so soft it took her breath away. As did the thought that Liam would love to see her in this…and she would love to wear it for him.

Like magic, there was a knock at the door.

Her heart was pounding hard and fast as she walked over. She'd opened it for Liam so many times in the past week. But this time everything was different.

His eyes held hers for a long moment, as though he was drinking her in after a long, long absence—even though it had been only a couple of hours. And when he whispered her name—*Christie*—it didn't simply sound like her name.

Tonight it sounded like the one thing she hadn't been able to stop hoping for, no matter how many times she tried…

* * *

Twenty years ago, everything in Liam's life had changed in an instant with a kick to the gut, the ripping of his heart.

But tonight, it was just the opposite. Because just looking at Christie, standing only inches away, was all it took for Liam to finally feel whole again.

While she'd been at the knitting group, he'd been trying to concentrate on the emails his lawyer had sent earlier that week. Concentration had never been a problem for Liam, even when he wasn't getting much sleep. Heck, in the past, a circus could have been going on all around him and he would have been focused on his task. On his goal.

But tonight he hadn't had a prayer.

How could he when he'd been checking the clock every other minute? When he'd been holding his breath waiting for footsteps outside his door, for the moment when Christie came back to him, so warm and pretty and sweet that he never wanted to let her go?

Waiting, he'd walked over to the window, thinking about how he hadn't been planning to stay in Summer Lake. Even if he decided to buy a string of inns, he'd been planning to run his business from Boston or New York City, close to funding and business partners. Only, he couldn't take Christie away from here. She was as much a part of the land, the water, the mountains as anyone whose family had been here for generations. And the thought of leaving her behind had every muscle in his body tightening.

Again and again, he'd found himself thinking back to their flight, to their conversation on the beach, to what she'd told him: *I love you.* And what he'd told her, something just as incredible: *I trust you.*

The rain had started coming down, a spring shower that would turn buds to leaves, dirt to grass, ice to lake water. The dark street was empty, the lights all along Main Street making it look like a movie set for an old black-and-white film like *Singing in the Rain*.

That was when he saw her running across the street, through the puddles, a bag clutched to her chest. A half-dozen emotions went through him.

The desire that had grown from the first moment he'd set eyes on her.

A surge of protectiveness. The knowledge that he would have swept the sky clear of rain if he could have to keep her dry and warm.

But strongest of all was the one emotion he'd never thought he'd be able to feel. Or recognize. But it was there, so strong, so powerful, he had to grip the edges of the window frame to steady himself.

The same emotion he felt right now as he stood in her doorway…and his entire life changed again.

All because of Christie.

* * *

For a long moment, Liam didn't move from the hallway, didn't come toward her, until suddenly, she was in his arms and he was kicking her door shut.

He carried her into the bedroom and laid her on

the bed as if she were the most delicate porcelain. She had never been looked at this way, as though she was the only person on earth who mattered.

"Kiss me," she said, and then he was gently, slowly moving to her, over her. His kisses were always spectacular, but this one was different. Almost as though it was a beginning to something more.

The next thing she knew, he was sitting up and she was in his lap. He brushed another kiss against her forehead, down to her cheekbones, before stopping at her earlobe. "I can't believe you're real, that you're here with me." His voice shook. "I can't believe you love me."

"I never had any other choice."

He threaded his hands into her hair, holding her still. She expected another kiss, wasn't at all surprised by the heat in his eyes. But she was thrown completely by the depth of emotion there.

"Liam? What is it? You can say anything to me. Anything at all."

"I know I can. But this—" He stopped, took a breath, actually closed his eyes as he steeled himself for whatever he was going to say to her.

Her heart was racing out of control. *Please. No. Don't say this is the end. That you're ready to leave again.* And then his eyes opened, a deep, rich brown as he gazed at her.

"I love you."

She thought her mouth might have fallen open, knew she was having a hard time finding enough oxygen to pull into her lungs. But before she could get a handle on anything—anything at all—he was kissing her again.

The kiss that followed the three words she hadn't thought she'd ever hear him say turned her brain to mush. He wasn't the only one who could hardly believe this was happening between them. Her brain was a lost cause...but her heart needed to know for sure.

She dragged her mouth from his. "Liam?"

It wasn't until the corners of his mouth moved up that she knew that she wasn't dreaming. "Do you want me to say it again?"

"Yes," she whispered, tracing her fingers over his jaw, along his cheekbones, over his lips.

He held her hand there, pressed a kiss to her fingertips that had her shivering with desire. With love. "I've never trusted anyone the way I trust you. I've never admired anyone the way I admire you." He moved her hand from his lips to his chest, holding it steady right over his heart. "And I've never loved anyone the way I love you."

* * *

After so many years of guarding his heart, it should have been harder to tell Christie how much he loved her. But she made it easy, her eyes shining down at him as he moved his fingers beneath the thin shoulder straps of her slip. The knitted slip he hadn't even realized she was wearing until now, because he hadn't been able to look away from her eyes.

God, she was gorgeous. Her skin was so soft, so pretty as it flushed beneath his every touch as she gave herself over to him.

For so long, he hadn't believed in love. But now, here, tonight, love was all he could feel. When Christie was in his arms, he could forget everything but her. Nothing else needed to matter.

And in the morning, when reality came rushing back, he'd try to figure out how to balance what he knew to be true about the world with this new love that he couldn't deny.

He pressed a kiss to the center of her chest, wanted to feel her heart beating beneath his lips. Her hands moved from his shoulders to thread through his hair.

"Liam?" He lifted his head and instantly read her desire. But there was something else there, something that had his own heartbeat hitching. "I want to be with you so badly, but I'm scared." She shifted, and for a split second, he was afraid she was going to move away. Instead, thank God, she pressed herself more tightly against him, as if she were trying to take shelter in his arms. "When I thought you didn't love me back, I knew I had to be prepared for all this to end. I kept telling myself that I didn't have expectations. Even though I was falling for you, it was easier somehow to know that it went only one way. I know it sounds strange, but it was safer. For me. For my heart. But now, if something happens—"

He kissed her before she could finish her sentence. "I love you." God, it felt good to say it. To *feel* it. "You love me." And her love—he still couldn't figure out how he'd been lucky enough to deserve it—meant absolutely everything to him. "Whatever comes, we'll figure it out. Together."

CHAPTER THIRTY-ONE

During the next week, as Christie worked to make sure the Tapping of the Maples Festival was the best it could possibly be, Liam helped her when she needed it and gave her enough kisses throughout the day to make her feel as though she was still flying through wonder with him—but otherwise, he was on the phone working on his own business endeavors.

She would never want her love to box him in. Still, she couldn't help but hope he'd factor her into his future plans.

And then, every night, when she was sure that she was too exhausted to do more than sink into a bath with a glass of wine, just being in Liam's arms was enough to chase away all thoughts of sleep and baths—unless he was there too, doing deliciously wicked things with her.

But it wasn't just how hard she was working, wasn't just her lack of sleep at night that had her so off-kilter during the busy week. It was the secret he'd trusted her with.

The secret he expected her to hold forever.

Liam had never trusted a woman enough to let himself love her. Not until now. She couldn't stand the thought of betraying his trust. But she was desperate to tell his mother what she thought of her—that Susan was an awful person for hurting her own child the way she'd hurt Liam, forcing him to carry her secret. And every day that frustration, that anger on his behalf, grew bigger and bigger. So big that Christie was very much afraid the day would come when she wouldn't be able to hold it all inside.

"Your work crew has arrived!"

Christie turned to see Calvin and Sarah; Calvin's sister, Jordan; and Sarah's mother, Denise, walking through the inn's front door. She'd been so busy this week she hadn't seen Calvin since they'd returned from their honeymoon.

Forcefully pushing aside her thoughts about Susan, she gave him a hug. "Thanks for coming to help, you guys."

"This is exciting," Jordan said. "My friends are all dying to tap a maple."

Calvin grinned. "We've been practicing making the perfect pancakes to eat with the syrup all week."

Surrounded by her friends, warmth flooded Christie. Summer Lake was beautiful, but that wasn't the only reason she'd fallen in love with this town. She'd fallen for the community almost as quickly as she'd fallen for the natural surroundings.

But she'd fallen even faster for Liam. Her body was so attuned to him that she could feel his presence before she saw him coming down the stairs.

He was smiling as Denise called out a greeting, and Sarah shot Christie a surprised glance. Christie had almost forgotten that he hadn't smiled when he first came here. It was still one of her greatest pleasures to tug a grin or, even better, a full-blown laugh out of him.

A few moments later, he was standing behind her and his arms were around her waist, pulling her against him, pressing a kiss to the top of her head.

Christie almost laughed at the way Calvin's eyes just about popped out of his head. Sarah and Denise simply looked pleased.

"Now that everyone's here, why don't we—" The words dried up in Christie's throat as Henry walked in the door…followed by Susan.

A burst of anger came so swiftly that Christie's hands actually fisted. It was only when she felt Liam tense behind her and pull her more tightly to him that she snapped out of her haze.

Henry was smiling as he asked, "Can you use a couple extra pairs of hands?"

Christie hoped the smile she gave Henry wasn't as

shaky as it felt. "Absolutely. Thanks for coming."

It was a relief to bury herself in details, to get everyone off and running. Sarah, bless her heart, ran interference with Susan, so that Christie didn't have to deal with the woman face-to-face. The problem was, she couldn't keep her distance forever. One day she was going to have to figure out how to sit down at a dinner table with Liam's mother...and not throw a drink in her face.

When everyone else was out putting up tents and moving the tapping equipment into the spots she'd marked on her map, Liam reached for her hand. "Come here, sweetheart."

It still gave her the shivers every time he called her that. And every time he said *I love you*, it felt brand new, as though she was hearing it, feeling it, for the very first time in her life.

"You're tired." He kissed her eyelids, first one, then the other, and she let herself sink against him. Just for a moment, and then she'd get back out there and take care of everything that needed to be done.

He pressed a soft kiss to her mouth before saying, "Everything is going according to plan. The festival is going to be a hit."

After what she'd been through to get it off the ground, she should be ecstatic. "I hope so."

"I know you have a lot of work to do, but I want to

show you something first." Liam led her by the hand out the front door of the inn and over to the gazebo.

She looked across the lake, over to the sugar bush, then back at the inn. She didn't get it at first, but then as he wrapped his arms around her again, her back to his front, and she felt his strength, his steady heartbeat, finally she saw it.

In the span of the few short weeks they'd known each other, the trees had gone from bare to budding to bright green leaves. The roses that had been hiding during the freezing days were almost ready to show off their pinks and whites and reds in the sunlight.

"It's going to be summer soon," he said, making sure that she didn't miss the miracles taking place right before her eyes. "As soon as the water's warm enough, I'm going to take you sailing. And when we tip over, we're going to get right back in."

She knew what he was trying to tell her: *I'm going to stay.*

"I love you," she said softly as she turned in his arms and slid her hands around his neck.

And as they stood there, forehead to forehead, in the place so many brides and grooms had stood before, Christie understood just how boundless and how wonderfully sweet love could be.

* * *

Henry couldn't take his eyes off Liam and Christie. "Remember the day we stood in that gazebo?"

Susan looked up with surprise from the table that she was trimming with fabric and followed his gaze to the gazebo, where Liam and Christie were holding each other. "Our wedding was one of the best days of my life."

Henry took in the wistful expression on his wife's face, her clear longing for what had once been. He longed for it too, had been trying for days to find a way back to that place they'd been so many years before. But Susan had returned from Lakeside Stitch and Knit on Monday night distant and out of sorts, and he hadn't been able to push past her walls yet. Seeing Christie and Liam so obviously in love gave him hope to try again. One more time.

"Mine too," he said, putting the staple gun he was holding on the table. He took Susan's hands in his. They were cold and, if he wasn't mistaken, trembling. "Susie." Her eyes widened at the nickname he hadn't used in far too long. "I love you."

"I love you too." The words were right, but her voice was desperate. "So, so much."

"Tell me what's wrong. Let me help fix it."

* * *

Oh God. She couldn't keep her hands from tensing in

his. This was her chance to tell him the truth. To confess everything, to lay bare her soul and hopefully wash it clean.

Henry had been trying so hard to reconnect, doing sweet things for her all week. Picking fresh flowers for the vase in the center of the kitchen table. Coming home with her favorite bread from the bakery.

If she told him about her affair, he'd pull away.

No, worse than that. He'd *hate* her.

She moved closer, loving the way his arms wrapped around her. She couldn't give this up, couldn't give him up. She just couldn't.

"I was just thinking about Wesley," she finally said. It was true; she'd been thinking all day that her youngest son should have been here, helping along with everyone else. That Wesley should never have run away in the first place. That he should have been brave enough to face them—and to remember that they all loved him, no matter what, no matter whom he loved. "I wish he'd come home."

Henry was silent for a long moment, and she got the distinct sense that he knew she wasn't saying everything she had to say. "I wish he was here too. He belongs here. With his family. His friends." She felt him shift, knew he was looking back toward Liam and Christie. "But it looks like there's going to be a wedding after all, doesn't it?"

Tears pricked her eyes. She was so glad her eldest son had found the love he deserved. And she prayed that nothing would come between Liam and Christie, that neither of them would ever experience this fear of losing the truest love they'd ever known…

CHAPTER THIRTY-TWO

The morning of the festival was full of sun and bright blue skies. The wind was still, the birds were chirping, and the flowers were blooming.

Everything was perfect.

At ten a.m. when the festival opened, there was no doubt in anyone's mind that it was a huge success. People had come from all around New York state to celebrate a new ritual of spring at Summer Lake.

Christie had worked toward this day for months. She was glad to see what fun everyone was having, both young and old, as they learned to tap the maple trees. Mr. Radin was conspicuously absent, of course, but she wouldn't have expected anything else.

But instead of basking in her success, she felt her gut churn. Because all the while, as she kept an eye on the festival proceedings and dealt with a handful of issues throughout the morning, she couldn't push away her memory of watching Liam sleep last night, the hard lines of his beautiful face softening as he relaxed into her arms.

She'd never loved anyone the way she loved him. And she simply couldn't stand beside him every day, couldn't lie with him in her arms every night, and know that his mother's secret continued to tear him apart.

Confident that everything was under control, she was glad for a few minutes to walk away from the crowds. Somehow, she needed to figure out how to take a full breath into her clenched and tight lungs. She was doing just that when she felt a buzzing along her spine and saw Susan coming toward her.

The breath Christie had been taking exploded in her chest. *You promised him you wouldn't say anything.*

Susan gave her a wobbly smile as she approached, but Christie couldn't smile back. Twenty years. That's how long it had been since Liam had caught his mother in a compromising position with another man. That's how long his relationship with his father had been fractured. That's how long he'd been eaten up inside by his promise.

"I'm so glad the weather is cooperating for your festival," Susan said.

Not trusting her voice, Christie simply nodded her agreement.

Liam's mother looked tired, more worn than Christie could remember seeing her. With anyone else, she would have asked if everything was all right, if she could help. But she didn't dare say those words to Susan. Not when she knew others might follow, harsh words that weren't her place to say.

"You're angry with me, aren't you, Christie?"

Her breath caught in her throat. She knew what she needed to do, knew the lie she needed to tell, that everything was fine. But Christie couldn't do it. Couldn't do anything but look Liam's mother square in the eyes. "Yes, I am."

Susan looked terribly fragile as she nodded her acceptance of the truth. "I'm sorry. So very sorry for the way I've behaved. I've never treated you as well as I should. I was too protective of Wesley. And then Liam. I wouldn't let myself see you for who you really are because I was afraid you were going to hurt my sons."

Christie barely kept her mouth from falling open. *This* was what Susan was apologizing for? For being somewhat cold and unwelcoming to her?

Blood rushed in her ears, louder this time, and her hands formed tight fists by her sides. She needed to turn away, needed to do a much better job of backing down. But, damn it, Liam had borne the pain of his mother's deep betrayal for twenty years already.

One more second was one too long.

"I'm not the one you should be apologizing to." Her words were flat and so much colder than Susan's had ever been to her.

Susan went perfectly still. "What are you talking about?"

"Liam. And the secret he's been keeping from his father. The one you're making him keep."

Christie wasn't glad to see his mother turn a nasty shade of greenish white. She wasn't doing this because she wanted to see Susan put in her place. It was simply instinct to protect the man she loved from the one person who'd hurt him the most. Not just once, but again and again with her continued demand for his silence.

Susan didn't pretend she didn't know what Christie was talking about. She didn't defend herself either. Instead, she stood there looking completely broken, tears cascading down her cheeks.

The sight of tears had always made Christie fold. But this time, she was immune to Susan's tears, even to the woman saying, "I was such a mess. My brother had died, and I wasn't thinking. I should never have had the affair."

Christie shook her head, even though she wanted to put her hands on Susan and shake her instead. "But you did." That was all it took for everything Christie had told herself she needed to keep inside—to hold on to Liam's trust—to break through the dam and come spilling out. "And when he caught you in the act, instead of being brave and owning up to your mistake, you asked a *child* to be your partner in crime. For a crime he didn't have any part of. You hurt him so badly, Susan. You changed him by teaching him all the wrong things about relationships. About women. And he's paid for your mistake his entire adult life." She all but bared her teeth at the crying woman. "You're not going to let him pay any longer."

"Oh God." Susan's hands were over her mouth, and she was sobbing so hard that it was hard to understand her. "The accident afterward was all my fault. That's why he has that scar."

"The scar on the outside doesn't matter. That one has healed. But you could never stand to see it, could you? Not when it reminded you of everything you did wrong." There was no point in holding back now. Not that she could have, even if she'd wanted to—Liam meant too much to her to not do everything she possibly could to help heal what was broken. "He loved you. God help him, he still does, despite what you did. But the secret you made him keep from the father he loves ripped a hole inside of him that's never even come close to closing."

"He won't talk to me."

"Of course not," Christie said bluntly. "Why would he when every conversation is lined with betrayal? With secrets. With lies."

"Oh God," Susan said again.

"But if that's ever going to change, you're going to have to try again and keep trying." Christie paused, let her fists unclench. Her fingernails had been digging into her palms. "Start now." She could feel her own tears coming. "Love your son. Please just love your son."

"I do love him. I've always loved him."

"Then go find him. If the only thing you can say right now is *I love you*, that's a hundred times better than continuing to say nothing at all."

"How have I been so wrong for so long?" Susan sobbed. "About everything?"

Christie had messed up plenty in the past. But she was starting to see that it wasn't the past that should be holding any of them back. It was the future they should be looking forward to. And every single beautiful moment in the present that they should be cherishing.

Just as she'd cherished every moment with Liam. Every smile. Every kiss. Every time he held her in his arms. Every time he'd told her he believed in her, even when she forgot to believe in herself.

"I know you've lost so many years," Christie said in a voice that came out barely above a whisper around the huge lump in her throat. "Don't lose any more. Please try. Please just keep telling him how much you love him. Even if he doesn't want to listen, even if he pushes you away, he needs to know that you're sorry.

And that you don't need him to keep your secret anymore."

"I was going to tell Henry today. I swear I was."

Christie didn't know what was going to happen between Liam's parents. Of course, she hoped they'd work through their issues, but—"Your son needs you first."

Susan took a breath, one that shook her entire frame. "I know." And then she turned and ran toward the inn, to find her son, the man who needed her love now just as much as he'd needed it when he was fourteen.

Liam was more important to Christie than any festival. He was more important to her than her job at the inn. If it meant helping him move forward with his family, she was willing to risk losing him, was willing to risk her job and any future she could have had in Summer Lake.

All her life, she'd thought she was such an open book. But now she realized that she'd always been holding something back. Until Liam had cracked open the final part of her shell, so she could love more purely, more wholly than she ever had before. At least this time around when she had to start over somewhere new, she'd know that she hadn't held back any part of her heart.

Which was why she had just risked it all, risked the

job, the town, the friends she loved.

For love.

Liam deserved true happiness, the kind that would come only when he and his mother were honest with each other. It might not happen today, but at least the painful silence he'd kept for two decades would end.

Still, for all Christie's clear-cut reasons for what she'd done, and despite how much she believed in each one, she could feel her own heart breaking, one painful beat at a time. Because she knew Liam. Knew without a doubt that by being unable to keep her promise and his secret, the man she loved was already gone. Even if he didn't know it yet.

But he would as soon as his mother found him.

And as Christie stood on the edge of the sugar bush with people laughing all around her and small children playing tag, she knew it wouldn't matter that she'd broken her promise to Liam out of love.

He'd stop loving her anyway.

CHAPTER THIRTY-THREE

"Liam, honey, we need to talk."

He looked up at his mother from the registration counter, where he was putting away the file on a new guest that had just checked in. And in an instant, he knew.

Christie had broken her promise.

He'd told himself he could trust her. That if there was a woman on earth whom he could hand his heart, his fears, over to, it was Christie.

But he'd been wrong.

"We don't need to do this," he said.

He had been playing this game with his mother for long enough to know that his only chance to get out of the big emotional scene she clearly wanted to have in order to assuage her own guilt was to nip it in the bud. To act like it didn't matter to him. Because it didn't, damn it. He was over something that happened when he was fourteen years old.

She stopped, faltering as she came toward him. She shook her head, opened her mouth, but nothing came out. And he thought maybe, just maybe, he was safe. But then she put her head in her hands, and he saw the frailty of her shoulders. Shoulders that were shaking from fear. From sorrow.

He shouldn't feel pity for her. Shouldn't feel anything at all. But Christie had changed him. He'd let his heart lead him for the first time in nearly twenty years. And now he couldn't figure out how to close down the pathways to his heart this fast.

His mother lifted her head, looked directly at him, holding his gaze with such focus he couldn't pull his away. "I love you." Her mouth wobbled, and fresh tears came. "I love you so much, Liam. I always have. From the first moment I held you in my arms when you were a baby. When I watched you grow up into such an incredible child and into a young man."

She took a step toward him, and he couldn't contain the urge to flinch.

Seeing it, she almost crumbled to the ground, catching herself on the side of a chair a split second before he moved to help her. "Sit down, Susan." He tucked a pillow behind her shoulders, made sure she was steady before he stepped away, putting much-needed distance between them.

"I remember the first time you called me that instead of Mom," she whispered. "You were in the hospital after the car crash, and they told me you were awake. All night long, I'd prayed for the chance to rewind time, to take back what I'd done, to make it so you wouldn't see what you'd seen. But when I saw you lying there with bandages over part of your face, I knew none of those prayers were ever going to be answered. Your father was there. You called him Dad, just like you always had. And then you said Susan instead of Mom." Her breath hitched in her chest. "And I knew you would never forgive me." She reached out and grabbed his hands, holding them so tightly he couldn't let go. "I knew what I did was wrong. Every minute of every single day I've known it, but I was so scared. Scared of losing everything. But I lost everything anyway, didn't I? You. Your father's love. And any self-respect I might have had." Into his continued silence came, "I ruined your life, Liam. I'm so sorry."

He hated the thought that she could possibly have had that much power over him. "You didn't ruin my life."

"I taught you about lies. I taught you about secrets. I've seen you with women over the years, the way you hold yourself back. The way you never let any of them touch your heart." She paused, and he knew what was coming. "Until Christie."

He couldn't keep his fingers in her grip any longer. "If you want to talk, fine. We'll talk. But keep Christie out of it."

"She loves you."

"What the hell do you know about love?" Years of repressed anger banged and bumped up against the walls he'd built to contain them.

It was the first time he'd ever spoken to her like that, and she looked shocked, but then, instead of falling apart even more, she actually straightened up a bit in the chair. "I can take it," she said, "whatever you've got to say to me. You must be so angry with me."

"It all happened a long time ago." Even though, when he closed his eyes, he could see the whole scene with his mother and Roy as though it were yesterday.

"Please, Liam," she begged. "I'd rather you yelled and screamed at me than look right through me."

"I'm not the one you should be apologizing to. I'm not the one you should be coming clean with."

He left her sitting on the chair…alone. Just the way he'd been since he was a teenager. Just the way he was going to be again once he undid the mistake he'd made with Christie. The mistake of thinking he could let himself trust her.

And love her.

* * *

Christie hadn't moved from her spot by the maple tree in the farthest corner of the bush. She was glad she was wearing a bright red jacket over her sweater and jeans. She wanted it to be easy for Liam to find her. Not because she wanted to get their breakup over with sooner—that wouldn't make it hurt any less; she wasn't nearly stupid enough to believe that—but because she knew how much he must be reeling right now.

She just wanted to make life better for him. Now. In the future. And then one day, maybe he'd wake up and realize that he missed her.

Or…he wouldn't.

She watched him as he approached, her heart breaking even further apart with every step he took—his expression proving without a doubt that she was right about the way everything was going to end between them. She had less than thirty seconds to try to pull herself together. And even though she needed more like thirty years to accept that Liam was already gone, she'd use every last store of her strength for what was coming. Because the last thing Liam needed was one more woman crying. One more woman begging for his forgiveness.

Besides, she wouldn't let herself be sorry about giving her heart for his.

And then, there he was, close enough that she could reach out and touch him. Close enough that he could pull her into his arms and kiss her. Close enough that he could tell her everything was going to be okay.

Instead, he looked at her as if he was berating himself for ever trusting her in the first place.

"You promised to keep what I told you between us."

"I thought I could." A tear fell before she could fight it back. "But I couldn't. I love you too much to keep it." Her words were soft, but they didn't waver. Hopefully, Liam would find a way to patch things up with his mother and finally let out all the love he was holding inside.

"You're the first woman I've trusted since I was a kid. If you really loved me, you wouldn't have said anything to her."

But that's where he was wrong. She'd already lost so much that there was no point in stopping herself now. "That promise you made to her has hurt you from the first moment you made it. I kept Wesley's secret for only a few weeks, and even that was too much. It took something out of me that I shouldn't have had to give up. Just like your mother should never have asked you to give up a piece of your soul for her mistake."

But he clearly didn't want to hear her, and she understood why, even as he said, "You should have respected my wishes. Period. It doesn't matter what your reason is."

She knew what he was doing, that all he wanted was for her to stop loving him, that he wanted to finish putting up his walls and walk away. But though she knew it was the last thing he wanted her to do, she reached out, took his hand, and held it. She couldn't stop her eyes from closing at the pleasure of feeling his warmth, of knowing his touch this one last time. Every second with Liam had been precious.

And she would never regret a single one, regardless of the way they were ending.

"Sometimes loving someone means breaking a promise that will only hurt them if it's kept." She steeled herself to reopen her eyes, to hold his gaze, to keep the tears back. "You're more important than any promise I could ever give you."

Where there had been warmth and love in his eyes just hours ago, now there was nothing. Not even anger. So she finally let go of his hand. But she had to say it one more time, while he was still standing with her.

"Whatever you think, Liam, I love you. I'm pretty sure I loved you from that first moment I saw you at Sarah and Calvin's wedding." She made a sound that could have been a laugh, but that was impossible now. "I was crying then, wasn't I?" She wiped her tears away. "At least I make consistent first and last impressions."

She was that babbling open book she'd always been, but she'd never been able to hold back with Liam. She couldn't do it now even if it meant saving what little strength she had left to move forward. But she could force herself to take a step away, even as the cold penetrated not only her coat but also her flesh, her bones. Her heart.

"I won't make you choose," she said. "This is your home. You should be able to find someone to run the inn within a couple of weeks." She looked over his shoulder at festival attendees struggling with their syrup tapper. "I need to go help with that machine. I'll have a report for you on the festival attendance by close of business tomorrow."

And then she forced herself to move past him, to squash the part of her praying he'd call her name, come after her, and tell her not to go.

She knew that was never going to happen.

And it didn't.

CHAPTER THIRTY-FOUR

Christie had wanted to run, to flee, to hide. She'd been tempted—so very tempted—to leave the festival grounds and lock herself in her bedroom to curl up on her bed and cry for all she'd just lost.

Instead, she forced herself to stay and follow through on what she'd set out to do in a way she never had before.

Saving the festival had helped bring her and Liam together. Now, even though her actions had ripped them apart, she hoped that taking care of a million and one details today and tonight would help her get through to tomorrow in one piece.

Even without Liam's love.

She was standing a hundred yards from the bustling activity, working to open a cardboard box of empty maple syrup containers when she heard, "Christie!"

How was it, she thought as she turned to face Wesley, that he'd managed not only to come back just as abruptly as he'd left, but with the worst possible timing to boot?

"I'm sorry for leaving the way I did," he said, honest regret evident in his tone, his expression.

An hour ago, she would simply have accepted his apology. She would have told him not to worry about it, that he'd had to do what was right for him. But the dam had already broken with both Susan and Liam, so how could she possibly hold back with Wesley?

"You should be sorry. You left me here to deal with everything. To run the inn by myself." She gestured to the crowd of happy people with a jerk of her arm. "To get this festival off the ground by myself."

"I know I shouldn't have treated you like that, but everything looks like it's going so great. You pulled off the festival beautifully. Just like I knew you would."

"Do you really think that's all you left me with? Just the festival? Just the inn?" She could see his surprise at her harsh questions. She'd never spoken to him like this, had never really let loose her true feelings with anyone until Liam. With Liam, she simply hadn't been able to hold back the love she felt. "You left me to deal with telling everyone the wedding was off. I thought you were going to be there beside me, that we were going to tell everyone together."

She could see the flush of shame grow deeper beneath his tanned skin. "You're right. I was a coward. I wasn't thinking about anyone but myself."

"Dealing with people whispering, wondering about

me, wasn't the worst, Wesley. Even the way your mother looked at me, talked to me like I'd driven her baby away, wasn't the worst." She paused, tried to gulp in air as swift pain nailed her in the chest. "Your brother came home. Liam didn't get your letter. He didn't know the wedding had been canceled."

"Oh shit." Wesley grimaced. "I told him it was my fault, that he shouldn't take it out on you, but if he didn't get the letter..."

"Summer Lake was supposed to be a safe haven for my heart. If I could have stopped myself from dreaming those dreams again, I would have."

"What dreams?"

"I love him."

Wesley blinked at her, obviously more confused now than ever. "Wait, what are you talking about? Who do you love?"

"Your brother." She wiped away a rogue tear. "I love your brother with all my heart."

"Liam?" Wesley ran a hand through his dark hair, leaving it standing on end. "You're in love with Liam?"

"You know me," she said sarcastically. "Always falling for those dark, mysterious types."

"No," he protested. "Liam's not like that. I mean, he is, but down deep inside he's not like those other guys you dated. He's a good man. One of the best I've ever known."

"You don't need to tell me how good he is. I know." So good that one day, when Liam could finally let himself love again, the woman, the children he loved, were never going to doubt his love for a single second.

How she envied them.

And how she longed to know that kind of love for herself. Just once.

There had been moments in his arms when she'd thought he was almost there, when he'd looked into her eyes and she'd seen clear into his soul, when he'd said, *I love you.*

But his love for her had never been whole. Because *he* wasn't whole.

"I should have known," Wesley was saying slowly, softly. "If anyone could reach my brother, it would be you."

"Wrong." She couldn't disguise the raw pain behind the one short word. "He doesn't love me back. Do you want to know why?" She didn't wait for him to reply. "Because I suck at keeping secrets. His." She paused, guilt knocking into her as she admitted, "Yours too."

Wesley paled. "I trusted you."

Now it was her turn to say, "I'm sorry. I tried to keep the truth from him, but he was so worried about you. He loves you so much that his fear for you was tearing him apart." Her words had fallen to a faint whisper. "And I loved him too much to keep any secrets from him at all."

She waited for Wesley to be angry with her, like Liam had been, for spilling his secret. Instead, he pinched his eyes closed with his fingertips. "Talk about screwing up. I should never have asked you to keep that secret, Christie. I know it's no defense, but when you found John and me, I flat out panicked."

The way he immediately owned up to the complications he'd caused softened Christie's response. "I know." Finally, she gave in to the instinct to throw her arms around him. "How are you feeling about everything now?"

He smiled down at her, that gentle, sweet smile that she'd always loved, from the first time she'd looked across the nude-drawing class and found a kindred spirit who thought the whole thing was goofy. "Better. So much better. I'm not going to hide anymore. I don't want my life to be a lie anymore. Not to myself or anyone else."

She found a smile for him. "Good. We all love you, Wesley. Everyone in your family. This town. And especially your best friend, who wishes you had confided in her a long, long time ago. Which is why you need to know—your mother overheard my conversation with Liam, the one where I told him your secret. So your parents both know. And they both love you and wish you hadn't run, that you'd trusted them with the truth."

Relief blanketed his face, and he covered her hand with his own. "Thank you, Christie. For everything. For being my friend all these years. For being my friend, even now that I've made things so difficult for you."

A baby cried in the distance. A cloud moved to cover the sun. And a wave of exhaustion hit her hard, sweeping through her from head to toe.

She saw Dorothy and Helen over his shoulder, knew they'd spotted him. Christie couldn't stand here while everyone in town exclaimed over his return. But she couldn't leave the festival either, not when the responsibility for its success—or failure—rested entirely on her shoulders.

"I'm happy you're home," she said. "And I'm even happier that you're happy. But I've got to do my rounds to make sure everything is still going smoothly." With that, she headed for the biggest group of strangers she could find and hoped—prayed—that they would need her help with something.

* * *

The inn's dock was strangely empty. Everyone was in the sugar bush at the festival. Liam was going to head back in a few minutes, couldn't live with himself if he let Christie shoulder the responsibility for the event all by herself. But he'd needed to get away just long enough to pull himself together.

He quickly uncovered and untied the nearest rowboat. The oars were cold and squeaky from a winter and spring of non-use. These past three weeks that he'd been home, the ice had melted from the surface of the water, with only small patches left floating here and there.

Liam's heart had been like this lake when he'd arrived for Wesley's wedding. Frozen solid, but for so much longer than one winter and the beginning of one spring. Christie's smile, her gentleness, her love, the heat of her kisses, the way she gave herself over to him so completely when they were making love—they had all been more warmth than his ice could combat.

He pushed away from the dock, the cold water enveloping the hull of the wooden rowboat as the town got smaller. But after fifteen minutes of hard rowing, he had to face facts.

This time around, he couldn't close himself off, wasn't having any luck making a decision about what he would and wouldn't feel and then simply following through on it. Everything that had worked for him in the past was failing him.

Because he loved Christie.

Secrets. Trust. He'd thought those were the most important things of all. But now he knew better.

Only love mattered.

And he'd just thrown it away.

* * *

Wesley stood at the foot of the dock and watched Liam row toward him. His big brother had always been larger than life. Wesley had always looked up to him.

When they were teenagers and Liam had changed after the car crash, Wesley had wished he could have back the brother who had been so happy, so much fun when they were kids. But Wesley had been holding too tightly to his own secrets to dare ask anyone else for theirs.

Rowing in with his back to shore, Liam didn't see him until he was at the dock and Wesley leaned over to pull him alongside and tie up the rowboat.

"Where the hell did you go, Wes?" Liam looked simultaneously relieved and irritated. "I've been trying to track you down for weeks."

"Sorry about that." And Wesley was, sorrier than his brother knew. Especially because he'd had a hand in tearing apart the love between his brother and his best friend. "Now that I'm back, I promise I'll tell you everything you want to know."

But Liam didn't look particularly happy about that

vow. "You should have told me everything a long time ago."

"I know you're angry with me, but—"

Liam all but jumped out of the rowboat. "Do you think I would have cared that you're gay? Do you think that would have bothered me even the slightest bit? Don't you realize the only thing that could possibly bother me is that you kept something so important from me for so damn long, and I couldn't be there to support you?"

"Remember how Mom was after her brother died?" Wesley said instead of answering his brother's questions. "And then when they found out it was AIDS? She didn't get out of bed for days, and she was so fragile for so long after that." Wesley tried to explain everything he'd been forcing himself to dissect for the past three weeks. "I was confused, and I didn't want to put you in the position of having to lie to Mom and Dad."

"I would have helped you figure things out," Liam told him. "Don't you know I've always been there for you? Don't you know that I still am, even now when I'm so angry with you that I can hardly see straight?"

"I'm not the only one who screwed up." Wesley loved his big brother enough to go out on a limb. The limb he should have gone out on a long, long time ago. "You've been making excuses and pushing all of us away for too long. I know you're angry with me for disappearing the way I did, but I'm mad too. You're upset that I didn't confide in you. But you didn't confide in me either! I know I wasn't brave enough to ask you for answers when we were kids, but neither of us is a kid anymore." He watched his brother carefully, knew that the time had come to find out the truth. "I've been gone for three weeks, Liam. But you've been gone for twenty years. What happened between you and Mom when we were teenagers?"

Finally, Liam told him.

CHAPTER THIRTY-FIVE

Susan found Henry in one of the smaller barns, hammering on the leg of a wooden table that had broken off under the weight of the tapping equipment.

"Henry." His name shook, fell from her lips.

And he knew. The time had come for the final secrets, the final lies, to be revealed.

"I had an affair. Twenty years ago, after my brother died. With Roy." His wife looked ragged. She was crying, but he could see that she'd been crying long before now.

"I know."

Her shocked gasp resonated through the room. "*You knew?* But you never…you never said anything to me." Her words came out barely above a whisper. Raw and ragged. "You never did anything that made me suspect."

"You might not remember the past very clearly, but I do." His voice shook now from the force of the emotions pushing up from his gut, his chest, through his windpipe. "Your twin brother had died, and you went from being the strong, capable, loving woman I'd married to a brittle shell. I did everything I could to try to help you, but you were lost to me. To your sons. To everyone who cared about you."

"I never meant—" A sob choked her words short. "Roy didn't mean anything to me."

"I know that. Just as I knew it then. Being with people who loved you hurt too much. So you jumped into the arms of a man who didn't care about anything more than his next affair." It hadn't been hard for Henry to piece two and two together—and to get the other man to confess. "And I know it never went beyond that one time. I forgave you for that a long time ago."

In all the ways he'd thought this conversation would play out over the years, he'd never imagined that he'd tell her she was forgiven and she'd break down and cry harder.

"Liam…"

He could barely make out his son's name. "What about Liam? Is something wrong?"

"He saw me. I made him promise not to tell you."

Thirty-five years ago, Henry had taken one look at Susan and known he would love her forever. Only, no one could have told him forever wasn't nearly as long as he'd assumed it would be.

He'd loved her—so damned much—that he'd tried

to convince himself it was enough. For nearly twenty years, he'd told himself one version or another of that lie. But his love could never be enough. He saw that now. Just as he finally let in all the anger, the frustration, the hurt that he'd forced himself to push away for two decades.

"I loved you." He heard the past tense at the same time she did. "How could you, Susan?"

She flinched at the way he said her name. His heart broke looking at her, but he wouldn't let himself go and pull her into his arms.

"I thought I could look the other way when you came back to me," he continued. "But that was when I thought it was just between us." He looked down at her hand, her diamond ring still gone. She'd taken it off when they were sanding the floor. Watching her take off that ring three weeks ago had felt like a prophecy of doom. But now he knew that everything had broken a long time ago, when she'd made all the wrong choices with their son. All to save herself.

"I wanted to tell you so many times, but I couldn't risk losing you."

"I know why you cheated, Susan. I even told myself I understood. But I'll never understand how you could ask a fourteen-year-old boy to keep a secret like that." He took a step closer to her. "I'm his father, for God's sake! You forced him to lie to me. You made it so he couldn't look me in the eye." His voice boomed at her, his breath blowing her hair back from her face. He'd always thought she was the most beautiful person he'd ever seen. But he wasn't sure he'd ever be able to see her beauty again. "The affair was forgivable. What you did to our son isn't."

And then he walked out of the barn, leaving his wife behind.

* * *

"Sweet girl, come here."

For hours, Christie had been on autopilot, running the festival. Her grief, her exhaustion, must be making her hear things. But the arms pulling her close were warm. And real.

"Mom."

She breathed in her mother's familiar scent and closed her eyes as she let herself be held by someone who would never desert her. And when she looked up from her mother's shoulder, she saw her father and four sisters and their husbands and kids. Her family had come, after all.

They'd waited weeks for her to clean up her messes, just as she'd asked them to. And yet, here she was, more of a mess than she'd ever been.

She knew what they were going to say. They were going to tell her to come home with them. To let them all take care of her. And oh, how big a temptation it was to give up every stride she'd taken to become a strong person over the past months.

She forced herself to pull out of her mother's arms and smile at the people she loved so dearly. "I'm so glad you're all here. You guys are going to love tapping a maple. Come with me and I'll show you how."

CHAPTER THIRTY-SIX

Liam's brother had dozens of questions—about their mother, about what had happened at the inn, about what had happened between him and Christie. But only Christie mattered now.

"Man the inn," he told Wesley. "I need to go and beg Christie to take me back."

He thought he saw his brother smile, but he was already heading up the dock toward the forest. Toward the woman he loved.

He quickly spotted her working to help a family with small children get situated behind the maple syrup tapping equipment. A little boy fell, and she knelt beside him, brushing the dirt off his pants, talking animatedly to him until he stopped crying. The child's parents looked at her gratefully, but she was wholly focused on the little boy's welfare and happiness.

Just as she'd been wholly focused on his own.

God, how he loved her. Since that first moment he'd seen her at Sarah and Calvin's wedding with tears streaming down her face and her hand over her heart.

And every moment since.

He could still hear her words echoing not only in his head, but also deep inside his heart. *Sometimes loving someone means breaking a promise that will only hurt them if it's kept.* His beautiful Christie. So sweet. So wise.

And so much stronger than anyone ever gave her credit for. Especially him.

He'd give anything to share her life, to be strong for her and let her be strong right back. Here he'd thought he wasn't afraid of anything, when all along, she was the truly brave one. The dragon slayer who would face down the hottest flames, the biggest dangers, to protect the people she loved.

He wanted to call her name, wanted to beg her to forgive him, to take him back, right then and there. But as she turned to take care of yet another family who needed her help, he realized that right now, she needed his support far more than she needed his pleas for forgiveness.

As he attended to various issues that cropped up at the festival throughout the rest of the afternoon, she gave no outward sign that she saw him. But she made sure that they were on opposite sides of the festival, moving away from him whenever he came too close. He kept seeing her with the same large group of people and eventually realized that they must be her family based on resemblance and how effortless and comfortable she was with them all. He wanted so badly to meet them, to thank her mother and father for raising such an incredible woman. But he knew better than to do it just then.

Christie was hurt. Angry. And she had every right to be. He'd gotten everything wrong.

Everything.

As night began to fall, he made sure every last festivalgoer got back to their car all right in the dark. Then, in case it rained, he wanted to make sure the tapping equipment was put away and covered for the rental company to come pick up Monday morning. But Christie was already there, kneeling beside one of the tappers, wiping it down with a wet rag.

He couldn't stop himself from watching her. And from wishing he'd understood what love was really about before he threw it all away.

Her hand stilled on the equipment as she realized he was standing behind her. The moon was bright enough that he could watch her slowly pull air into her lungs and then let it out before she said, "Thank you for your help today."

He'd gone and stomped on her heart and she was thanking him for helping with the festival? He didn't even come close to deserving this woman. "You don't need to thank me for anything, sweet—" The endearment was halfway out before he saw Christie flinch.

The tiny movement pierced straight through his heart.

He knew she wanted him to leave her alone. But how could he bring himself to leave her? And how could he ever let her go, if that was what she really wanted from him now?

He tried again. "I saw that your family came."

Her mouth almost tipped up into a smile. "They wanted to surprise me."

"I'm glad they were here for you, Christie."

For the first time, she met his gaze. Her chin was lifted, her shoulders back. Here was the stunningly strong woman who had fought the Preservation Council, who had believed in herself and her festival. The woman who had always been such a big part of his brother's life. The woman everyone in town cared for and wanted to see happy.

The woman he would never stop loving.

"I am too," she said. "I've missed them." She looked pale. And tired. But still so beautiful he could hardly believe his eyes.

"Have you eaten today?"

She covered the tapper, then stood and wiped her hands on her jeans. "I appreciate your concern, but you don't have to take care of me," she said softly. "I already know how to take care of myself. I've always known. But before now, I haven't wanted to make the hard decisions about when to stay. And when to go."

It killed Liam to stand there and let her walk away. He couldn't do it. "Christie, I—"

She stopped him with nothing more than a look over her shoulder. "Have you and your mother spoken?"

"She came and found me and tried to talk about things."

She studied his face, looking deep, the way she always did. "But nothing has changed between the two of you, has it?"

He knew his answer wasn't the one she wanted, but he had to give it to her anyway. Because it was the truth. "No, it hasn't."

She didn't look surprised. "Wesley is going to cover for me for a few days. I've got some things to take care of."

All he wanted was to run after her as she walked away, to beg her forgiveness. But he knew now that wouldn't be enough. Christie wasn't leaving because their broken relationship was beyond repair. She was leaving because of problems that had nothing to with her and him—and everything to do with the way he had dealt with his family for so long.

She wasn't the only one who hadn't wanted to make the hard decisions about when to stay and when to go. He'd done exactly the same thing.

And in that instant, he understood that there was

only one way he could prove his love to Christie, only one path to having a solid, loving relationship: He needed to deal with the demons that had been eating away at him for twenty years.

His gut clenched, tightened even further, at the thought of seeking out his mother. He had to speak with her soon.

But first, he'd go make his apologies to his father, who had only ever wanted to love his son.

⋆ ⋆ ⋆

Liam found Henry in his workshop, surrounded by saws and hammers but not using any of them. His father looked crushed. Shaken. So shaken that Liam knew without a doubt that his mother had finally told him everything.

"I'm sorry I pushed you away," Liam said without preamble. "I didn't know what else to do. I worried that if I was around you too much, one day her secret would slip out. You loved her. Wesley and I both saw how much. I didn't want to be responsible for anything happening to your marriage."

Henry walked across the workshop and pulled him into a hug. And Liam didn't want to move away. Not when he and his dad had twenty years of lost hugs to make up for.

Finally, his father said, "I wish you hadn't felt like

you needed to protect me. But you've always been so honest. Such a good person—even when you were a little boy, you were helping the other kids at school, protecting your little brother from bullies." Henry grimaced. "I've always known what happened that afternoon. What she did. If only I had confronted her right away, then it would all have come to light and you wouldn't have had to live with her secret for so long. Will you ever forgive me?"

"There's nothing to forgive. You're the best father I could ever have asked for."

"No, I wasn't. Not even close. But I'd very much like to be, if you're open to letting me try again."

"I am," Liam said. "Of course I am. But what is going to happen with you and Susan?"

His father's face shuttered. "I don't know." He sighed, deep and long. "The only thing I know for sure right now is that no matter what happens, I don't want you to feel responsible in any way for my marriage. All I want is for you to be happy."

"I'm going to talk to her. I have to finally confront the mess we've been in for so long." Because if he didn't, Christie might never consider coming back to him. And he would do anything to persuade her to give him another chance.

"I don't know that I deserve the privilege of giving you advice," his father said, "but can I give you some anyway?"

Every muscle in his body tight, Liam nodded. "I'll take whatever you've got."

"With every new house I build, somewhere in the middle of it all, I look around at the mess and disarray, and the easiest thing is to let it overwhelm me. To let it defeat me. But what I always work like hell to make myself see is the potential for what's coming. The new building that will soon stand tall. Proud. Of course, this is also right when clients worry that everything's going wrong, that we'll never be able to turn the piles of wood and shingles and cement and tile into a home. But there's no use in trying to placate them. It's better to be honest. To tell them, yes, things are messy, bordering on being out of control—and I'm sticking to my vision anyway, along with my hope that, with focus and determination, all is going to go well." He held his son's gaze. "You're focused, Liam. And you're determined. Let yourself be honest too. Getting things out in the open won't necessarily make them any less messy. But at least everything will finally be laid out on the table. And then if you ever decide that you want to rebuild, you can do it on a solid foundation."

* * *

Liam's mother was in the house, standing at the kitchen counter, staring out the window above the sink into the darkness. When he walked in, she turned to him, and he could see she was still crying, the tear tracks fresh on her cheeks.

Black. White. That was the way he'd seen the world since he was fourteen. He'd never looked for the shades of gray. Even as a child, he'd liked what he liked and disliked what he didn't.

But standing in the kitchen of the house he'd grown up in, the same kitchen where his mother had asked him to keep her secret, he wondered if things were ever really completely black and white.

Yes, his mother had cheated on his father.

Yes, Liam had climbed into her car and crashed into a tree in a foiled, childish attempt to forget what he'd seen.

But if he'd known that one day in the future he'd find a love like Christie's—then didn't that mean it had all been worth living through?

Just to be with her.

"Liam?" His mother's voice shook on his name.

"I don't really want to forgive you," he told her, taking his father's advice to tell the truth, no matter how messy, how complicated. "But I'll do anything for Christie. Even put what happened behind us with the hope that forgiveness will come someday."

"I'm so sorry."

He nodded. "I know." And, for the first time, he

truly did.

He wasn't going to solve things with his mother today. But they'd made a start. At long last.

* * *

Liam made it back to the inn just as Christie was coming out with her suitcase. As she stood on the inn's front porch, her delicate beauty that he'd been so aware of from the first moment he'd set eyes on her was made even more beautiful by the moonlight that illuminated her features.

"I'll be back to help with the wedding this weekend," she told him.

Then what? Would she leave again? And the next time, would it be forever?

"I talked with my father tonight. About—" The words choked in his throat, but he made himself push them out. "About everything."

Her expression softened. "That's good." The edges of her lips moved up, almost making a smile. "Really, really good."

"I also talked to Sus—to my mother."

Christie's eyes widened at that news, and in the moonlight, he swore he could see tears. A moment later, as she blinked, two tears fell from her eyelashes to her cheeks. *"Liam."*

She whispered his name, and there was so much

love in it, he could feel it wrap around him, almost warm enough to chase away the chill of the wind blowing across the lake.

Liam had never begged a woman for anything. Not for attention. Not for love.

Until now.

"Please don't go." When she didn't put the suitcase down, he said, "Earlier today, you said nothing had changed, that you couldn't stay until I worked things out with my parents. I'm trying. I swear to you, I'm trying."

He watched myriad emotions move across her face: hope, longing, love. Then she said, "Why? Why are you trying?"

He didn't have to think about his answer. "Because I don't want to lose you."

A cloud drifted in front of the moon, making it impossible for him to see her expression. "Wesley knows to call me with any problems while I'm away this week." She moved her suitcase into her other hand. "Good night, Liam."

As she walked away, the only thread of hope he had to hold on to was that she'd said *good night*.

And not *good-bye*.

CHAPTER THIRTY-SEVEN

Wesley called Christie's cell early the next morning. At first, she thought he was calling to ask for help with something at the inn. But he never even brought that up.

"Liam loves you."

Three words. That was all it took to pierce her already shattered heart. "You needed time to go away," she reminded him. "To think about your life and what you wanted from it. Now I'm asking you for the same thing." And then she hung up to do some more of that thinking.

Only, Wesley continued to call every day without fail. And Christie knew why: Her friend cared about her. He cared about his brother. He wanted to see them happy. And, preferably, together.

After that first conversation, Christie let Wesley's calls go through to voice mail. Because she truly did have a lot to think about. Namely that for her entire life, she'd been running when things got too complicated. Not because she was weak or afraid or unable to take care of herself. But because she'd never had a reason to stay—and she'd never had anything important to lose.

Liam had been important right from the first moment he'd spoken to her, touched her, looked into her eyes and connected with her despite all the reasons not to. This time around, he'd been her reason to run.

But he was also her reason to go back.

And to stay.

* * *

She returned to Summer Lake early Saturday morning, just in time to witness the first outdoor wedding of spring. She was happy for the couple, who had just said their *I do's* and kissed in front of their applauding family and friends. And still, she was crying, just like she always did at weddings. Because there was nothing she loved more than a happy ending.

Even if she hadn't yet managed one for herself.

As the bride, the groom, and their guests all moved inside for the reception, she stepped beneath the roof of the gazebo and onto a wooden floor covered in rose petals—where *forever* had been declared so many times before—when—

"Christie." Slowly, she turned to face Liam. "I missed you."

She'd never known how to lie. She definitely didn't

know how to do it now. "I missed you too." So much that her heart had broken a little more every time she thought about the distance between them.

She could almost feel his relief, could certainly see it in his face. She was about to tell him everything she felt when he spoke first. "You were right."

Her heart was thundering in her chest. "About what?"

"About going." Finally, he crossed the distance between them, coming close enough that she knew he'd catch her if she fell. "I gave you so many reasons to leave me. So many reasons to stop loving me. All I wanted was to find one to make you stay. Just one. That was why I talked to my mother that night. Because I knew you wanted me to. Because you thought I needed to. Because I knew you'd leave if I didn't. But you left anyway."

Her chest had never felt so tight, so constricted. "I didn't want to go. Leaving you was the hardest thing I've ever done."

"When I was a teenager, I didn't understand that loving someone could mean having to break a promise. I've made and remade that mistake over and over for twenty years, but you were wise enough to know better than to keep a secret that was going to tear someone apart. That was already tearing *me* apart. The first time I saw you, I thought you looked so delicate.

But you're the strongest person I've ever met. So strong that you'll sacrifice anything for the ones you love." He paused, his gaze sweeping over her. Sweeping through her, deep into her heart. "Even yourself."

She felt tears come again, but she didn't want anything to blur her vision of the beautiful man standing before her.

"It was a hell of a week," he said softly. "Probably the worst one since I was fourteen. But all I could think was that maybe, just maybe, if I kept at it, if I kept trying to forgive her a little more, then somehow you'd know and you'd come back."

"I told you I was coming back."

"Not just for the weekend. For good. But somewhere along the way, I realized I wasn't just talking with my mother for you anymore. I was trying to fix things in my family for me too."

She couldn't stand apart from him another second. She reached for him, wrapped her arms around his broad shoulders. And held on tight, wishing she'd never, ever have to let go of him again.

But he held her even tighter as he said, "You were gone, but I could feel your love behind me every step of the way, sweetheart."

She didn't bother to try to stop her tears as she pulled back to tell him, "It still is."

He slid his hands across her shoulders and down

her arms, until he was holding her hands in his. And then he was getting down on one knee and looking up at her. "You taught me to trust again. And to love with all of my heart. Please stay, not only because you love your job and your friends and this town—but also because you want to live forever with me. Here. Together." She'd never seen him look so intense—or so full of love—as he said, "Marry me, Christie. Please, be my wife. And I promise to love you more than any man has ever loved a woman."

She had to join him on her knees so that they were eye to eye. Heart to heart. "You say I taught you so many things, but what about everything I've learned from you? For so long I was afraid to trust my heart, but it led me to you. You showed me a world I've only glimpsed from the outside, that I was too afraid to explore. That day out on your beach, with your plane, you believed in me in a way no one else ever has."

"You would have gotten on an airplane eventually, even without me."

"Maybe, but it wouldn't have been nearly as special. Nothing is as good without you, Liam. When I'm with you, everything is brighter, sweeter." She smiled. "I spent the week planning a round-the-world trip that I should have taken a long time ago, because being with you has shown me that I can't put off what I want—what I need—another moment." She intercepted the pain moving across his face by placing his hands over her heart. "I want you, Liam. I need you."

"But you just said you're leaving."

"You know how I'm always saying and doing things no one else would? Well, it turns out I couldn't give up hope when anyone else would have." She smiled even wider, feeling the joy of being with the man she loved in every cell. "I bought *two* round-the-world tickets. One for me. And one for you. Although now it looks like we're going to have to see a whole lot of stuff really fast, before my legal name changes and my ticket isn't valid anymore."

Liam's eyes were shining as he tested out her future married name. "Christie Kane. God, that sounds good."

"It really does."

"So is that a yes?"

Christie whispered, "Yes."

And then she leaned in close to seal it with a kiss.

EPILOGUE

Two weeks later…

Wesley threw them a heck of a going-away party at the inn. Christie's and Liam's bags were packed, and they were due to fly to London that night on the red-eye. For the next several months, the world was theirs, ready to be explored, hand in hand.

She looked around the room at her friends, then out the window at the lake. "All this time, I've been wanting to see the world. So why do I suddenly wish we could just take our bags back upstairs and stay right here?"

Liam smiled at his fiancée. "It will still be here when we come back."

It wasn't just a promise; it was something he knew from experience. He'd tried to leave Summer Lake behind, but he'd never succeeded. Christie was going to love the Eiffel Tower, the Tower of London, the beaches of Thailand—but he knew that nothing would ever take the place in her heart held by this small Adirondack town.

He wanted to say all of this to her, but before he could, his mother approached them. His parents were currently living apart. After the festival, Henry had moved out of the house he'd built and was renting a cottage on William Sullivan's property. Henry had come in earlier to say his good-byes, but he'd left before he and Susan could run the risk of bumping into each other in the inn's event room.

"This has been a lovely party," Susan said. It was far too easy to see the sorrow behind her smile. "I'm so happy for both of you. We all are."

Liam and his mother had been meeting every few days for coffee out on her porch. He knew how glad Christie was to see them trying to forge a new relationship. And he was glad, a million times over, to see Christie face his mother with none of the anger that had been eating her up before.

"Your father and I have been talking," Susan said. "Not a lot, but more than we were last week." Christie squeezed his hand as his mother added, "I'm hopeful that we'll be able to make a new start. One day soon."

Jean came to say good-bye next, kissing both of them on the cheek, one after the other.

"I'll take good care of your grandson," Christie said.

Jean smiled. "I never had any doubt of that," she said in her serene way, as if she had expected them to fall in love all along. "Loving with all our hearts is what

Kanes do. That's how I knew you were one of us, honey—because you've always been willing to risk everything for love."

Christie blinked back a rush of tears as Wesley moved into their small circle and pointedly looked at his watch. "Time to go, lovebirds."

He was their chauffeur for the night, having offered to drop them at the airport on his way to visit John for a couple of days. Christie had been training Alice to run the inn while she was gone, and this would be her first trial run by herself.

After hugging everyone good-bye—with Christie solemnly promising Sarah and Calvin they'd be home with plenty of time to spare before they had their baby—the three of them headed off down the forested road to Albany International Airport.

During the drive, Liam and Wesley kept Christie laughing with their stories of growing up on the lake. There was nothing Liam loved more than seeing her smile and knowing he could make her laugh—everywhere, including in the bed they shared.

Wesley was just pulling up to the curb to let them out at Departures when he said, "I forgot to tell you guys. The plumbing contractor finally looked at that problem you've been having with noises and cold in your bedroom."

Liam and Christie looked at each other. "It's been silent and warm for the past two weeks." She smiled, and Liam knew what she was thinking, that the problems with the bedroom had gone away when they'd declared their love to each other, a love with no secrets in the way. His grandmother had told him all about what had happened on her honeymoon, and even Jean seemed to believe that their love had healed old wounds.

"What did he tell you was wrong?" Liam asked his brother.

"Nothing."

Christie laughed. "Did he say anything about a ghost?"

Wesley clearly didn't know how to respond to that. "Uh, no. Should he have?"

Christie simply said, "Ask your grandmother about it." They hugged good-bye, and then she turned, flipping her silky hair over her shoulder as she headed in to the check-in area.

And as Liam followed her inside—he still couldn't take his eyes off of her and knew he never would—he gave silent thanks, just as he had at least a million times in the past two weeks, that he'd found such an extraordinary woman to love at Summer Lake.

* * * * *

ABOUT THE AUTHOR

Having sold more than 6 million books, Bella Andre's novels have been #1 bestsellers around the world and have appeared on the *New York Times* and *USA Today* bestseller lists 33 times. She has been the #1 Ranked Author on a top 10 list that included Nora Roberts, JK Rowling, James Patterson and Steven King, and Publishers Weekly named Oak Press (the publishing company she created to publish her own books) the Fastest-Growing Independent Publisher in the US. After signing a groundbreaking 7-figure print-only deal with Harlequin MIRA, Bella's "The Sullivans" series has been released in paperback in the US, Canada, and Australia.

Known for "sensual, empowered stories enveloped in heady romance" (Publishers Weekly), her books have been Cosmopolitan Magazine "Red Hot Reads" twice and have been translated into ten languages. Winner of the Award of Excellence, The Washington Post called her "One of the top writers in America" and she has been featured by Entertainment Weekly, NPR, USA Today, Forbes, The Wall Street Journal, and TIME Magazine. A graduate of Stanford University, she has given keynote speeches at publishing conferences from Copenhagen to Berlin to San Francisco, including a standing-room-only keynote at Book Expo America in New York City.

Bella also writes the *New York Times* bestselling "Four Weddings and a Fiasco" series as Lucy Kevin. Her sweet contemporary romances also include the USA Today bestselling Walker Island series written as Lucy Kevin.

If not behind her computer, you can find her reading her favorite authors, hiking, swimming or laughing. Married with two children, Bella splits her time between the Northern California wine country and a 100 year old log cabin in the Adirondacks.

For a complete listing of books, as well as excerpts and contests, and to connect with Bella:

Sign up for Bella's newsletter:

BellaAndre.com/Newsletter

Visit Bella's website at:

www.BellaAndre.com

Follow Bella on Twitter at:

twitter.com/bellaandre

Join Bella on Facebook at:

facebook.com/bellaandrefans

Follow Bella on Instagram:

instagram.com/bellaandrebooks

Made in the USA
Monee, IL
17 October 2020